TWILA MASON

DESPERATE HEARTS BOOK 2

Step by Step
Desperate Hearts: Book 2
Red Adept Publishing, LLC
104 Bugenfield Court
Garner, NC 27529
https://RedAdeptPublishing.com/
Copyright © 2026 by Twila Mason. All rights reserved.

---

1.   http://StreetlightGraphics.com

To my husband, for never letting me give up on my dreams

Chapter 1
Chrissy

The bedroom door slammed behind Chrissy Hardin with more force than she'd meant it to, but she didn't care. She tossed her purse on the nightstand and let out a growl as she plopped onto her bed.

"Rough day?"

Chrissy brushed her blond hair from her face and turned to see her roommate, Donna, curled up on the beanbag in the corner, reading a book. "That's an understatement. It took everything I have not to quit."

Donna slipped in a bookmark and set the book down, giving Chrissy her undivided attention. "Anything specific?"

Chrissy crossed the room and sat in the computer chair next to Donna, even though the space they shared was small enough to easily have the conversation from anywhere. "Well, for starters, I'd like to tell Mr. Davis where he can shove his sales quota."

"He gave you that lecture again?" Donna folded her arms across her chest.

"Yes. And we don't even have an actual sales quota we're supposed to meet. There's no commission." Chrissy shook her head, and a strand of her hair tangled around her name tag. She unclipped the red rectangle and flung it across the room to her bed.

"So what's his deal?"

"He says ever since I took over the shoe department, the sales have dropped. But he also cut back on special discounts around the same time. It can't possibly be his fault, though. It's always my fault."

Donna grimaced. "Sounds like a real jerk."

"He is. I wish I could quit." Chrissy propped her elbow on the desk and rested her chin in her hand.

"But you can't," Donna said matter-of-factly. "At least, not until you have another job lined up. And there are jerks everywhere, I'm afraid."

"I hate feeling stuck."

Donna shrugged. "It sucks, but what can we do?"

"I don't know. I guess after thirty-one years of being alive, I'm tired of feeling like I never get past square one." Chrissy sighed, her frustration giving way to melancholy.

"It took a lot of work to get to that square one, though."

Chrissy huffed. "That's even more pathetic."

Donna gripped Chrissy's knee, her brown eyes locking on to Chrissy's. "Stop. You can't be pathetic because then that would mean I'm pathetic. All of us are in the same boat here. I'd hate to have to beat you up for calling me pathetic."

"You're right." Chrissy couldn't help but grin at Donna's playful threat.

"I know I'm right." Donna stood and stretched. "Group is in ten. You should bring it up in there."

Group therapy was the perfect place to discuss her struggles, but Chrissy couldn't shake the feeling that she was being ungrateful. She was judging herself, so the others in group would judge her too. But she had to do something. Spring in Chicago was magical, one of her favorite times of year, but even the chirping birds and budding trees on her walk home from work hadn't lifted her spirits. She knew she should be grateful for having a job and a routine, the security of knowing what each day would be like. Just eighteen months ago it was a completely different story. But she couldn't shake the growing restlessness and stagnant feeling. The city was coming alive after a long winter, and she longed to do the same.

Chrissy's phone buzzed in her purse, and she walked over to get it.

"I'm going to head on down. See you there." Donna walked out into the hallway, securing her brown hair into a bun.

Chrissy watched her go and made a mental note to add having Donna as her roommate to her gratitude list that night.

She fished her phone from her purse, frowning at the unknown number as she sat on the edge of her bed. *Should I answer it?* Since the beginning of her recovery journey, unknown numbers made her jumpy. One phone call with the wrong person could trigger an avalanche of disaster. She had to remain vigilant.

Her mental struggle went on too long, and the phone went silent.

Whew.

Another buzz, and a message popped up on the screen. "Hello. This is Madison from the Office of Cultural Affairs. I'm looking for Christine Hardin regarding her contract. If you could, please give me a call back at your earliest convenience."

Chrissy stared at the screen, her mouth agape, then dialed the number as her heart threatened to race out of her chest. It had been a year since she'd signed her contract with the city. As the phone rang, she prayed Madison had good news. She wasn't sure she could handle bad news.

"Office of Cultural Affairs, Madison speaking. How may I help you?"

"Hi. I missed a call from you." Chrissy inhaled deeply, trying to soothe her nerves.

"What's your name?"

"Oh, sorry. I'm Chrissy, I mean Christine Hardin." She smacked herself on the forehead. *Could I be any more awkward?*

"Oh, yes. Thank you for calling me back, Christine. I'm happy to let you know the mural project is slated to begin next month."

"Really?" Relief flooded through Chrissy. "That's amazing news."

"I know you signed on to the project months ago, so I need to confirm that you're still available."

"Yes!" She cleared her throat and tried again, calmer. "Yes. I am available to start whenever." Her eyes dropped to the retail-store badge on the bed beside her. "I just need two weeks' notice."

"Great. You'll have to come in and fill out some more paperwork for payroll and such. I don't have an email on file for you, so text me your email address, and we can coordinate a day and time that works for you."

"Okay. Sounds great. I'll do that right now."

"I'll talk to you soon."

"Thank you. Bye." Chrissy texted her email address to Madison and laid her phone on the bed beside her.

This is real. It's finally happening.

She jumped as the alarm for group therapy blared from her phone. She shut it off, cursing it under her breath even though she knew she'd never be on time for anything without her alarms.

As she shut the bedroom door behind her and headed for the stairs, there was an unusual spring in her step. For once, she was heading into group with more than just the normal "I survived another day sober" good news. She had the best news of her life and couldn't wait to share. She might even volunteer to go first.

Chapter 2
Adam

Shoving away from his desk, Adam Rochester grabbed his jacket and headed for the door, his stomach growling. A glance at his watch let him know it was already two o'clock. He'd worked through lunch. Again.

He punched the elevator button and slipped on his jacket, wondering if he should have just ordered in. No. If he wanted to actually enjoy his food, he would have to get out of the office and away from his computer.

When the elevator door opened, he suppressed a groan as his boss, Mr. Lyones, zeroed in on him.

"Adam. Just the man I needed to see." Mr. Lyones stepped from the elevator and clapped Adam on the shoulder. "Follow me to my office. I have something I need to discuss with you." Adam opened his mouth to protest, but his boss continued. "It will only take a minute."

Not one to say no to his boss, Adam followed the short yet formidable man to his swanky corner office.

Mr. Lyones sat down and motioned to the chair across from him. "Have a seat."

Adam did as he was told. "What can I do for you, sir?"

"Do you remember the mural project for that warehouse down by the farmer's market?"

"Yes."

"Then you probably remember that we hired a girl Liam insisted was right for the job."

Adam nodded. Of course he remembered. They'd hired his friend's sister. He hadn't met her, but he had heard Luke talk about her off and on.

Mr. Lyones leaned forward and laced his fingers together on his desk. "Before I start, this doesn't leave this room. Understand?" He waited for Adam to nod then continued. "I personally don't like the idea of hiring a girl who has no track record. She's never painted anything large scale before, let alone a mural. But we both know that whatever the Worthington family wants, the Worthington family gets. If Liam is insistent this girl do the job, then that's who we have do the job. Besides, it's his warehouse she'll be potentially ruining, and it's his sponsorship dollars we might be wasting."

"Surely the people overseeing the project will make sure that doesn't happen," Adam said. *Lord knows the city has plenty of layers of oversight for every project*, he added to himself.

"That's my hope." Mr. Lyones's mouth curled into what Adam might have considered a grin if he thought the man capable. "I'd like you to oversee the project for me."

Adam blinked. "Me? But, sir, Cultural Affairs usually handles that kind of thing, not Economic Development. Surely there's someone better suited—"

"I know what your job is, Mr. Rochester. I'm the one who hired you. And I'm telling you that as economic development coordinator, you will be overseeing the beautification of the farmer's market area. Yes, Cultural Affairs oversees art for art's sake, but this art is under your umbrella. From now on, all murals involved in beautification will be handled by the Economic Development Office because their purpose is to develop a particular part of the city. Making that warehouse more appealing so we can boost the numbers at the farmer's market is developing the economy of the area, is it not?"

Adam swallowed. "I-It is, sir."

"Good. Now, I need you to watch over this project like a hawk. Check in daily if you have to. Keep everything on schedule and on budget. The faster and cheaper it gets done, the better. We are already a year behind schedule."

"Yes, sir. Consider it done." Adam forced his mouth into a placating smile.

"I knew I could count on you." Mr. Lyones stood. "I have a meeting with the mayor I can't be late to. I'll forward you the details of the mural project."

Adam sprang to his feet and followed his boss into the hall. "I won't let you down."

"I'm sure you won't. Especially with performance reviews coming up."

Adam stared at Mr. Lyones as he walked away, resisting the urge to flip him off behind his back. Years of being dedicated to his job and doing everything that was ever asked of him didn't matter. Nothing was ever enough for his boss.

"Now I have to babysit a mural project," he grumbled to himself as he made his way back to his office. As if he didn't have enough work to do. And the real kicker was that if he did a great job, all he would have accomplished was ensuring he would have to babysit the future murals too.

He sank down in his chair and pulled up the menu for City Club Café. A quick, late lunch while he checked emails would have to suffice.

Maybe one of these days I'll tell Mr. Lyones where he can shove this job.

Chapter 3
Chrissy

A month later, the aging three-story brick wall loomed over Chrissy, taunting her. Challenging her to conquer it while laughing that she thought she even had a chance. She dug her neon-yellow fingernails into her palms, using their bite to hold in the tears burning beneath her eyelids.

"You can do this," she told herself, swiping her sleeve at the sweat beading under her blond bangs. The chilled early-spring air rustled her messy bun, providing a kiss of relief from the sun's heat radiating from the brick. "You have to. The future depends on it. Time to sink or swim."

She glanced down for the hundredth time at the paper in her trembling hand. A cheerful sketch of Chicago's skyline as seen from the Chicago River graced the page. Not only did she hold the final approved mural design, she also held her future. Her chance to start over after years of nothing but utter failure. With a resolved inhale, she picked up her paintbrush and swirled it in the can of paint. As she made the first swipe, a mix between a laugh and sigh of relief escaped her, and she stared at the streak of shiny green against the aged brick. She'd done it. She'd taken the first baby step toward a brighter future. Time to chase those dreams.

Her apprehension quieted with each stroke. Maybe she could actually paint this giant mural and make a name for herself, giving herself the fresh start she craved. As the minutes ticked by, a quiet confidence began to take root inside her.

"You really just jumped right in, huh?"

Chrissy yelped, and the can of green paint slipped from her hand, crashing to the ground as she spun around.

"Whoa, easy. I didn't mean to startle you." A man in a gray suit extended his hand, his warm brown eyes crinkling in the corners. "Nice to meet you again, Christine."

One of Chrissy's hands lay over her hammering heart as she shook his hand with the other. "I'm sorry, but have we met before?"

A hint of something flashed across his eyes as he dropped her hand. "Uh, yeah, actually. I'm Adam Rochester. I work for the city of Chicago. I'm the guy who signed your contract."

Chrissy sucked in her breath. "Oh, of course. I'm so sorry. I'm usually really good with faces. There were just so many guys in nice suits in that office..."

"We all kind of blend together?" he said with a slight grimace.

"No, I... Well, to be honest, it was all pretty intimidating, so I spent most of the time looking down." She took in his sandy hair and the smattering of freckles across his nose. *How could I forget that sexy surfer-boy face?* Heat filled her cheeks, and before she could help it, her insecurity forced her eyes to the ground. What she found there only made matters worse. "Oh my gosh. The paint," she said, her voice squeaky.

Adam followed her line of sight, and she cringed, anticipating his wrath upon seeing the green splatters all over his undoubtedly expensive suit and leather shoes.

"Well, that's what I get for startling people, I guess."

Her eyes shot to his. "You're not going to fire me?"

"What?" He looked at her like she'd grown a second head. "Why would I fire you?"

"Because I haven't even made it through the first day of painting, and I've already screwed up." Her chest tightened, and she clenched her fists to stave off the rising self-loathing.

His expression softened with a sympathetic look that would make Chrissy squirm under normal circumstances, but at that moment it fed her hope. She hated other people's pity, but she would take it if it saved her job. "It's just pants and shoes. I'll survive."

"Oh." Chrissy blinked, the storm of emotions within her dissipating into confusion. "Are you sure? I'm really sorry, and I promise I'll make it up to you somehow."

"No worries." He turned his attention to the brick wall behind her with a nod of approval. "Not a bad start."

Chrissy's mood lifted, and she turned to admire her work. "Thanks. It's not much yet, but I hope it will be. I hope I can make the city proud."

"I have no doubts. But you're definitely going to need some scaffolding. I'll have someone bring one by today." He turned, scanning the area around them. "You're supposed to have an assistant. Did they not show up?"

"I haven't seen anyone except the guys who delivered the trailer of materials." She motioned to the trailer sitting across one end of the narrow street running along the wall. No one was supposed to use the private dead-end drive anyway, but the trailer made sure no one would be running her over.

Adam frowned toward the trailer. "It's extremely important we stay on schedule." He shifted his attention back to her. "On that note, I wanted to ask if you're okay with overtime. You'd be financially compensated, of course. I know your contract states a flat fee for the commission, but I can arrange a bonus for completion ahead of schedule."

Chrissy chewed her lip for a moment. She wanted nothing more than to impress Adam and prove she was the right person for the job, but she also had to stick to her schedule. "Yeah, I can do some overtime. But on Tuesdays and Thursdays I have to leave by five at the latest."

"Every Tuesday and Thursday?" His forehead creased, letting her know that wasn't the answer he was looking for. "Can you move things around?"

"It's not really something I can control, unfortunately." *Please don't ask for details.* She hated being cryptic, but the last thing she wanted to tell her brand-new employer was that she had required group therapy twice a week. She knew she shouldn't be ashamed of something that helped her keep her life on the straight and narrow, but she was also realistic about the stigma surrounding being an addict in recovery. "I can come in early on those days, though, if that helps."

Adam studied her for a second then nodded. "That works. But no cutting corners just to finish early for the bonus. The work still has to meet the requirements."

"Of course. My name is going on this thing, so I'm going to do my absolute best. I swear." She clasped her hands together at her chest but pulled them apart when she realized it looked like she was begging. Even if she felt that desperate, she didn't want to make it quite so obvious.

Adam's phone rang in his pocket, and he pulled it out, sucking air through his teeth. "I better take this. I'll check on your assistant and see what's going on there. Keep up the good work, and I'll see you around."

Chrissy waved as he walked away toward the gravel lot beyond the trailer. It was a shame those pants got ruined because the way they hugged his backside brought the heat back to her cheeks. She chastised herself. *In my wildest dreams, maybe,* she thought. *No man like that would ever have anything to do with damaged goods like me.*

"Not bad for a first day." Chrissy congratulated herself as she wiped her hands on her painting overalls. She couldn't help but smile as she scanned the wall and admired her unexpected progress. One third of the outlining done on the first day. She might've gotten even further if her barely five-foot frame could've stretched a little more. That scaffold Adam mentioned would definitely come in handy.

Honk, honk.

She turned to see her brother, Luke, waving as he drove by, music thumping from his party bus as multicolored lights shone from the windows.

"Thank you," she whispered as he drove from her sight. Without him, some other lucky artist would be standing in her place. Someone else would be living her dream and starting a new life.

She put the last crate of supplies in the box trailer and snapped the padlock shut, officially finished with her first day as a paid artist and what she hoped was a new beginning. Turning to head to the bus stop, she paused, the beauty of the city taking her breath away. The radiant setting sun shimmered red and gold behind the skyscrapers, the towering buildings made into navy-blue silhouettes. The reflection of the beautiful scenery twinkled on the rippling river below. Too bad the city wanted a daytime mural because this was a sunset to die for. Maybe she could paint a sunset next, if she was lucky enough to get another job.

Basking in the warm glow, she felt hope trickle into her wounded heart. Hope for a future free of the demons that lurked in the shadows, waiting for her to fail and fall back into their snares. She had hope that she'd stumbled upon a better path for her life rather than the broken one she'd been navigating so far. For the first time, she could see a way not only forward, but upward. All she had to do was keep her eye on the prize and avoid any distractions and temptations.

Chapter 4
Adam

Pulling up in front of the dry cleaners after work, Adam gathered his paint-splattered pants and shoes from the passenger seat and inspected the damage again. He had hidden his irritation well, something he had a lot of practice with. Though he had only just met Chrissy, it was obvious she would respond better to a gentle approach, which was a relief. From the start, he'd made it his mission to be the opposite of his boss. Most people were much more receptive to taking direction from someone they respected rather than feared. And striking fear wasn't something he enjoyed. But with some people, he had to use a tougher approach, and he always hated it. He'd rather leave being an asshole to his boss.

As his finger traced over the splatters, his lips curled up, a curiosity given she had destroyed a thousand-dollar suit. He should have been grumbling and irritated, especially since the suit was one of his favorites, but there was something about her that he couldn't quite pinpoint. It had been easy to push away his irritation as she apologized, especially since her apology was obviously sincere. Sincerity was a rare thing in his world. And the odd combination of insecurity and fierce determination in her expression had left him wanting to know her story.

The jarring ring of his phone snapped him out of his thoughts. "Get ahold of yourself," he said as he gave himself a mental slap. As if the universe was reading his thoughts, Luke Hardin's name popped up on his screen. Adam inhaled and tapped his Bluetooth earpiece. "Hey, Luke. What's up?"

"Hey, man. I was just wondering if you knew how Chrissy's first day went," Luke said.

"I'm not entirely sure. I stopped by this morning, but I've been swamped, so I haven't checked in with her since then."

A sigh whooshed through the phone. "She said she'd call me when she gets home, but she would tell me it was great even if it was horrible. I don't know if it's a big-sister thing or what, but she always tries to sugarcoat stuff. I figured you'd tell me the truth. Curiosity got the better of me earlier, so I drove by, and it looked like she got a lot done. She was still there, so she must have worked kind of late."

I guess she took the talk about overtime to heart.

"I plan on stopping by tomorrow to check on the scaffolding that's supposed to be delivered, so I'll let you know what I find out." He couldn't tell Luke that he had to stop by to check on the mural once per day minimum because his job depended on it. Mr. Lyones had sworn Adam to secrecy so no one would know he questioned Liam's judgement. No one wanted the richest family in Chicago as enemies.

"That'd be great. Thanks. I better go. I have to pick up another party."

"All right. Enjoy. Before you know it, you'll be in the nine-to-five alongside me."

"I'm actually looking forward to it, believe it or not. Talk to you later."

As soon as Luke hung up, Adam's screen lit up with Mr. Lyones's name.

"Great." Adam accepted the call. "Hello."

"How did the first day go? Did she show up?"

"Yes. It went quite well, actually. She agreed to overtime and has made excellent progress already."

"What's this I hear about scaffolding?"

Adam cringed. Of course Mr. Lyones had heard about the scaffolding. It was like he had eyes and ears everywhere. "It was delayed, but it should be delivered first thing in the morning. Don't worry, sir, I have everything under control."

"I hope so. And remember, this stays between me and you."

The line went dead, and Adam took his earpiece out. He'd been looking forward to Luke coming to work in the office from the moment he heard the city had offered him a job. After all, Luke was his best friend. As with everything else, though, the city was taking their sweet time with Luke's contract. Maybe it wouldn't be so bad if they waited just a little longer. Long enough for the mural to be finished.

After flipping through the channels for what felt like the hundredth time, Adam gave up and tossed the remote on the cushion beside him. Not even three hundred channels on a giant screen could capture his attention. No matter what he did, he couldn't get his brain to focus on anything for more than a few minutes. Mr. Lyones was already unhappy with the mural project thanks to the scaffold delays and the no-show assistant. All Adam could think about was making sure everything went smoothly for the remainder of the project. He needed his boss to be happy when all was said and done.

An idea popped into his head, and Adam picked up his phone to check his email. Scrolling back through several weeks, he found the email with Chrissy's contact information, and before he could talk himself out of it, he typed her number into his messages.

"Hi, Christine. This is Adam from the city. I realized we hadn't given you any information on who to contact if you have issues. I apologize for that oversight. It's something you should've had before your first day, so I wanted to make sure you had it before your second. You can text or call this number whenever you need anything."

Adam hit send, hoping he hadn't just made a huge mistake by giving her his cell phone number. He usually reserved his desk number for people he didn't know, but if he was supposed to monitor the project as closely as possible, he reasoned she needed a way to reach him at all times.

A typing bubble appeared, and he stared at the phone, waiting to see what she said.

"Okay. Thank you."

Adam's shoulders fell. *Well, that was anticlimactic.* He wasn't sure what else he had been expecting.

"Today went well?" he asked.

"Yes, I think so."

"Good."

Apparently, she's not much of a texter. He got up and went to the bedroom to put his phone on the charger. *I sure hope it did,* he thought. He knew he needed the project to go well, but he had a feeling Chrissy needed it even more.

Chapter 5

Chrissy

"Who are you?" Chrissy shouted, the bravado in her voice in stark contrast to the thundering of her pulse. She clutched her Mace, her finger ready on the trigger as the intruder moved around in the supply trailer.

Bang.

On instinct, Chrissy ducked, scanning the area in search of danger. Instead, a muffled curse word echoed from inside the trailer.

"Ouch. Stupid piece of..." the intruder mumbled as he backed out of the trailer, carrying a box of drop cloths.

"Who are you?" Chrissy asked again.

He glanced her way but ignored her as he retrieved some paint from the trailer.

"You better stop right there if you know what's good for you." Chrissy extended her Mace-wielding hand toward the mystery man.

He turned in her direction, his dark eyes boring into hers. With his tanned skin, dark buzzed hair, and slight beard, he looked like the type of criminal whose mugshot would be popular on social media. "Oh yeah? Who says?"

"Me. I'm the artist, and those are my supplies. That's property of the city, and you better drop it." She squared her shoulders, trying her best to keep her cool composure as her traitorous body wanted to run.

The man sauntered toward her as if he had every confidence in the world. "And just what are you gonna do if I don't listen?"

Chrissy gulped as he drew nearer, and she pulled her cell phone from her pocket. "I'm calling the cops."

He reached for her phone, and she jumped backward, sending him stumbling to regain his balance. She held up her Mace as her anger fueled her bravery once again. "You better stay the hell back, or I'll mace you. Don't you think for one second that I won't. I promise you I will."

"Stop. Don't call the cops. I'm not a bad guy. I swear," he said, pleading, his swagger suddenly nowhere to be found.

Chrissy snorted. "Yeah, sure. I totally believe you."

He held his hands up in surrender. "I swear. My name is Damien, and I was hired to be your assistant."

"Who hired you?"

"A buddy of mine knows some guys that work for the city. He hooked me up through this guy, Adam. I didn't catch his last name. He's one of the suits."

Chrissy watched him. His story checked out, but something about the whole situation still made her leery. His fear when she mentioned cops screamed of a previous record, a guilty conscience, or both. She scrolled through her contacts and hit a number.

"Are you still calling the cops?"

Chrissy held up a finger as the phone rang.

Adam's voice came through the line. "Hello, Christine. How are you this morning?"

Chrissy eyed Damien as she spoke. "Well, I'm not sure. There's a guy here getting stuff out of the trailer. He says his name is Damien and that he's my assistant. I just wanted to see if he's legit or if I need to mace him."

"I did, indeed, hire a Damien as your assistant. He was recommended by a friend of mine here in the office. No need to mace him," Adam said, his voice thick with a suppressed chuckle.

"Fine, I'll put the Mace away." She stifled a grin as Damien breathed a sigh of relief.

"On that note," Adam said, "I want you to know that if you ever have any problems with anything, just give me a call. Any time. I'm your go-to guy, okay?"

Chrissy froze, her mind transporting her back to all those lonely years spent longing to have someone, anyone, to call. Even though her brain knew Adam was only talking about the mural, her heart still rejoiced at the thought of having a go-to person at long last.

"Christine?" A hint of concern came to Adam's voice.

She cleared her throat and shook the silly daydreams from her head. "Yeah, sorry. I'm here. I'll call you if I need anything. And please, call me Chrissy."

As she slipped her phone back into her pocket, the cockiness returned to Damien's face. "See? Now can you put the Mace away and finally let me get back to work?"

"I'd love nothing more than to get to work." Chrissy tucked her Mace into her pocket and stalked toward the trailer. "You know, all you had to do was tell me who you were right away, and we could've avoided all of that."

"I tried. You didn't believe me."

Chrissy scoffed. "That was after you ignored me, strutted over here with a threatening look, and tried to take my phone. How was I supposed to believe anything you said then?"

Damien's jaw clenched. "I was trying to get you to leave me alone so I could work."

"If you want to work so bad, where were you yesterday?"

He gave a low whistle. "So hostile. I can see I'm going to have my work cut out for me with you."

"Well, maybe I wouldn't be so hostile if you hadn't shown up a day late and acted like a cocky thief." She put a fist on her hip.

He studied her for a moment, a sly smile spreading over his face before he clicked his tongue. "You're feisty. I like feisty."

The way he looked at her, like he was undressing her with his eyes, made the hair on her neck stand at attention. "I'm here to work and do a good job. I honestly don't care whether you like me or not."

"And what if I do? You're kind of cute, especially when you're mad."

She shrugged. "Then you're crap out of luck, I'm afraid. Go bark up another tree."

"So you're gonna write me off from the start?"

"Look, Damien. I'm here to do my job, and I need you to do yours. It's nothing personal." *Why is this conversation even happening?* She'd only known the guy a total of five minutes, and he'd been a jerk every second.

"If you'd give me a chance, you'd see I'm a decent guy. You might even like me."

"How about we just focus on the scaffold so I can get to work?" She spun on her heels and began gathering the supplies she needed for the rest of the mural outline. She kept her back to the clanking metal poles while she tucked her long wavy hair into a messy bun.

Within minutes, Damien had the scaffold assembled. "Here you go, princess. Your throne is ready to sit all high and mighty on."

"Excuse me?"

"You know, your throne. So you can look down on us peasants and judge us. I know your type. Pretty little artist working for the city thinks she's better than the throwaway hired to be her slave." He smirked as if he had her pegged.

Chrissy's temper flared hotter than the spring sun on the pavement. "You don't know one single thing about me. Just because I'm not flirting, you think I'm a snob? So far I haven't seen anything but hostility from you. And for your information, I'm the farthest thing from a princess. Not one single day in my life has been cushy. Now, are we going to have a problem? Because I'll gladly give Adam a call and have you replaced by the end of the day."

His dark eyes smoldered as they locked onto her hardened blue ones. Her heart seized for a beat at the danger she found lurking there, and her hand instinctively crept toward her Mace.

In a flash, he turned the charm back on and extended a hand. "There's no need for that. How about we call a truce and start over? Forget this morning ever happened."

Her brain screamed for her to call Adam, but that would be the second time within a half hour. She refused to act like a damsel in distress. She'd dealt with Damien's type before and would do it again. And she'd take care of herself like she had all her life.

When she hesitated, his shoulders slouched, and he seemed to finally drop the act and be himself. "Look, I really need this job. I'm trying to straighten my life out, and sometimes I forget I don't have to be a tough guy all the time. Can we please start over?"

All the anger left her body. She knew all about trying to get back on track.

"Okay. Truce," she said, accepting his handshake. *But I never forget.*

Adam

Adam grumbled as he wove his way through rush-hour traffic to the mural site. Stupid, pointless meetings had eaten up his entire day like gluttonous pigs, preventing him from keeping an eye on the mural project like he was supposed to.

The tires crunched on the gray gravel as he pulled into the vacant lot next to the warehouse. His shoulders relaxed as he stepped out and saw Chrissy perched on the scaffold in front of the wall, having made great progress.

At the slam of his car door, Chrissy turned his way, her smile brighter than the sun setting behind him.

"Still hard at work, I see," he said as he approached the scaffold.

"I was so close to finishing the outline I just couldn't bring myself to stop." Chrissy turned and scanned over her work. "I just have a few more lines, and I'll be done. Did you need something?"

"No. Go ahead. I can wait."

"Okay, great. It'll only take a minute."

Adam rocked on his heels and clasped his hands together, glancing around for something to do so he wouldn't be so awkward. He looked toward the trailer in time to see Damien step from the shadows and pick up a bucket of water.

Damien stopped when he saw Adam and smirked. "You must be the suit."

Adam ran a hand down the front of his navy suit jacket and straightened his spine. "If you mean the person overseeing this project, then yes, I am."

"Did she tattle on me again and get me fired?" Damien jutted a thumb toward Chrissy and then moved to dump the paint-muddied water in the storm drain.

Adam worked his jaw before answering, reminding himself to be professional. "No, but you'll get yourself fired if you dump that water in the storm drain. We have protocols in place for the proper disposal of chemicals."

Damien opened his mouth, but Chrissy popped over the side of the scaffold and climbed down.

"Hey, Adam. I'm done now. What did you need?" Her words came out breathy as she shined a bright smile his way.

Adam couldn't help but smile back, feeding off her energy. Everything about this woman was sunshine through a storm cloud. "I didn't need anything specific. Just checking in on how everything is coming along. Making sure everything is going okay for you." He glanced over to Damien, who grumbled and put the bucket in the trailer, sloshing water onto the ground.

Chrissy followed Adam's glare. "Oh. Yeah, everything is going good. It was a rocky start this morning, but everything's cool now."

Adam's features relaxed as he returned his attention to Chrissy, and he hoped she couldn't read how worried he'd been. As much as he told himself his concern had been related to keeping the project going, he couldn't deny part of him *was* worrying about Chrissy. "Good. Remember, you can call me any time for any reason."

Chrissy nodded and dug at the ground with the toe of her sneakers. "I remember. I'll try not to bug you too much, though."

"Don't worry about bugging me. It's my job to make sure you have everything you need to make your job go as smoothly as possible." And so he could make sure his job was safe in the process.

"Thanks. Honestly, as long as I have paint and a scaffold, I'm good." She held her arms out wide as she stood in front of the wall. "The fact that I'm getting to paint a giant mural for the city is more than enough. It's everything I've always wanted. Anything else is just icing on the cake."

"The icing is the best part, though." Adam grinned. Realizing he was being flirtatious, he scolded himself. *Not only is she Luke's sister, you're also her boss.*

An alarm went off in Chrissy's pocket. "Oh, shoot." She scanned the worksite. "I need to get all this cleaned up so I can go."

"I can help," Adam said.

"I got it, boss man," Damien said, picking up the last of the supplies Chrissy had been using.

"Thanks," Chrissy said to Damien. Then she turned to Adam. "Sorry to run off, but I can't be late."

"No worries. I need to get going as well. See you tomorrow. Keep up the good work."

As Adam walked to his car, thoughts of Chrissy swirled in his mind. Every time he saw her, he left wanting to know more about her. Something about her messy bun and faded denim overalls drew him in like a moth to a flame in the most inexplicable way. A quirky dash of chaos in direct opposition to his boring and ordered world. Babysitting the mural was turning out to be much less painful than he had anticipated.

His phone rang, Mr. Lyones's name popping up on the screen. A timely reminder that he needed to stop getting distracted and focus on the task at hand.

Chapter 6
Chrissy

"Look at my big sister, painting the biggest mural in the city."

Chrissy spun around at the sound of Luke's voice, a huge grin taking over her face. She swirled her paintbrush in the water pail, sloshing gray water over the side, and bounded over to Luke and his little brother-in-law, Ben.

"Hey, guys. What a nice surprise to see you two here."

Luke beamed at her over the temporary fencing. "We had to come see it for ourselves. You've got quite the audience here."

Chrissy followed Luke's gaze around the farmer's market, noticing for the first time how many people had stopped to watch her work. "Oh, wow. Now I'm feeling a little stage fright."

"Sorry, I figured you knew. I should've kept my mouth shut." Luke offered an apologetic grimace as he ran a hand through his dark hair.

"No, it's fine. Luckily, I'll only have an audience on Saturdays." She searched the crowd past Luke for his wife. "Where's Aria?"

"She had some homework she had to do." Luke jutted a thumb at Ben. "Ben and I went to do laundry and decided to stop by here on our way home. She doesn't know we're here, or she would've come too."

"I really hope she gets a chance to come see it," Chrissy said, turning to look toward the mural so Luke wouldn't see her disappointment. In the short time they'd known each other, she'd grown to think of Aria as a sister.

"Don't worry, she'll come as soon as she can. Hey, we were about to go hit up the food trucks. Want us to grab you something?" Luke asked.

"Oh, that's okay. I packed a lunch."

"You sure?" asked Ben, his blond curls bouncing as he shook his head. "I don't see how you can stand working while you smell all that food. My stomach is about to eat itself."

Chrissy laughed. With him being a growing thirteen-year-old boy already towering over her, Ben's stomach was always about to eat itself. "I get so in the zone, I don't even notice anything else around me. Not even the smells."

"I don't think anything could make me not smell the food trucks," Ben said.

Luke chuckled. "I guess I better go get Ben some food. Are you sure you don't want anything?"

"I'm sure." A lump formed in her throat as she peered up at her brother. "Luke, I just want to thank you again for getting me this job. This whole thing has been amazing so far. Way better than selling shoes, that's for sure."

Luke shrugged. "All I did was put your talents in front of the right people. Your work speaks for itself. You're extremely talented and deserve this job." He scanned the mural behind her. "I know you're nowhere near done, but this is already looking great. I have no doubt the city will hire you again. They have several more revitalization plans for this area and some of the other up-and-coming neighborhoods. I hope you like being busy."

Chrissy rose up on her toes to give Luke a hug, unable to keep all her gratitude wrangled up inside any longer. "Thank you so much."

"Another one?" Damien's voice ruined the joyous moment like a bug landing in a glass of lemonade.

Chrissy let go of Luke and turned to Damien. "Another what?"

"At least this guy isn't so stuffy. Still a pretty boy, though." Damien scanned Luke's green T-shirt and khaki shorts with a sneer.

"Excuse me?" Chrissy's blood pressure rose as she put a fist on her hip.

"Who are you, and what exactly are you implying?" Luke asked as he took a step toward Damien.

Damien smirked. "I'm the slave for the princess. And you know exactly what I mean. Seems the princess has a type."

Chrissy stepped even with Luke. "I told you I'm not a princess. And for your information, this is my brother."

"Brother, huh?" Damien's brow shot up as he looked between Chrissy and Luke, no doubt seeing the lack of resemblance. Luke had told her she took after their mom while he favored their dad. "Whatever you say."

As Damien stalked off, Luke turned to Chrissy and jerked his head toward Damien. "What's his problem? Need me to take care of it?"

Chrissy shook her head as she watched Damien. "No, it's fine. He just has an attitude toward guys that look like they have money."

Luke gave himself a once-over with a huff. "I didn't realize shorts and a T-shirt were fancy. I just left a laundromat, for crying out loud. Pretty sure people with lots of money don't go to laundromats."

"Yeah, but you carry yourself like you have money. Not in the snobby way, but in the classy way. I'm pretty sure he equates self-respect with snobbery. I'm not groveling at his feet, so he calls me princess."

Luke frowned over at the trailer as if he could see Damien sitting on the other side. "Well, I don't like the guy one bit. You be careful around him. Call me if you need anything."

Chrissy gave him a mock salute. "Yes, sir. I'll call you and Adam if I have any problems. Now, you and Ben better get to the food trucks before they sell out. I'll be fine."

After goodbyes, she watched them disappear into the crowd, and her heart filled with immense gratitude that she'd been given a second chance at life. Without it, she never would've gotten to know how good a person her little brother grew up to be.

Adam

Adam swore under his breath as he threaded his way through the crowds. He always avoided the farmer's market like the plague, as rubbing shoulders with sweaty strangers in a cacophony of sounds and smells was like his personal version of hell. Yet there he was, fighting his way through the throngs and toward the mural.

"Adam?"

Adam searched the crowd for the source of his name and found Luke waving. He wove his way over, heaving a sigh of relief when he got to the small clearing where Luke stood.

Luke clapped him on the shoulder. "I'm surprised to see you here, man. I know how you are with crowds. Speaking of which, you don't look too hot. Are you okay?"

Adam tried to laugh off Luke's comment, but the sound came out a mixture of a humorless snort and panic. "I mean, I've been better. That's for sure."

"So why are you here?" Someone stumbled into Luke's shoulder, and he said, "Oh, and this is my brother-in-law, Ben."

Adam nodded at the young boy chewing a mouthful of barbecue. "Nice to meet you, Ben." Then he turned back to Luke, his brain taking a second to remember why he was torturing himself in the crowds. "I'm here to check on the mural."

"Why would you torture yourself to check on a project? You have people to do that for you." Luke narrowed his eyes, and Adam swallowed and waited. "It's that Damien guy, isn't it?"

Adam blinked, confused by Luke's question. "What do you mean?"

Luke's lip curled in a snarl. "I had the displeasure of meeting him just now. That guy's attitude rubs me the wrong way. I thought maybe I was just being an overprotective brother, but you don't like him either, do you?"

Adam didn't bother hiding his hostility. "No, I can't say that I do. I've offered to fire him, but I think Chrissy's afraid of hurting his feelings or something."

Luke nodded. "Yeah, that sounds like Chrissy. Despite everything, she's got a heart of gold."

Luke's phrasing piqued Adam's curiosity. *Despite everything? What's "everything"?*

Luke glanced at his watch and gave Adam another pat on the back. "We better get going before Aria freaks out. I'm already going to get a lecture about keeping my phone charged." He nodded toward the mural. "Keep an eye on that guy, will you? I don't trust him around my sister."

"Will do." Adam watched Luke and Ben weave through the crowd as guilt settled in his stomach like a brick. While he wasn't lying to Luke, he hated hiding the complete truth. Yes, Adam would keep an eye on Damien. But Adam couldn't tell Luke he was also keeping an eye on Chrissy as an unknown artist. A risk factor. As much as he wanted to tell Luke what was at stake for Chrissy, he couldn't. And for reasons he refused to think about, Adam really hoped things went well for Chrissy as much as for himself.

Just then, a girl walked by selling daisies, the bright-yellow and white flowers conjuring images of the glow surrounding Chrissy when she smiled. Before his rational brain could stop him, he bought the whole basket.

Chapter 7
Chrissy

Leaning against the brick wall in the shade of the scaffold, Chrissy people-watched as she chewed her sandwich. She imagined their backstories as they milled about buying expensive artisan breads and handwoven alpaca-fur rugs. A young man dressed like a hipster lumberjack laughed with a young woman in an olive-green jumper and a floppy brown hat. *Do they know how perfect they appear to the outside world?* She imagined their social media plastered with perfect smiles and celebrity-style pictures. People like the family dressed as if they were set to go sailing on a yacht after lunch fascinated her. *I bet they've never had a stomach so empty it stopped recognizing hunger signals.* She wondered if they were as happy as they appeared, or if they hid skeletons behind the designer clothes in their closets. And she wondered if it was possible for someone like her, who had started at nothing, to ever reach that level of success.

She dipped a baby carrot in some ranch and bit down with a satisfying crunch. When she looked back at the crowd, a flash of white and yellow rising above the sea of heads caught her attention. Squinting, she realized someone was holding a bouquet of daisies over their head as a group of people pressed against them. A soft smile curled her lips as she imagined the man struggling against the mob of people just so he could bring a bouquet to his wife. After a moment, the man broke through the crowd and put a hand on his chest as he panted, his sandy hair looking curiously familiar. If she didn't know any better, she would've sworn it was Adam standing at the edge of the crowd and looking primed for a panic attack.

The man straightened himself and ran a hand through his hair then started in her direction. Her jaw dropped as she saw it was, indeed, Adam walking toward her, wearing jeans and an orange polo.

"Hi," he said as he neared. "Man, that crowd is thick today."

"So I noticed. I thought you were going to be trampled there for a second."

"You saw that, huh?" Adam cringed.

Chrissy nodded, biting her lip to hold back her grin. "Sure did. Are you okay?"

Adam let out a nervous laugh. "Yeah, I am now. I, uh... I don't do so well with crowds, actually. That was kind of a nightmare."

"You must really like daisies, then."

"Oh, a-actually..." Adam stammered. "These are for you."

"For me?" Chrissy's eyebrows shot up.

"Yeah, I hope that's okay. I was... Well, I got stuck in a crowd, so I stopped at a stall for a breather, and they were selling flowers. I saw the daisies, and they made me think of you, so I got them. I mean, you're out here working on a Saturday so the city can use it for publicity, so I felt like I owed you something. Flowers seemed like a decent start."

Seeing a high-powered businessman ramble and squirm as he held out flowers for her made her heart flutter. She took the bouquet, giddiness bubbling inside her. "You don't owe me anything for doing my job, but thanks. They're gorgeous." She retrieved an empty jar from the trailer, filled it with clean water, then arranged the flowers.

He palmed his forehead. "I didn't even think about a vase or anything. Good thing you're resourceful."

"A useful byproduct of my crappy childhood." She cringed mentally at the slip of the tongue. Great. Now he definitely knew she had a dark past. "But seriously, you don't owe me anything. I'll paint every day of the week if you want me to with no complaints. Damien might not like it, though."

Adam frowned at Damien's name. "Speaking of Damien, where is he?"

"On his lunch break." Seeing the dislike for Damien from both Luke and Adam made her question her own instincts. Maybe she was being too nice in giving him the benefit of the doubt. But then again, she knew what it felt like to have no one give you a chance. Sure, he could be a jerk, but that was also a common coping mechanism for insecurity. Most of the time he was tolerable.

"Have you had lunch yet? I could pick up something for you." Adam tipped his head toward the line of food trucks at the edge of the market.

"I was just finishing up, actually. And thanks for the offer, but I don't think I could let you suffer through those crowds just to get me lunch."

Adam laughed with a nod then squinted against the sun as he looked over the crowd. "Thanks for that. Though if you really needed something, I could try. Or just pull out my phone and have it delivered. Yeah, that sounds like a better option."

"Where's your suit, boss man?" Damien dropped his trash in a trash can and leaned against the trailer.

Adam set his mouth in a hard line as he turned toward Damien. "It's Saturday."

"Ah, that's right. We're the only ones that have to work." Damien huffed as he shifted his weight to the other foot.

"You're free to go if you want. No one is stopping you from leaving. And I'm here on official business, so I am working too." Adam stared at Damien as if daring him to give Adam a reason to fire him.

Instead, Damien huffed again and disappeared into the trailer. "Whatever."

Adam turned his attention back to Chrissy. "As you know, we had you work during the farmer's market to garner some interest in the mural and our revitalization plans. One of my colleagues happens to be married to a photographer and had the idea for her to take some pictures of the artistic process. The pictures will go up on the website but also might be used for brochures and fundraising purposes. Would you be okay with that?"

Chrissy scanned her paint-smeared, faded overalls and her green-and-pink floral shirt. Her hand flew to her messy bun and sweat-plastered bangs. "But I look a mess."

Adam eyed her. "I think you look perfect. Besides, if you were painting in a fancy dress, it wouldn't be believable. So what do you say?"

Chrissy's stomach filled with riotous butterflies at the thought of a photo shoot, but she wanted more than anything to become a well-known artist. Part of that dream meant being thrust into the spotlight, ready or not. She nodded, ready to fake it until she made it. "Sure. I'll try my best."

Adam

Adam shielded his eyes with his hand as he peered up at Chrissy perched atop the scaffold. She was in her element, gliding the paintbrush over the bricks in effortless perfection. He'd been to the jobsite several times, but until that moment he'd never had the chance to watch her paint beyond a couple of brushstrokes. The star in a colorful ballet, she exuded a peace and radiance like never before.

Sheila, the photographer, crossed in front of him for a better angle. "This was a great idea, Adam. The camera loves her." She cupped her hand around her mouth and shouted up toward Chrissy. "Hey, Chrissy! Do you have anything you can paint down lower? I'd like to get some shots without the scaffold for variety. Maybe some close-ups of your hand while you paint too."

"Oh, sure. Let me finish this up, and I'll hop down," Chrissy said as she focused on the final swipes for a cloud. Finished, she swung a bucket over the edge. "Here you go, Damien."

Adam stepped forward to take it but stopped as Damien came from the side and grabbed the bucket. "That's my job, boss man."

Adam counted to five before answering, a trick he used to keep his cool during insufferable meetings. By the time he'd finished counting, Chrissy had jumped from the last rung onto the pavement.

"I can get started on some of the detail work on the buildings. Would that be good for the pictures?" Chrissy asked Sheila.

Sheila eyed the area of the mural Chrissy motioned to and nodded. "Yeah, that should work. I'd like a section with some good contrast for the close-ups."

Adam watched as Chrissy set to work with the clicking of a camera shutter as her soundtrack. Never in a million years would he have thought watching someone paint could be so enthralling.

"I never would've thought to use purple and orange for a building," he said, stepping closer to get a better view.

Chrissy flashed him a smile as bright as the daisies sitting in her jar. "You can't be too literal with the colors. You know the building is gray, but it doesn't always *look* gray. Purple hues hide in the shadows, and the sun shining on the edge of a window gives a bright-orange glow. The variety in colors gives the building a depth you just won't get if you paint the whole thing gray. See?"

He looked from the building she'd layered color on to the flat gray rectangle beside it. "Definitely. It really makes it pop out at you."

"Hey, why don't you guys turn around and let me get a couple of pictures?" Sheila made a spinning motion with her finger. "Some behind-the-scenes kind of stuff of more than just the painting."

"Oh. Okay." Adam gave a nervous laugh as they turned and smiled for the camera.

After several shots, Sheila lowered her camera. "Great. That's a wrap. I think I filled my SD card. I'll get a couple edited tonight for you to use right away, but I'll try to get the rest within a week."

"Sounds good." Adam gave her a handshake then turned to Chrissy as Sheila walked away. "I think that's enough for a Saturday. How about dinner to celebrate surviving the photo shoot? I know having your picture taken a hundred times was the last thing you wanted to do, so thank you."

Chrissy looked down at her toe as she dug it into the pavement. "Thanks for the offer, but I really need to get home. I have plans with my roommate. Sorry."

Adam clenched his jaw as he gave himself a swift mental kick in the butt. He should've known better. "Yeah, of course. It's fine. I just don't want you to think I'm the boss from hell or anything. I promise I won't make you work another Saturday."

Chrissy shrugged and peeked up at him through her lashes. "I kind of like working Saturdays. They're good for people-watching. And you're far from a boss from hell. You've been pretty great, actually."

"Good. The last thing I want is to make you miserable on the job." His chest seized as he realized how much he wanted to keep spending time with her, which let him know loud and clear that what he really needed was some distance. "I guess I'll see you Monday, then."

"Looking forward to it," she said, blushing a pale pink.

As Adam walked to his car, he refused to acknowledge the fact that he was looking forward to Monday too. It had been years since he'd felt the beginnings of a crush take hold, and it terrified him. He couldn't let his mind go there. It was just another job, albeit one that could make or break his career, and he would treat it as such. And more importantly, he wouldn't allow himself to entertain any thoughts of romance ever again. He'd had his chance, and he blew it. At thirty-three years old, his life was set on a certain path, and he would remain on that path. He would merely do his due diligence overseeing the work by an unknown artist and then move on. Sure, the artist happened to be cute and sincere, and talking to her awakened things he never thought he'd feel again, but nothing would ever come from it. It couldn't. Not if he wanted to keep his heart and career safe.

Chapter 8
Chrissy

"It really is you."

Chrissy knew that voice. She spun around and gasped, her heart rejoicing as her brain struggled to make sense of the woman before her. It couldn't be possible that she was actually seeing her best friend from the Sacred Hearts Children's Home. "Lilly?"

Lilly set a box on the scaffold step and swooped Chrissy into a hug.

"It really is you," Chrissy said, echoing Lilly's words as Lilly's red curls threatened to suffocate her. "I thought the paint fumes made me hallucinate."

Both women giggled as they stepped apart. Lilly swept her gaze over Chrissy. "You look good. When I saw Chrissy Hardin on the order sheet, I just had to hand deliver it to see with my own eyes if it was really you."

"Order sheet?"

Lilly grabbed the box and held it out for Chrissy to see. "I own a bakery. A Luke Hardin ordered a cake for you. I thought the address was odd, but it makes sense now. And the requested decorations make a lot more sense too."

Chrissy peered through the cellophane window on the top of the box. A kaleidoscope of colors had been splattered across the cake, which was topped with the word "Congratulations."

"So who is Luke?" Lilly asked, wiggling her eyebrows as her green eyes sparkled.

Chrissy grimaced at the suggestive gesture. "Ew, no. He's my brother."

Lilly gasped. "Brother? But I thought you were an only child?"

"Yeah, so did I until almost two years ago. I saw Luke's name in my mom's obituary. Apparently, after I went into the system, she sobered up, and our parents were able to keep the next kid. He's a good guy with no record, so I never saw his name until she died."

Lilly's jaw dropped. "You have a brother. That must be amazing."

Chrissy tilted her hand back and forth in a so-so gesture. "It's been a little rocky. He had no idea I even existed or that our mom ever did drugs, so it started out kind of rough. But he was the one who got me this job, and we've been spending some more time together. Slow and steady wins the race, right?"

Lilly gave a vigorous nod and put her hands on Chrissy's shoulders. "Absolutely. It's only the beginning. I'm so happy for you."

Chrissy reached her hand up and laid it over Lilly's, and a sizable ring snagged her attention. She pulled Lilly's hand in front of her to get a better look. The decent-sized princess-cut emerald glistened in the sunshine, and Chrissy gave a low whistle. "I'm assuming you're married with a rock like this on your ring finger."

Lilly's freckled cheeks flushed. "Yes. For the second time, actually, but that's a story for another day. This time, I got it perfectly right with Zach. He's so good to me."

Chrissy recalled teenaged Lilly spending hours creating vision boards for her future wedding and married life, planning the creation of the family she'd never had. She pulled Lilly into a hug. "I'm so happy for you, Lil."

They stood embracing in silence, their sisterhood forged through trauma connecting them in ways words were unworthy of.

"Am I interrupting?"

Chrissy startled at the low rumble of Damien's voice and pulled away from Lilly.

Lilly extended her hand to Damien. "Hello. I'm Lilly with The Gilded Lilly, the sweetest bakery in town."

"Must be the friendliest in town too." Damien looked from Chrissy to Lilly and back with a questioning look.

"Did you need something?" Chrissy's voice came out with more of an edge than she intended, but she was tired of Damien assuming she was sleeping with everyone she touched.

He rolled his shoulder and worked his jaw. "I was just wondering if you needed any more paint hauled up on the scaffold."

"Oh." Chrissy thought for a moment, trying to regain her bearings. "Yeah, I'll need some more of the blue, but I should be good on the others."

Damien gave her a salute and winked at Lilly before walking to the trailer.

"Who is that?" Lilly asked, peering over Chrissy's shoulder.

"That's Damien. He's my assistant. He helps me move the scaffold and lug all the supplies around."

"Well, he looks exactly like the kind of trouble you used to get into back in the day." Lilly looked away from Damien and raised her brow at Chrissy.

Chrissy's hands shot up in defense, and she shook her head. "Oh, no. Nothing is happening there, and nothing will. I've been there, done that, and have the scars to prove it. Honestly, it's hardly even tempting with how much of a jerk he is sometimes. He's trouble with a capital *T*. I don't want anything to do with my old life, and that includes fraternizing with that type of guy."

"So where does that leave me?" Lilly crossed her arms over her chest and grinned, her eyes sparkling playfully.

"Other than you, obviously. You were the best part of my old life, and I need you in my new one. I've never been more happy to get a cake." Chrissy sighed, her heart elated to see her old friend. "Man, it's been so long. Over a decade."

"Way too long." A chipper tune rang from Lilly's pocket, interrupting their moment. "That would be my assistant, Ruth. I better go before she blows a gasket wondering why I've been gone so long."

"Oh, yeah, I need to get back to painting too. Do you maybe want to exchange contact info?" Chrissy hoped she didn't come off as desperate, but she honestly was. She couldn't let this friendship slip away again.

Lilly pulled Chrissy into a long, firm hug. "Of course. Let's not wait another ten years before we see each other again. We need a girls' night so we can catch up on a decade of gossip."

"That sounds perfect."

After exchanging numbers, Chrissy watched Lilly leave with a slight panic building in her chest. *You have her number. You'll see her again.*

Lilly had been the one and only person Chrissy had ever formed a real bond with until she'd met Luke, Aria, and Ben two years ago. They were supposed to tackle life together. Then Chrissy had fallen in with the wrong crowd and screwed it all up. Lilly had been a hard loss. One she'd never forgiven herself for.

Chrissy knocked on Luke's door and waited, giggling at the commotion she heard through the window beside her.

Luke pulled open the door, his face wild and his hair disheveled. "Oh, hey, Chrissy."

"Am I interrupting something?" She peeked around him and saw Aria sitting on the ground, her dark hair shrouding her as she doubled over in laughter.

Luke glanced back at Aria with a twinkle in his eye. "No, you just missed it." He stepped aside and waved Chrissy inside. "Come on in.

Once Aria can breathe again, she can regale you with the tale of Luke versus the robin."

Chrissy's mouth twitched up at the corners. "I'm assuming the bird won?"

"Definitely," said Ben from the couch.

Luke puffed out his chest as he took a seat at the table. "I'd like to say it was a tie, thank you very much."

Aria climbed to her feet, wiping her face with her sleeve. "I wish you could've seen it. Oh man, that was funny. Luke went outside to check the garden, and apparently a robin built a nest out there. It was dive-bombing him, so he ran inside, but... but..." Aria struggled to contain her giggles, forcing herself to take deep breaths. "But then it followed him inside. After about twenty minutes we managed to chase it back out, but whew. That was hilarious."

"Sounds like I missed quite a show." Chrissy set down the cake box as she joined Luke at the table. "I wanted to stop by and say thanks for the cake. There's no way I can eat it all, so I brought it to share."

Ben appeared instantly and plopped down next to Chrissy, pulling the box toward himself. "Oh, it's from Gilded Lilly too. Sweet."

"Of course." Luke got up to get plates and forks while Aria started cutting the cake with a knife. "Now that I've had their cake, I can't eat anything else. Unless Aria makes it, of course."

"Nice save," Aria said with a wink.

Watching the playful banter between Luke and Aria never got old. Chrissy marveled at how in sync they always seemed, moving together so fluidly, as if they could read each other's minds and knew the other's next move. As happy as she was for her brother that he'd found the true love of his life, it caused a pang of sadness and envy in her heart. Having that kind of relationship for herself would be more amazing than anything she could ever hope for. But it would take a miracle for her to find someone brave enough to see her in her entirety and not run away from the brokenness they found.

"So how's the mural going? Sorry I haven't had a chance to make it out there yet," Aria said as she set a plate in front of Chrissy.

"That's okay. I know you have a ton of stuff going on with college and everything. The mural is coming along well, I guess. I've finished the outlining and base colors for everything. Now I'm working on the layers and details." Chrissy shoveled a forkful of cake in her mouth, beyond ready for a taste after looking at it for half of the day.

"Wow. You're moving right along with it." Aria took a bite of her own.

Chrissy shrugged a shoulder. "Those parts go pretty fast. Kind of like decorating a cake. It's the little details that take the longest, but they're the key between it being good or being great." She tapped the cake box. "And I actually have another reason to love this cake."

"Oh yeah?" Luke asked.

Chrissy nodded, a nostalgic elation filling her at the thought of her long-lost friend. "Yep. Lilly, the owner, is actually my best friend from the children's home. She saw my name on the order and personally delivered it so she could see if it was really me."

Luke, Aria, and Ben all gaped at her.

Aria's face broke into a huge grin. "Seriously? Wow, what a small world. That's amazing. You must've been so excited."

"Yeah, I was shocked at first. I haven't seen her since we aged out of the home. Neither of us had a phone, so we couldn't exchange numbers. I gave her my address when I left, but I didn't stay there long and couldn't tell her I moved. She was my ride or die back then. She kept me out of a lot of trouble, and that's saying a lot considering the amount of trouble I ended up getting into." Chrissy giggled at her trip down memory lane.

"Well, I guess that's why I was forced to make a detour to her bakery a couple of years ago. Who would've guessed that a hangry pregnant lady would lead to me connecting my long-lost sister with her long-lost best friend?"

"The world works in mysterious ways," Aria quipped.

"It sure does." Chrissy savored the creamy sweetness of the cake and wondered what else the world had in store for her. Who else fate would bring into her life. Hopefully Lilly would be the only person from her past to make an appearance in Chrissy's new life, but Chrissy had to admit she hoped the world might bring more pleasant surprises. Like someone she could share life with the way Luke got to share it with Aria. Her therapist told her no romantic relationships for at least a year once she began her recovery, a benchmark she had since surpassed, but she had sworn off men forever. Maybe the idea of romance could still be on the table.

Luke finished his cake and put his plate in the sink. "Sorry to run off, but I promised Ben I'd take him to the gym tonight."

Ben grabbed his gym bag and stood by the door, almost bouncing with anticipation. "I'm going to try increasing my bench press weights."

"That's fine. I need to get going soon anyway so I can make it back by curfew," Chrissy said.

Luke and Ben said their goodbyes, and as the door swung shut behind them, Aria focused on Chrissy. "Is everything okay? It seemed like your mind wandered off there for a minute."

Chrissy bit her lip, unsure whether she should expose her foolish dreams. But Aria had always been a safe space for her, so she took the leap. "Now that I'm feeling more secure in my sobriety, I guess I've been thinking further into the future. Like maybe it's not impossible to think I might, you know, meet someone someday. Romantically. Do you think that's stupid?"

"Of course not. Why would that be stupid?"

Chrissy shrugged, blinking back tears. "Because who would want damaged goods like me?"

Aria pulled her into a hug. "Oh, honey, you're not damaged goods." She let go and held Chrissy at arm's length. "You're one of the strongest people I know. Look at how far you've come and how hard you've worked to get there. You're a rock star, and any guy would be lucky to have someone like you be their partner."

"You really think so?" It seemed like such a far-fetched idea it might as well be in outer space.

"I know so."

If Aria could speak with such confidence about Chrissy's potential future, perhaps there actually was hope. Maybe Chrissy could let herself start to dream a little bigger.

An image of Adam handing her flowers popped into her head. No. He was her boss and off-limits. Painting the mural was the key to her future, and she couldn't let anything compromise that.

Chapter 9
Chrissy

Tires crunching on gravel drew Chrissy's attention away from the cans of paint she'd been organizing. Her pulse kicked up a notch at the sight of Adam climbing out of his sleek black BMW, earning her a mental scolding. *He's your boss,* she reminded herself.

"Good morning," she called out as he drew nearer. "What brings you by so early?"

He slipped the Bluetooth earpiece from his ear and handed her a paper cup. "Good morning."

Chrissy sipped the steamy liquid. "Mmm... What is this?"

"Caramel macchiato. I didn't know what you drank, so I got you the same thing I got. Do you like it?"

She took another sip. "It's like caffeinated dessert in a cup. What's not to like?"

He chuckled then eyed her. "I just got off the phone with the principal at one of the charter schools in the area, Chicago Legacy Academy. Have you heard of it?"

"No, not really. Should I have?" Chrissy frowned, not sure what any of this had to do with her.

"No, just wondering. Anyway, they heard about the mural, and they were wondering if they could bring the high school art students by."

Her frown deepened. "They don't have to ask permission. Anyone can walk by and watch."

Adam rubbed the back of his head. "They meant to make it a field trip. Watching you work is part of it, but they want to come inside the fence and talk with you and all that jazz."

She recoiled and pointed to herself. "What? Why would they want to talk to me?"

"Because you're the artist who's painting the biggest mural in the city. That's kind of a big deal, especially to art students. I wanted to run it by you first, though, before I gave them an answer."

As her brain processed his request, she scanned the area, taking in the cans of paint, the scaffold, and the mural. Everything he said was factual, yet it still seemed so surreal and far-fetched. "I don't know. It seems kind of... fraudulent, I guess. They're going to come here expecting a professional to impart some great wisdom or something, but they'll just get me."

At once Adam's cheerful demeanor vanished, and he took on a wounded look. "It's not *just* you. You *are* a professional, Chrissy. Look at the wall beside you. Who painted that?"

"Me."

"Exactly. You're officially a professional artist. And you have more wisdom to impart than you think. You never know how you might impact or inspire someone."

So much passion filled his words, as if he truly believed them, and in turn, some of that belief trickled through her crippling self-doubt. "Okay, I'll do it. I'll try my best."

Triumph lit Adam's face. "Awesome. You'll do great. I'll call them back and set up the time. It'll probably be tomorrow morning, but I'll text you the confirmed details. And don't worry, I'll be here the whole time. I better get going for now, though."

"All right. I'll see you later." His brisk walk back to his car ended all too soon for Chrissy. Once again, she sent a silent thank-you to his tailor.

No amount of swallowing could clear the lump of anxiety from Chrissy's throat. She tugged at the sleeves of her emerald blouse and smoothed her indigo jeans. Though Adam insisted her normal attire was fine, she'd opted for her nicest outfit that was still casual, hoping it struck a balance between "nice" and "so nice it looks like she's trying too hard."

"Ready to be a show pony for the boss man?" Damien cocked his head toward the bus pulling into the gravel lot.

"It's not like that," Chrissy said, Damien's words like a cheese grater on her already raw nerves.

"Sure looks it, with the pictures and now this. Seems like he keeps finding stuff you don't want to do and making you do it anyway."

Chrissy pulled her attention from the bus and bristled. "Okay, first of all, this field trip wasn't Adam's idea. The principal called him, not the other way around. And second, Adam isn't forcing me to do these things. He always gives me a choice. Am I uncomfortable doing this? Yes, most definitely. But I'm choosing to push myself out of my comfort zone, because if I don't then nothing will ever change. I want to be a well-known artist, and with that comes putting myself out there in ways I'm not used to. Now if you'll excuse me, I have some kids to inspire."

With a huff, she spun on her heels and marched toward the gate. She squared her shoulders, mentally brushing off Damien's remark, and planted a smile on her face broad enough to cover her nerves.

Two dozen teenagers entered the gate and lined up along the fence, giving Chrissy the impression of a firing squad. Adam stood behind them and flashed Chrissy a double thumbs-up. She gave him a slight nod, biting her lip to hide her mischievous smirk, and clapped her hands together. "Welcome, everyone, and thanks for coming. I know you came to talk to me, but I have to start off by mentioning the guy spearheading the project. Why don't you join me, Adam?"

She fought to contain a giggle at Adam's shocked face as he shook his head. Two dozen people swiveling in his direction stopped his protest dead in its tracks, and he turned on a shaky smile. With no other choice, he stepped forward and joined her in front of the firing squad.

"I figured I'd share the spotlight," she whispered with a wink. Before he could reply, she turned her attention to the students. "I'm the painter, but without Mr. Rochester this project wouldn't exist. Feel free to ask him any questions you might have about the business side of things."

The humph from beside her was clearly meant only for her ears and elicited another giggle for her to bite back.

"Going back to the art side of things, I know you're all art students, but I wanted to see what career paths you all are aiming for. Anyone care to share?"

Crickets. All right, new strategy.

"Are any of you wanting to be an art teacher?"

Five hands went up.

"Okay, how about aiming to be a professional artist?"

A dozen hands went up, but one in particular caught her eye. The tall, slender girl at the end inched her hand up in front of her as if raising it too fast or too high would end in certain death. Her long brown hair hung around her like a veil, the sun catching on the purple highlights scattered throughout. Chrissy knew that stance, knew the crippling self-doubt so profound it became a physical force of pain.

Adam nudged Chrissy's arm. "Everything okay?"

She tore her attention away from the girl and blinked back the painful memories. "Sorry, I thought I saw someone I knew. Anyway, those are the two main career paths, but it only covers a little over half of you. What about the rest of you?"

A boy Chrissy would've pegged as a football player raised his hand. "I want to be an art historian."

She never would have seen that coming. "Wow. That would be fascinating. Anyone else?" Nothing. "That's okay, and it's okay if you don't know yet. I've been out of school for over ten years, and I just now figured out what I want to be when I grow up."

A couple of chuckles from the kids served as wind in her sails. "Okay, so I figured I'd start by walking you all through the entire process from concept drawings to actually painting. Feel free to ask any questions along the way. Also, I want to point out that every artist has their own ways of doing things, so what I tell you isn't set in stone."

After a while, the kids broke off into groups to do the assignment from their art teacher, and Chrissy sucked in what felt like her first breath in over an hour. Between presenting, answering questions, and giving a painting demonstration, her brain was mush, ground to a pulp by a freight train driven by her nerves.

Adam sidled up beside her and handed her an ice-cold bottle of water. "You did great."

She took the water and gulped down half the bottle before turning to him. "Thanks. I just hope something I said was useful. I felt like a rambling idiot."

Adam's kind eyes locked onto hers. "You're far from an idiot. I think you did a fantastic job. You'd never guess it was your first time doing something like this."

"Thanks." Chrissy shied away from the compliment and scanned over the students. At the edge of the groups, the girl with purple highlights sat alone. "I'll be right back," Chrissy said to Adam.

Walking toward the girl, Chrissy couldn't help but feel as if she approached her younger self. She was probably overstepping, but the instant kinship she felt spurred her forward. As she drew closer, she searched for a conversation starter. Then the girl shifted and gave her the answer.

"Nice shoes," Chrissy said.

The girl looked around her then pointed to her chest. "Me?"

"Yeah. I love high-tops. I wore my fancier shoes for today, but usually you can find me in my worn-out high-tops." She eased down, joining the girl on the curb. "What's your name?"

She eyed Chrissy for a moment with a look Chrissy knew all too well. The girl was trying to figure out Chrissy's motive. Finally, the girl spoke. "Abilene."

"Abilene. I don't think I've heard that name before. It's pretty."

Abilene's sad features brightened just a tad. "Thanks."

"So you want to be an artist, huh?"

Abilene shrugged. "It sounds nice and all, but it probably won't ever happen."

"Why do you say that?"

The girl stared at the ground. "Because people like me don't get what we want." She looked toward a group of girls whispering together. "No one thinks I can do anything right. And I don't have any money for art school."

Chrissy's heart broke for the sad girl sitting beside her. "Well, I barely finished high school, and now I'm painting the biggest mural in the city. One thing I've learned is that a fancy art school means nothing if you don't have passion and talent. Anyone can be an artist if they want it bad enough."

Abilene tucked her brown-and-purple hair behind her ear and peeked up at Chrissy. "Is that true?"

"Yep. Every single word of it. I had a horrible childhood, and I have issues with learning, so school wasn't exactly great for me. Art is the one thing that pulled me through it all, and look where it took me." Chrissy peered up at the mural.

"So I actually have a chance?" Abilene asked.

"Absolutely."

The principal blew a whistle, signaling the end of the field trip. Abilene and Chrissy stood and began walking toward the fence.

"Thank you," Abilene said. "What you said, it... it means a lot."

"Can I see your notebook and pen?"

"Sure." Abilene handed over a purple notebook covered in doodles.

Chrissy's adrenaline coursed through her veins as she jotted down her phone number. Maybe she was breaking some unwritten rule, but this girl was worth it. "Here. Text or call me whenever you need to."

Abilene's dark eyes widened. "Are you serious?"

"One hundred percent. I'd love to mentor you in any way I can. I don't have all the answers, but I know what it's like to struggle."

Abilene did the last thing Chrissy expected and pulled her in for a brief squeeze of a hug, then she sprinted to catch up with her classmates.

Adam appeared beside her as she watched Abilene disappear onto the bus. "What was that all about?" he asked.

"That was me hopefully inspiring a young girl to follow her dreams even when the world tells her she can't. Giving her the kind words I needed to hear when I was her age." Old wounds were ripped open and raw as her mind traveled down a pothole-riddled memory lane.

"I'm proud of you," Adam said. "That couldn't have been easy."

Chrissy sniffled and watched the bus as it pulled away. "I wish I could do more."

Adam's hand rested on her shoulder. "What you did was amazing. Knowing someone believes in you can make a huge difference."

Chrissy nodded, not willing to put into words just how true his statement was. Without Aria's belief in her, Chrissy wasn't sure she would've had the courage to begin her journey to recovery. Aria and Luke believed in her until she could learn to believe in herself. She would do the same for Abilene.

"Maybe I could start a mentorship program or something. Once I get more established as an artist, of course. Do you think that's possible?"

"Of course it's possible." Adam sounded so sure.

"You don't think it's too far-fetched?" Chrissy felt silly for even entertaining the idea.

"No. I don't think it's far-fetched at all." Adam shook his head. "You sell yourself way too short, Chrissy."

The sincerity on Adam's face gave her pause. He truly believed what he was saying. So much so she started to believe it herself. And the look he gave her at that very moment made her wonder if maybe she could ask for more out of life.

"Am I allowed to come out now?" Damien's voice came from the supply trailer, making Chrissy jump.

"Oh, yeah. Everyone is gone." Chrissy hoped he couldn't tell she'd forgotten he was there at all. Or how she resented him for ruining the moment between her and Adam. Not that she had any business having moments with Adam.

Damien hauled himself off the boxes he'd been lounging on. "Good. It's getting hot in here."

"No one said you had to hide in there." She refused to let his sour attitude dampen her mood.

A strange look flashed on Damien's face for a second. "It's just some legal mumbo jumbo. No biggie. We getting back to work now?"

"Yep." She studied him as he moved about and avoided eye contact. Legal mumbo jumbo. In her world, that translated to having a record, and only a few things came to mind that would prevent him from being around the field trip. But then, with a record like that, he wouldn't be hired by the city. *Here I go, blowing things out of proportion again.* She shook the thoughts from her head and got to work.

Chapter 10

Chrissy

Hopping down from the scaffold, Chrissy scanned over the morning's progress. "Not too shabby, if I say so myself."

"Looks good to me, but what do I know? I'm just the help," Damien said.

"Let's break for lunch." Chrissy walked over to the trailer and grabbed her lunch box, ignoring Damien's sour mood.

"Looks like I made it just in time," said a voice behind Chrissy.

"Aria?" Chrissy turned and rushed over to her sister-in-law, pulling her in for a hug. "I'm surprised to see you here."

"One of my professors canceled class, and my brain can't handle studying or writing any more right now. What better way to utilize my unexpected free time than to visit my favorite sister-in-law?" Aria grinned as she tucked her sleek dark hair behind her ear.

Chrissy laughed. "I'm your only sister-in-law."

"You're still my favorite." Shifting her focus to the wall, Aria gave a low whistle as she scanned over the painting. "Wow. That's a lot bigger than I imagined."

Chrissy followed her line of sight. "You're telling me. When I first started, I was so intimidated I almost couldn't even pick up the brush."

"But you did. And now look at it. It's amazing already."

Both women stood looking over the painting in silent togetherness for a few moments before Aria broke the silence. "I brought a bacon, avocado, and pepper jack sandwich for you. It's Ben's new favorite combo, and he keeps bugging me to have you try it."

"Well then, I guess I better." Chrissy giggled, imagining Ben's persistent badgering. "I usually eat under the scaffold, but we can go around the corner to the bench if you want."

"Here is fine."

As they settled in the shade of the scaffold, the cool brick soothed Chrissy's scorching back. It was too hot for her long sleeves, but she couldn't bring herself to wear short sleeves and expose her past. "It's amazing how much of a difference some shade can make."

"I bet." Aria pulled two sandwiches from her lunch bag and handed one to Chrissy. "It's been a really warm spring so far. Make sure you're taking care of yourself out here."

"I'm trying to." Chrissy took a long drink of water. "You know, all these long hours painting has been giving me a lot of time to think. One of the things I keep coming back to is how different my life was just two years ago. I wanted to make sure I've thanked you for everything you've done for me."

Aria shook her head. "There's no need to thank me."

"Yes, there is. I didn't exactly make a great first impression, but you helped me anyway. If you hadn't slipped me that phone number... Well, honestly I can't let my brain go down that path. That hotline changed my life. It gave me the tools to get clean and start on a new path away from my demons. It led me away from that destruction. Every day that I'm here, I think about how close I came to not having a future at all. You saved my life."

"No, Chrissy, you did that."

"But you believed in me enough to give me hope. Without that, I don't know if I would've had the courage to try. That one phone call led me not just to the rehab clinic but to all the other programs that have helped me and still are. And without you advocating for me, I'm not sure Luke would've given me a chance to be in his life." Her throat closed at the thought.

Aria swiped at a stray tear. "Yes, he would have. It might've taken ten times longer thanks to his stubborn streak, but eventually he would've."

Chrissy's tearful giggle matched Aria's. "Well, I appreciate you speeding things along, for sure." She paused then looked around in awe. "I still can't believe it's real. That this is actually my life."

"Enjoy that feeling. Bask in its warmth for as long as you can. You deserve it." Aria leaned back against the leg of the scaffold and pointed her sandwich at Chrissy. "But stop giving everyone else the credit. People might've helped you out along the way, but you are the one who brought yourself this far. I know firsthand that it doesn't matter how much help you give someone. What matters is what they do with it, and you've grabbed it and run like the wind."

The simple silver urn that once held Aria's mom's ashes flashed into Chrissy's mind. Though Chrissy had never met the woman, she felt like she had. Chrissy had lived the same tortured life and had been headed toward her own bitter end on the streets. But then Chrissy had reached out and grabbed onto the olive branch of hope as if her life depended on it. Because it did. And that one single choice made all the difference. She'd wallowed in bed alone, writhing in agony as her body went through withdrawals. It was her dedication that saw her through her time in the halfway house. Her choice to transition to a sober living facility once her time in the halfway house was up had kept her on the straight and narrow. Even though she longed for the day she didn't need the extra support, she'd had the strength to admit she still needed it. She alone had done all the emotional and mental legwork in her recovery.

A smile curled her lips as the feeling of being indebted to others dissipated like the morning fog floating above the river. "You're right. I did that, didn't I?"

"Damn right, you did. And you'll keep on doing it until you have everything you've ever dreamed of. You can do it." Aria held up her water bottle.

Chrissy tapped her own bottle on Aria's, her heart filling with hope and determination. "Cheers to that."

Aria was right. Chrissy would keep pushing herself and making choices that furthered her recovery. While she used to get high to escape the realities of her life, therapy had helped her see she had the power to change her trajectory. To create a life she didn't need to escape from. Step one was to do everything in her power to ensure the mural was a huge success. Nothing and no one would get in her way. Zero distractions. And that included nipping her growing infatuation with Adam in the bud before it threw a wrench in her plans.

Chapter 11

Chrissy

Sweat trickled down Chrissy's back and pooled between her breasts as she fanned herself with a rag.

"It sure is a hot one today," Damien said behind her as he tapped her arm with a bottle of water.

She turned and took the bottle, the icy water from the cooler dripping down her arm. "Thanks. I definitely underestimated how much heat a giant brick wall can give off." She held the bottle to her forehead before taking a drink.

"You could try wearing less clothes."

Chrissy coughed and sputtered on her water. "Excuse me?"

Damien tugged at the fabric of her yellow peasant top. "You're wearing long sleeves and overalls. You could try a tank top and not be so hot. Maybe some shorts." He grabbed the hem of his black tank top and pulled it over his head. "See? I'm feeling cooler already."

Chrissy turned away, refusing to let him see how much he irritated her. "I'm pretty sure you aren't supposed to be shirtless at work."

"Why? Do I make you flustered?"

The cockiness in his voice grated on her nerves. "Far from it. But you said yourself how much you need this job. I'd hate for you to lose it over something so stupid as having your shirt off."

"You really mean that, don't you?" Damien's voice held surprise.

She took another drink and faced him. "Yes, I do. We might not see eye to eye much, but I know what it's like to struggle and really need a job. I'd never wish that on anyone."

He stared at her as if trying to read her past.

Uncomfortable under his gaze, she swigged the last of her water and headed for the scaffolding. "Let's get back to work. If I can get the base color for the sky finished today, maybe we can leave early."

"Sounds good." Damien grabbed a bucket of light-blue paint and hoisted it to the top of the scaffolding, using a pulley system. "It's a good thing you're not afraid of heights."

She peered down from her vantage point three stories high as she grabbed the bucket. "Trust me, I've seen a lot scarier things than tall scaffolding."

He shot her a curious look, and she cursed herself for oversharing. Especially with Damien. She might help him keep his job, but she was smart enough to know better than to trust him with something as important as her past.

Adam

Pulling into the gravel lot, Adam realized the resentment he'd once had at babysitting the mural was nowhere to be found. But he refused to even entertain the thought of why excitement had taken its place.

Chrissy climbed down as he walked up and ran her arm across her forehead, smearing black paint along her hairline. "Hey, Adam. What's up?"

"You got a little something." He suppressed a smile as he pulled a handkerchief from his pocket and offered it to her. He motioned across her forehead.

"Oh. Whoops." She wiped at the paint. "Did I get it?"

"Yeah, most of it."

She held the handkerchief out for him, but he put up a hand. "You keep it. I'm sure you'll need it again before the project is over."

"Oh, okay. Thanks."

"I thought only old guys carried handkerchiefs," Damien said as he stepped around the trailer.

Adam groaned internally at the sound of Damien's voice. "If you must know, it came with the suit. And I carry it for occasions just like this one."

Damien shrugged his bare shoulder. "Still seems like a crusty old-man thing."

Adam counted to five before responding, something he seemed to do a lot whenever Damien was concerned. "Everyone is entitled to their own opinion." He turned his attention back to Chrissy, who looked as uncomfortable as he felt. "Anyway, how are things going? I see you've made excellent progress today."

Chrissy brightened, and she turned toward the mural. "Yes, I can't believe I got so far today, even though I knocked over a can of paint and made us waste thirty minutes. We got it all cleaned up, though, and Damien dug through all the paint in the trailer and found a similar color, so crisis averted."

"Good. I'm glad Damien has been a help." He swallowed the bitter taste left in his mouth by those words.

Damien crossed his arms against his bare chest, and Adam wanted to smack the smug look from his face.

Adam cleared his throat. "I'm going to need you to put a shirt on, though."

Damien puffed his chest. "Why? Am I threatening your manhood?"

Another count to five. "No, but you are violating rules for appropriate workplace conduct."

Damien stared at Adam for a couple of seconds as if thinking about challenging him but then pulled on his black tank. "There. Is that better, Mr. Conduct?"

"Yes, it is."

Damien scoffed and shook his head. "Man, you suits and your rules. Is every job with you guys like this, or is it just because of Miss Prissy Chrissy over there?"

Screw counting to five. "W-Watch it, now. If you're going to make this a hostile work environment, then you're done."

"She's going to have heat stroke dressing like a nun," Damien said, his eyes wild as he took a step toward Chrissy.

Chrissy sprang forward. "I'm not dressing like a nun. I just don't want everything hanging out for the world to see. It's called modesty."

Damien sneered. "Like I didn't notice the saint hanging around your neck?"

Chrissy's hand flew to her necklace as her mouth gaped open.

"Enough," said Adam, his voice raised and stern. "I think you should go, Damien. Your check will be mailed to you."

Damien stalked over to the scaffold and slapped one of the poles. "Damn it. I'm getting fired for taking off my shirt? I need this job, man. What am I going to do now? Ugh. How could I be so stupid?"

"Wait," Chrissy said, making them both look her way. She studied Damien a moment before turning to Adam. "Don't fire him."

Adam blinked, unsure he'd heard her correctly. "What? But he's being too hostile and making this an unsafe work environment."

She cut her eyes to Damien again. "It's hot, and we're all cranky. And I know what it's like to really need a job. I think we should give him another chance. If there're any problems, I'll call you right away."

Adam clenched his jaw, torn between kicking the guy to the curb and following Chrissy's wishes. The thought of Chrissy seeing him as an inconsiderate jerk made his stomach twist. "Fine." He turned to Damien, his features hard. "It's your lucky day. You should thank her."

Chrissy brushed her hand on Adam's forearm. "Thanks, Adam."

"Promise you'll call me if there's even the slightest problem."

"Yes, sir." Chrissy gave him a mock salute.

Adam had a sinking feeling in his chest as he walked away. When he glanced back, the evil gleam in Damien's eyes made his skin crawl.

Chapter 12
Chrissy

Through all her grunting and straining, Chrissy only managed to move the scaffold an inch. Maybe coming to work on a Saturday without telling Damien wasn't the best idea.

"So much for getting ahead," she grumbled as she slumped against the scaffold.

"Need some help?"

Chrissy's head rose, as did her spirits. "Lilly? What are you doing here?"

Lilly waved a hand in front of her apron then jutted a thumb toward the farmer's market. "Ruth usually does the farmer's market booth, but she's not feeling too great today, so it's my turn. What are you doing here alone? Isn't Damien supposed to be moving the scaffold for you?"

Chrissy gave a sheepish grin. "Yeah, he's supposed to, but I didn't tell him I'm working today."

"Oh?" Lilly's brows shot up.

"He got kind of mad about working last Saturday, and the tension has been pretty high between him and the guy overseeing the project. I figured I would just come by myself without telling either of them to try to keep the peace. I planned on working on the ground so I wouldn't need the scaffold, but I didn't think about needing to move it so I could get to that part of the mural."

"I bet we can move it." Lilly grabbed ahold of one end and nodded toward the other. "You get that end. Remember to lift with your legs. Do we need to go your way or mine?"

"My way. I need to work on the area behind it on your side." Chrissy gripped the metal bars.

"Okay. Ready? On the count of three. One. Two. Three."

Mustering all her strength, Chrissy lifted the scaffold an inch off the ground and waddled backward several feet. "Okay, that's good."

They set the structure down with a clank, and Chrissy joined Lilly to inspect the exposed area of the mural. "We did it."

Lilly brushed her hands together and gave Chrissy a triumphant grin. "Of course we did. We don't need a man to get things done." She turned and inspected the growing crowd. "I better get back to the booth. Come over and get me if you need anything."

"Thanks for your help. This patch of the mural should last me all day, though."

"Okay. But you can still come over, even if you just want to chat. Plus, I have muffins."

Lilly's singsong tone on her last sentence made Chrissy giggle. "I might take you up on that."

She watched Lilly jog back to the bright-pink tent for the bakery, where a line of people was already perusing the goodies on the tables. Her friend's words rolled around in her brain as she began painting. "We don't need a man." All of her life, Chrissy had been on her own, bouncing from one foster home to another until her "troubled kid" label landed her in the children's home. She'd grown accustomed to ignoring her own needs, especially her needs regarding relationships. For her entire life, not a single person had stayed around long enough to form any sort of attachment.

Except Lilly. The day Lilly moved into the home was a day Chrissy would never forget. That bouncy, spunky redhead tore into the room and into Chrissy's life like a tornado, mixing up the lonely, boring days with her larger-than-life personality. For an introverted kid like Chrissy, Lilly's extroverted vibrancy was a ray of sunshine bursting through a dreary fog. Chrissy came to life that day, and they became inseparable.

At least until the cruel reality of life tore them apart. Chrissy had aged out first, giving Lilly her address at the transition house with hopes of reuniting. But without Lilly by her side, Chrissy spiraled into a depression she self-medicated, and that began her path of destructive behaviors. By the time Lilly aged out, Chrissy had gotten herself kicked out of the transition program and ruined her chance at a new start.

Lilly might have been right about not needing a man, but there was no doubt Chrissy had needed Lilly. No amount of denial could change that fact. But the thought of needing someone with such desperation terrified her. *Am I strong enough to survive on my own?*

If she'd asked herself that a year ago, the answer would've been a resounding no. But now, after rehab, lots of soul-searching, and therapy, she was stronger than she'd ever been. It was all her. She pushed up the sleeve of her orange shirt and ran a finger over her broken-chain tattoo. Proof that regardless of her past, she now carried the strength to survive on her own.

She scanned the ever-growing crowd at the farmer's market, taking in the people conversing and interacting with one another. Just because she could survive on her own, it didn't mean she had to. She didn't want to. Maybe it was okay to open her heart to more people. To let people in and even depend on those close to her. Having connections with other people seemed to be the key difference between surviving and living. She was going to live, damn it.

The booth for The Gilded Lilly proved easy to find, the hot-pink tent serving as a shining beacon, but getting through the throng of customers was another story. For once, her stunted growth courtesy of her addict mother came in handy as she slipped through the tiny openings between people, weaving her way toward the front of the booth.

"Hey, get to the back of the line and wait like everyone else," a voice yelled as a hand gripped her shoulder.

"Oh, uh, no. I wasn't cutting," Chrissy stammered as she peered at a middle-aged woman with her forehead scrunched in anger.

"Chrissy, thank goodness you made it." Lilly's voice called out above the crowd. She reached across the table and beckoned Chrissy with a big wave of her arm. "Let her through. She's my assistant."

With a grumble, the woman let her go, and Chrissy finished weaving through the crowd.

Once Chrissy was inside the tent, Lilly draped an apron over her neck and whispered, "Sorry, it was the first thing I thought of. You can go sit in the truck and pretend to work if you want."

Chrissy tied the apron around her waist and beamed at her friend. "I'm here to serve, boss."

Relief and gratitude filled Lilly's face. "Oh, gosh. Thank you so much. I'm swamped." She reached behind her and grabbed a laminated paper. "Here's the price sheet. There's a calculator in the cash box, there under the table. You don't have to do sales tax or any of that. If the price says five dollars, they pay five dollars."

"Seems simple enough," Chrissy said as she reached for the calculator.

Lilly pulled Chrissy into a tight hug and then held her at arm's length. "Thank you so much."

"I'm glad I can help." Chrissy hoped those wouldn't be her famous last words as she turned toward the crowd. She took a deep breath and jumped feetfirst into her new job as a merchant.

An hour later, Chrissy collapsed into a white metal folding chair next to Lilly. "I swear we must've sold a million muffins and cookies."

Lilly fanned herself with a paper bag, the curls piled up on her head wiggling in the breeze. "That morning rush is something else, huh? I'm going to have to give Ruth a bonus and send one of the girls out here with her. I can't believe she's been doing this on her own all this time without a word of complaint."

Lilly reached under the table and pulled out two blueberry muffins, offering one to Chrissy. "If my memory serves me, you always had a sweet tooth. Am I right?"

Chrissy took the muffin and offered her a crooked grin. "We both did." She sank her teeth into the muffin and moaned as the sweet crumbly goodness met her tongue. "Oh my gosh, this is heaven."

Lilly dismissed the praise with a wave of her hand, but she straightened her spine and beamed. "Thanks. I spent a couple of years perfecting the recipe, and I think it's just about perfect now. You'd be surprised at how soggy muffins can get with real blueberries."

They munched in silence for a bit, relishing the lull in activity, until Chrissy couldn't hold back her curiosity any longer.

"So Ruth sounds like a good worker, especially if she never complained about doing this alone. How did you two meet?"

Lilly nodded as she finished chewing. "Yeah, she's a terrific assistant. My right-hand woman. I met her in college in one of my philosophy classes, of all places. It was a morning class, and I almost always brought my breakfast to class with me. One morning I had an apple turnover, and she asked me where I bought it. When I told her I made it, her eyes almost popped out of her head. I started bringing something for her, too, and she was so impressed with everything I made. It was actually her idea for me to open a bakery, but that always seemed like too big of a dream, you know? Then I met my first husband, Steven, and the whole world of opportunities seemed to open up for me. He actually bought The Gilded Lilly for me as a wedding present, but it was named Mitchell's Muffins back then."

"Why Mitchell's Muffins?"

"That was Steven's last name, and mine for a while, obviously. Now I'm Lillian Bryant. I never really liked Mitchell's Muffins anyway, but it definitely didn't feel right to use it after Steven's death." Lilly stared down at her muffin with a mix of wistfulness and pain etched on her face. At once, she tossed the remainder of her muffin in the trash and stood. "Anyway, when I finally opened my doors, Ruth was there to lend a hand. I'd given her recipes over the years, and she really caught the baking bug, so she became my assistant. For over six years now she's helped me build this business from the ground up."

"Wow. It sounds like you two are really good friends." While Chrissy was glad to hear that Lilly hadn't been as alone as she had over the years, she couldn't help the slight pang of jealousy toward her. While Chrissy had been self-destructing, Lilly had built herself a wonderful life full of loving people. But as she had learned in group therapy, jealousy wasn't a very productive emotion unless she channeled it into something to better her own life. She would be happy for Lilly and use her as a source of inspiration.

"We've been through a lot together." A timer buzzed at a nearby booth, bringing Lilly's attention to her watch, and she sucked in a breath. "Oh my goodness, look at the time. I didn't mean for you to get stuck here helping me and not get any of your work done."

Chrissy stood and threw away her muffin wrapper. "I'm ahead of schedule anyway. Besides, I needed a snack, and where better to get one than from my incredibly talented bakery-owning friend?"

Indeed, as the muffin nourished her body, the time spent with Lilly nourished her soul. Not only did Chrissy have family in her life, actual, real, blood-related family, she also had her best friend back. Her brief jealousy dissipated as she realized she had the beginnings of the wonderful life filled with loving people that she'd been envious of. Undeniable proof that she was, in fact, lovable as a sister and a friend. Maybe finding someone to love her the way Luke loved Aria wasn't just a pipe dream after all. Maybe she could have it all.

Chapter 13
Chrissy

Staring up at the spackled ceiling, Chrissy groaned as sleep eluded her yet again. Since the day she began working on the mural, it seemed her mind never wanted to settle down. Her talk with Lilly didn't help matters any, filling her with hopes and daydreams of possibilities. Every time she closed her eyes, images of the life she wanted clashed with images of her past. From the day she was born with drugs in her system until her overdose, life had thrown every curveball imaginable her way. For so long she'd traveled on a broken path riddled with potholes and shrapnel at every step. If only she could just hop onto a smooth and shiny path. To jump ahead to where all her struggles were behind her. Fast-forward to a time when she didn't live paycheck to paycheck. To when she didn't have moments of weakness where she craved the numbness drugs had once provided. If only life could be that easy. But easy or not, she kept going. Step by step, it got easier to push herself forward. She had people in her life who believed in her, and she refused to let them down. Or let herself down.

She pulled back the curtain and peered up at the sky through the window beside her bed, searching for a star to wish upon. But her life was far from a fairy tale, and instead of a star, all she found was light pollution.

Buzz.

Chrissy closed the curtain and looked over at her phone on the bedside table, her heart skipping a beat when she saw a message from Adam asking if she was awake. She grabbed the phone and pulled up her messages, but her thumb froze over his name. The thrill of late-night texting with Adam gave her pause. She shouldn't be reacting like a teen seeing her crush's name on her screen. *He is my boss.* Letting her fantasies go too far could ruin everything she had worked so hard for. It was stupid anyway. She was nothing but an employee to him.

But the smiles and flirtations. The flowers. No. It couldn't be real. Her love-starved heart had merely taken his niceness and twisted it into something more out of sheer desperation. And she couldn't put her future in jeopardy over her silly imagination.

She clicked on his name and edited his contact information to read "Adam/BOSS" so she would be reminded of that fact every time his name popped up on her screen.

"There," she said to herself.

Then she opened his message and typed her reply. "Yes. Did you need something?"

"I hope I didn't wake you up."

A soft smile curled her lips. "Unfortunately, no. Couldn't sleep."

"Okay, good." Immediately the text bubble popped up again. "I meant good I didn't wake you, not good that you can't sleep."

She chuckled and glanced over at her roommate to make sure she wasn't disturbed. "I knew what you meant."

"Okay, good. Again. Anyway, a little bird told me you worked on the mural today."

She chewed her lip as she typed. "Yeah. I hope that's okay."

"Of course it is, but I don't want you to think you have to. Last Saturday was for promotion."

"No, I wanted to. I promise. And I didn't work too hard."

"Good."

She watched the text bubble pop up and go away several times, as if he wanted to say something but wasn't sure how. "Was there anything else?"

A text finally popped up. "Actually, I was wondering if you're free tomorrow? I know it's your one day off this week, so I totally understand if you say no."

All her resolve to remain professional melted away, even as she stared at the word "boss" by his name. *Is he asking me out on a date? Me?* No. A successful, handsome guy who could get anyone he set his sights on couldn't be asking her on a date. It had to be work related. But if he was asking to meet on a Sunday, it probably wasn't good news. "Is something wrong with the mural?"

"No. Nothing is wrong." Then another reply. "I just thought we could chat in a less formal setting. Get to know each other a bit. The city has been finalizing some new projects, and I think we might be working together quite a bit in the near future. I have some unofficial news."

Her heart flip-flopped, unsure if it should rise at the talk of future work or fall at finding out he wasn't asking her on a date. It was better that it wasn't a date, anyway. "I don't have any plans for tomorrow."

"Great. How about I pick you up around noon for lunch?"

Panic shot through her veins. "Noon is good, but I'll meet you at the mural." She would die of shame if he found out where she lived. She had hoped to use Luke's mailing address, but it went against the rules and could get her kicked out. Instead, she just had to cross her fingers that no one decided to pay attention to the address in her file, especially Adam. Deep down she knew getting the help she needed was nothing to be ashamed of, but she didn't want him to see all of the skeletons in her closet.

"See you then."

She felt a buzz just as she locked her screen. She reopened her messages to find the words "Good night." She sent a "good night" back and laid her phone on her nightstand.

She stared up at the ceiling, but instead of the normal depression drowning her, motivation swelled in her chest. Instead of waiting for a better path in life to show up out of nowhere, she would go find it, scratching and clawing for it as she always had. She'd already come so far over the past year. She might not get the giant leap she wished for, but she was headed in the right direction, and that was good enough. And the mural was the biggest step yet. If the news Adam had was as big as he hinted, she might be closer to her future than she'd dared to imagine.

Chapter 14

Adam

Adam glanced at the time and then up and down the sidewalk. As much as he told himself this was strictly business, the nerves rattling around in his stomach didn't hear him. He pulled up his messages to see if he'd missed anything. Nope. He looked down the sidewalk again, and his heart kicked up a notch as Chrissy rounded the corner. Her billowy sky-blue blouse fluttered in the breeze and made her blue eyes even more radiant. She had ditched her trademark painting overalls and high-top sneakers for fitted khaki capris and brown leather sandals.

She jogged up to him, panting. "Sorry I'm late. There was a crazy guy on the bus who tried to pee on another guy. They got in a fight, so the bus driver had to pull over and call the cops. It was insane."

Adam balked at the thought of Chrissy being in the middle of that situation. "I'm glad you're safe."

"Thanks. There's never a dull moment on public transportation. So, what's the plan for today?"

"I figured the first stop would be grabbing some lunch. Unless you already ate." He motioned for her to join him as he began walking then hooked his thumb in his pocket to keep from reaching for her hand. *Get ahold of yourself,* he grumbled in his mind.

She fell in step alongside him. "No, I haven't eaten yet, since you'd mentioned lunch. When I was getting dressed this morning, I realized I had no clue what we were going to do. It's crazy because I don't usually agree to things without knowing the details. At least not anymore. I hope I dressed okay."

"You dressed perfectly. And I'm honored that you agreed even though I was cryptic." Despite himself, he raised a brow and gave a flirty grin.

She tucked her hair behind her ear, and her gaze fell to the ground. "So do you have plans, or are we just winging it?"

"A little bit of both. But first, we are going there." He pointed across the street to an oasis of a park tucked in the middle of sky-scrapers.

Chrissy drew in a breath as they crossed the street. "I didn't know there was a park so close to the mural. I would've been bringing my lunch here all this time."

"It started as a community garden type of thing." He led her down a gravel path to the garden area. Rows of cedar frames filled with rich soil lined the walkway. "This half of the park is for garden-ing for food. The city started it, but anyone can come and care for the plants or harvest the fruits and vegetables. And anyone can plant new stuff, as long as it's legal." His joke earned him a chuckle. He led her farther down the path, past play equipment to a picnic area. "The other half of the park is for leisure activities. There's the stan-dard stuff like a playground and picnic tables, but we also added the little pond."

He watched Chrissy drink in the picturesque view. Sun sparkled on the ripples crossing the pond as birds sang chipper tunes in the trees overhead. Spring flowers shone bright, scattered amongst the white rocks edging the water.

"This is gorgeous."

Adam puffed with pride. "Thanks. The park is part of the beau-tification project, so I was on the planning committee. Some of the guys wanted to scrap the pond due to logistics, but I felt the park just wouldn't be the same without it. It wasn't easy, but I knew it would be worth it. Not to brag, but I'm pretty sure I was right."

Chrissy's hair rustled as she gave an enthusiastic nod. "Oh, you were definitely right. And you deserve the bragging rights. I think this is my new favorite place."

Adam couldn't stop himself from grinning like a fool no matter how hard he tried. "I'm glad you like it. It's one of my favorites too. Now, how about lunch?"

Chrissy turned her head toward him but kept her sights on the pond. "But we just got here."

"I never said we had to leave."

Chrissy tore her eyes away from the view at last and narrowed them as she studied him. "What's got you looking like a possum eating grapes?"

Adam's smile fell away, and his forehead creased as he cocked his head to the side. "I'm sorry, what?"

Chrissy's cheeks flushed. "Never heard that saying, huh? Paulette used to say it all the time, so I forget it's not normal for everyone. I remember her talking about growing up in Mississippi, so I think maybe it's a Southern thing. Anyway, it just means you're looking pretty pleased with yourself or like you won the lottery."

"Huh. I'll have to remember that one. And I am pretty pleased with myself. Come on." He led her farther along the path to a gravel lot lined with food trucks. "Ta-da. Lunch in the park. One of the ways the city funds the community garden is by renting out spots for food trucks to set up. We have six different stations with water and electric hookup."

She nodded her approval. "Genius. I'm impressed."

Adam brushed off the compliment even as it boosted his sails. "It wasn't all me, but I'm proud to say I was part of the team. So, what do you want for lunch? It looks like we've got the Cheesy Pig and ToFunky for the main entrees today. What sounds better, tofu or a grilled cheese?"

"I can smell the cheese and bacon from here, so my vote is for the Cheesy Pig."

"You read my mind. Go snag a good spot by the lake, and I'll grab some food. Is lemonade from the Cup Full of Sunshine truck okay?"

Chrissy's hand flew to her tan leather purse. "I can get my own."

Adam pulled out his corporate card and wiggled it between his fingers. "This is technically a business lunch. I'll buy. Go get a seat before all the good ones are taken."

Chrissy

Chrissy moaned as gooey cheese and crisp bacon danced in her mouth. "This is heaven. Hands down the best grilled cheese I've ever had."

Adam wiped his mouth as he nodded. "I'm telling you, the best food I've ever had has always come from a food truck. It's like magic."

Magic. Her entire world at that moment was magic. Sitting under a weeping willow with the water glistening through its delicate green tendrils as birds chirped above them held more magic than every other moment of her life combined. She sipped her blackberry lemonade, attempting to swallow her emotions.

Adam sipped his tea. "I was thinking about the possum-eating-grapes thing, and I was wondering, who is Paulette?"

Chrissy froze, cursing herself for another slip of the tongue. She had to stop letting her guard down around Adam.

"She was just someone who took care of me quite a bit growing up." She hoped his mind would fill in the blanks with a scenario of someone with a normal life. Perhaps he would assume Paulette was a babysitter or daycare worker. She hazarded a peek at his face to see if it held more questions. The way he looked at her left her exposed, as if he could see past the carefully constructed walls to the little girl crying in the fetal position deep at her core. The little girl begged to be left alone in her sorrow, unencumbered by pressing questions.

Adam stared into his tea for a moment before clearing his throat. "I've been friends with Luke for a few years now. I don't know the backstory, but he told me about how he didn't know about you until around two years ago."

Chrissy squirmed. "Yeah, we didn't grow up together."

"I know Luke grew up with his parents. He doesn't really talk about what it was like for him, but I know about his sobriety tattoo. And I saw his reaction when he found out his dad died. I can make some guesses that it wasn't the best."

That was an understatement, and Chrissy's life had been even worse. But she wasn't ready to talk about that. Not to Adam. She scrambled for what to say to end the conversation without being rude.

"So is Paulette who raised you?" Adam asked.

Chrissy took a deep breath. "Kind of. But that was a long time ago, and I'd rather not talk about it right now."

Adam gave a quick nod. "Understood. I didn't mean to pry."

Chrissy hadn't realized how much tension had knotted her shoulders until it melted away, and it felt like her shoulders dropped three inches.

"Paulette sounds like an interesting person. Maybe someday you can tell me more about her. She must be great if she helped shape you into the amazing person you are today."

Chrissy huffed before she could stop herself.

"What?"

"I'm nothing special." As much as she tried to sound casual, sadness filled her voice.

"That depends on who you ask." His eyes softened like melting chocolate as he gave her the most heartfelt look she'd ever seen on a man.

She found herself suddenly craving dessert.

He broke eye contact first and cleared his throat then began gathering his trash. "How about we talk business so I'm not lying on my expense report?"

Chrissy nodded, magic swirling around her again as she let her heart see the man across from her. In their short time working together, he'd shown her more mercy and understanding than anyone else in her life other than Lilly. She hadn't realized a man like him could exist outside of a fairy tale. Her mind drifted back to the daisies he bought her and all the other gestures that seemed to hint at something beyond a work relationship. *Could it be possible that a Prince Charming like him could be interested in a lowly peasant like me?* Maybe she was drunk on the magic, but for once she let her heart run wild with the possibility of a happily ever after.

"Did you hear me?"

Chrissy blinked herself back to reality. "Huh? Oh. I'm sorry, I totally spaced out and didn't hear a word you said. It's just so beautiful right here, my mind went off into la-la land."

Instead of the scowl she expected, Adam chuckled. "I get it. I come here sometimes for the specific purpose of zoning out. This place can lull you into a trance."

"It sure can." *If he only knew,* she thought.

"Well, unless you want to try another food truck, would you like to go for a walk? What I want to talk about involves showing you something else, anyway."

"Let's go." She needed to get away from this magic before it set her up for a broken heart and ruined future.

Chapter 15

Adam

Adrenaline buzzed through Adam as they left the park. He crossed his fingers behind his back, hoping his news would make Chrissy as happy as he anticipated. "So, did you hear any of what I said back there?"

She let her face be hidden by her golden waves, free from the confines of her messy bun for the first time since they met. "No. I'm sorry."

"It's fine. I just didn't want to bore you with anything you already heard." He gave her a playful nudge with his elbow, and she rewarded him with a grin from behind her curtain of hair.

"No chance of that happening," she said.

"I'll start from the top, then. The tourism board is seeing a lot of positive things as a result of the beautification projects. It turns out tourists like pretty things. Who knew?" He rolled his eyes. "Anyway, those reports have encouraged the city to give the go-ahead to the rest of the projects, including the half-dozen murals they had proposed."

She peered up at him but said nothing.

"They absolutely loved the updated portfolio you submitted."

"Really?" Her mouth fell open.

The smile spreading on his face was unstoppable. "They were very impressed with the pictures of your current mural, and they loved the additional portraits you added. And the even better news is they loved your ideas and sketches for the future murals even more. The job is as good as yours."

She screeched to a halt and grabbed his arm. "Are you serious? You have to be joking."

He shook his head as he swelled with pride at making her so happy. "I'm not joking."

She jumped at him, throwing her arms around his neck and squeezing tight. "You have no idea how much this means to me."

Adam closed his arms around her and let his eyes slip shut, drinking in every sensation. He hadn't realized how much he missed having someone to hold, and Chrissy fit so perfectly in his arms. "I'm so happy for you, and I'm glad you're happy. A little part of me was afraid you'd be overwhelmed by so much work."

Chrissy pulled back, her face radiant. "Are you crazy? I need the work, and I want it. More than anything. I'll take every opportunity they want to give me."

He relished the warmth of her in his arms for a second more before making himself break away. He pointed across the street with a gleam in his eye. "How about some ice cream to celebrate? Well, technically it's frozen yogurt, but it's some of the best."

Minutes later, with frozen yogurt in hand, they continued their walk, inching closer to the big reveal. He took a bite of his red-velvet birthday-cake swirl and let the icy sweetness soothe his nerves. "How's yours?"

Chrissy made an *mmm* sound as she savored her bite of double-fudge brownie. "I've never had frozen yogurt before, but Yo Mama's Yogurt Mart will be my go-to place from now on. This is heavenly. Are all the flavors this good?"

Adam held his bowl toward her. "Here. Try mine and see for yourself."

"Are you sure?"

"I wouldn't offer if it wasn't okay."

She dipped her spoon into his bowl and took a bite. "Mmm. That's really good too. How do you know all the best places?"

"One of the perks of working for the city. I get to hear about all the new places before they even open."

They walked in silence as they ate, finishing their dessert just as they approached the riverfront walkway. Adam regretted getting two scoops as his stomach fluttered. He led Chrissy through the gate and stopped by a concrete wall.

"What do you think?" he asked as he turned toward her.

She shielded her eyes with her hand as she took in the view. Sunlight sparkled as it danced across the deep-blue water. The wind whipped her long hair around her face. "It's beautiful."

Watching her appreciate the beauty, he couldn't help but find her the most beautiful sight to behold. "Good. You'll be seeing a lot of it."

She whipped around and trapped her hair in her hand. "What do you mean?"

He let a broad grin take over his face as he waved his arm toward the concrete wall lining the walkway. "This big wall was put up to keep people from sneaking into concerts and other stuff that happens here on the riverfront. It works, but the problem is that it's kind of an eyesore. One way to make a giant slab of concrete pretty is to paint it. That's where you come in. The city added this wall to the list of murals right before you submitted your portfolio, so you'll be getting this one too."

Chrissy

Chrissy let her eyes travel the length of the concrete wall. "This thing is eight feet tall and has to be at least a hundred feet long. That would take forever to paint."

Adam beamed at her, clearly pleased with himself. "I hope you're okay with having your time booked for the next year or more on this project alone. Combined with the others, the city will have work lined up for you for several years. If you want it, of course."

Her eyes filled with tears of gratitude for the... Well, she'd lost count at this point. Her knees wobbled at the thought of how his news impacted her life. Painting the mural had turned out to be merely the beginning of a solid path for a better future. More than she had ever let herself hope for. She sank onto the concrete step and tucked her forehead into her knees.

Adam dropped down beside her and laid his fingertips on her arm. "Are you okay? Wh-What's wrong? I didn't mean to upset you."

She shook her head, her forehead rocking between her knees as she fought for words. "I'm not upset." She peeked a sideways glance at Adam's stricken face. Her chest ached as a wall around her heart crumbled to dust. She raked in a breath as she raised her head and looked out over the water. "Nothing is wrong. I'm just overwhelmed."

"You don't have to take the job. I won't be mad or anything if you decline. No one will. It's totally up to you."

"No, it's not that. I want the jobs. All of them. More than you could possibly know. I'm overwhelmed by how much my future just changed. Thank you." As she gazed at him, warmth and compassion emanating from his every pore, something stirred inside her for the first time in a decade. Desire. She craved that man's lips on hers so much her mouth watered. A longing awoke within her core, a sensation she'd long ago written off for dead.

His eyes darkened as they flicked toward her mouth, as if he also felt the intense electricity buzzing between them. He brushed her wild hair from her cheek, his fingertips leaving a trail of heat in their wake. His eyes dipped to her mouth again as his Adam's apple bobbed.

Chrissy's breath caught in her throat as he inched a little closer, his eyes questioning.

A cruising riverboat blared its horn, making them both jump. Chrissy yelped and then covered her mouth with her hand. She hazarded a sheepish grin at Adam as she giggled at herself. "That thing just about gave me a heart attack."

Adam let out a nervous chuckle as disappointment flashed across his features. "Yeah, it startled me too."

An awkward silence stretched between them, the moment ruined. Chrissy glared at the river cruise and sent a mental curse to the captain.

Adam cleared his throat as he peered out over the water. "I knew you wanted to paint, obviously, but I didn't realize how much it really meant to you."

Chrissy pulled her flyaway hair to one side and pinned it down with her hand. "It's my dream to make a living through my art. Knowing I can do that for at least a year, probably more, is beyond anything I dared to hope for."

"What is it about painting that you love so much?"

She contemplated his question for a moment, searching for the words to do her feelings justice. "I guess one of the things I love about art is finding the beauty in a moment and celebrating it."

She felt him studying her as she looked out over the river and to the sparkling windows in the buildings on the other side.

"But there's more to it than that. Isn't there?"

She cast a sidelong glance at him before looking back at the water. "I'm sure you're smart enough to have figured out by now that I haven't had an easy life. Especially since you know Luke and I grew up without knowing each other. Growing up in the foster care system isn't an ideal childhood. Paulette was the director of the Sacred Heart Children's Home I spent my teen years in. I'll spare you the gory details, but being able to find the beauty in the deepest, darkest moments is what kept me going. It's what pulled me through to the other side of things each and every time. All of my art—the paintings, sketches, everything—has been about celebrating life. It's therapeutic in a way."

"I'd love to see some of your other work."

Grief overtook her smile. "Unfortunately, I don't have any to show you other than the stuff you've already seen. I've never been able to keep any of it, for one reason or another." Her throat tightened as she imagined her art being tossed in the trash every time she had to leave it behind. "Once I get a place of my own without a roommate, I'd love to start painting for myself again. One of these days I'd love to experiment with darker artwork exploring the ugly and raw emotions that connect us all as humans, but I don't think I'm ready yet."

Adam moved his hand toward her knee but pulled it away and cleared his throat. "Thank you for trusting me with that. For what it's worth, I think you're extremely talented and anything you create will be amazing."

She shrugged, not believing his praise. "I don't know about all that, but I hope you're right. I don't have a lot to fall back on. I'm not exactly cut out for getting a college degree."

"Why do you say that?" He frowned down at her.

She sighed, not wanting to chase him away but unable to lie. "Things happened during my mom's pregnancy that left me with some... deficiencies, I guess you could say. Numbers and the written word have never been my friends. One of the reasons I like art so much is because there is no right or wrong. Art is subjective. You can't spell a painting wrong or add up two sketches wrong."

Adam stilled beside her, and she braced herself for the inevitable distancing. She didn't tell many people about her learning issues and honestly surprised herself by telling Adam. But she needed him to know so he could bow out before she let too many guards down. As he inhaled, she could almost hear the wheels turning in his head as he sought a way out of the awkwardness.

"I have a stutter."

Wait, what? Her eyes shot to him, and her brows knit together.

He glanced at her, the embarrassment on his face signaling his sincerity. "I'm pretty good at controlling it now, but it's taken a lot of work. As a kid, though, it was so bad it would take me almost five minutes to say a single sentence. I pretty much gave up on talking as a preteen. The other kids bullied me relentlessly whenever I was forced to talk. I actually flunked sixth grade because I hated school so much and just didn't even try."

Chrissy frowned at the ground, her brain struggling to reconcile the perfect man beside her with the image he painted. "Did your parents help you? You obviously didn't give up forever because look at you now."

His shoulders drooped. "They tried to help, but they didn't really know how."

She sensed there was more to the story surrounding his parents but didn't want to ask and derail his telling of it. "So what happened?"

"I had to do summer school after I flunked. They'd hired a new teacher, Mrs. Thomson, who happened to be married to a speech pathologist. What are the odds? I don't know why, but she took me on as her own personal project. That woman had the patience of a saint, never once groaning or rolling her eyes as I fought my way through a sentence. She taught me to speak slowly and deliberately so my brain had time to think before my mouth tried to form the words. There are certain words I avoid at all costs, and I learned replacements. Stress is a huge trigger, so I make sure to take a couple seconds to breathe before I speak, which is probably the most valuable tool she taught me. I use it literally multiple times a day, every day."

"Wow. I never would've guessed."

He nodded and peered at the river. "Most people don't know. After twenty years of practice, it's all second nature to me now. I still struggle with it, just not outwardly. If I get super stressed or exhausted it can get really bad, but I'm pretty good at avoiding that."

Chrissy studied his profile as he focused on a boat gliding through the water. Slight sandy stubble peppered his typically smooth jawline. The illusion of a perfect man vanished, but in its place, she saw something even better. Instead of impossible perfection he became genuine and vulnerable. Real and raw. Maybe there was a tiny chance he might not turn away from her if he learned the truth.

"Thank you for trusting me with that," she said.

He looked over, making eye contact at last. "It's only fair after you trusted me with yours."

Chrissy wanted to get lost in the depths of those dark eyes but forced herself to look back at the concrete wall. "I'm still in shock that I have work lined up for at least a year. It's all so surreal and more than I could've dared to ask for."

Adam laughed as he climbed to his feet, then he offered his hand to help her up. "I promise you it's real. Let's continue the walk, and I'll tell you the ideas the board has for this project."

She slipped her hand in his and let him pull her to her feet. She couldn't help but see the metaphor in how he'd also pulled her up and away from her past. And she was inching closer to making her dream a reality.

Chapter 16

Chrissy

Still floating on cloud nine from her day with Adam, Chrissy pushed open the bakery door, a charming bell dinging overhead. After she and Adam had said their goodbyes, Chrissy had found herself not wanting to go back home and ruin her good mood just yet, so she'd asked Lilly if she was up for a visit. When she stepped inside the bakery, her senses flooded with sweet, sugary smells and bright, cheerful colors, leaving no doubt she'd found the right place.

"I'll be right there!" a voice called from somewhere in the back. A woman with a blunt black bob appeared in the doorway, the name "Ruth" embroidered on her apron. "Hello. Welcome to The Gilded Lilly. What can I get for you?"

"Oh, actually I stopped by to see Lilly." Chrissy squirmed, self-conscious about her last-minute visit.

"You must be Chrissy. I've heard so much about you." Ruth gave Chrissy a friendly smile. She leaned through the doorway she'd just come through and shouted. "Hey, Lil! Chrissy is here."

Lilly appeared in the doorway at once, her flurry of red curls tied into a pile on the top of her head. "Hey. I was just finishing up some dishes. Sorry, I thought I could get them done before you got here."

"It's okay. I'm early." Chrissy motioned to the clock above the register.

"Come on back. We can talk while I finish up," Lilly said then turned to Ruth. "You can go ahead and lock up for the day."

"You got it, boss," Ruth said, slipping the apron over her head.

Chrissy wondered how much Lilly had told Ruth about her and hoped Lilly had left out the nitty-gritty details. She followed Lilly through the door and into a huge kitchen filled with shiny stainless steel. "Thanks for letting me stop by on such short notice."

Lilly stopped at the largest dishwasher Chrissy had ever seen and loaded a few more pans. "Are you kidding? You can stop by whenever you want." She studied Chrissy for a moment. "You look awfully happy today. I've never seen you with such a glow. What's up?"

"I'm just glad I finally get to catch up with my best friend after all these years." Chrissy could tell by the look on Lilly's face that she knew there was much more to the story. But she didn't dare tell Lilly about Adam. She couldn't take the chance of jinxing herself and bursting her bubble of hope by speaking the words out loud. And there was still that pesky problem of him being her boss. She wasn't willing to give up her budding career, but apparently her heart wasn't willing to give up its crush on Adam either. Instead of tackling any of that mess, she leaned against the counter next to the sink and looked around the kitchen, trying to divert Lilly's attention. "I still can't believe you own your own bakery. It's amazing. Teenage us never would've believed it."

Lilly grinned as she pushed buttons on the dishwasher. "I still can't believe it myself. Every once in a while, I stop and look around in awe of it all."

"Remember how we used to daydream about being able to control our own food?" A sad laugh escaped Chrissy at the memories.

"No more eating whatever the foster families or children's home served us, whether we liked it or not. No more hunger pains." Lilly paused, giving them a moment to sit in their shared grief, then motioned for Chrissy to follow her. "I think I took the food experimentation to the extreme, though."

Chrissy followed her up some stairs and into the second-floor apartment. The emerald-green couch and pink-and-green floral rug matched the pinks and greens of the bakery. "This place is so you. I love it."

"Thanks. Luckily, Zach is fine with my obsession with pink, and he refused to let me get rid of my favorite rug. I told him we could get something more manly, but he said he loved it because it reminds him of me." Lilly's hand went to her chest as she swooned.

"I'm so glad you're happy. Not that I ever doubted that you'd be successful. You were always the more disciplined one out of the two of us." Chrissy meant it. She really did. But that didn't stop a touch of jealousy and self-pity from gripping her chest.

"Meh, a lot of it is luck. It took a long time to get here." Lilly turned and sank into a chair at the dark wood table in her eat-in kitchen. "Have a seat and tell me what's been up with you."

Chrissy sat across from her and propped her chin in her palm. "Well, it's been rough, I'm not gonna lie. After I aged out... I guess you could say I went off the deep end. I'm still working on the whole food thing and figuring out what I like. After spending my whole childhood eating whatever was handed to me and getting smacked if I didn't, most of my adulthood has been spent homeless and eating whatever I could find."

"Oh, Chrissy, that's horrible."

"That's life." She shrugged, though her burning eyes belied her turmoil. "But things are looking up for me now. I met Luke and his wife, Aria. She swooped in during my darkest hour and gave me the tools to pull through. This new beginning, a relationship with Luke, the opportunity to establish myself as an artist, and my hope for a better future all stem from Aria's olive branch of kindness. I've been blessed to get into some programs to get my life on the right track."

Lilly reached for Chrissy's hand. "I have no doubt you'll get there. You've been a fighter since the day I met you. And so fiercely strong."

"I don't feel very strong." Talk about an understatement.

"Of course you are. Only a strong person can come through what you have and make a better life for themselves."

A tiny smile tugged at Chrissy's lips. "I guess you're right. And I've finally been able to control my food, even if I'm struggling. I don't know how it was for you, but that very first shopping trip was a completely overwhelming disaster. I didn't know anything about buying food or what I even liked."

"Yep. I was the same way. At first I just kind of copied what the other college kids were buying. Then I started getting one or two things that caught my eye."

Relief wasn't a strong enough word to describe the feeling coursing through Chrissy. Someone else understood exactly how daunting buying food could be. "I was bawling from my first disaster of a shopping trip when I went to hide at Luke's house. It's kind of become home base for me even though I don't live there. Aria grew up poor, too, so she took pity on me and used her perfected art of tough love to talk me off the proverbial ledge. She helped me make a template for a grocery list with basics to give me direction but let me fill in the blanks. Like for sandwiches I needed bread, meat, cheese, and condiments, but then I could choose white or wheat bread, turkey or ham, and so on."

"Aria sounds wonderfully helpful."

Chrissy nodded. "Oh, she definitely is. If I like something she cooks, I leave with the recipe and a shopping list. I'm finally gaining some confidence and branching out on my own with some stuff. I'm finding pretty much everything but fish tastes good."

Lilly giggled then sprang from her chair. "Oh, you're the perfect taste tester, then." She pulled a box from her refrigerator and set it on the table. "Want to try my new blueberry-lemon cheesecake? It's my first try at actually flavoring the cheesecake and not just doing swirls or throwing some toppings on."

"Are you kidding? Of course. That sounds delicious." Chrissy's mouth watered as Lilly set a slice onto a plate and handed it to her. The sweet, creamy cheesecake danced on her tongue with tart lemon and sweet blueberry. "This is the best thing I've ever had. You have to sell this."

Lilly clapped and squealed with glee. "It's so good, isn't it? I was so excited when I first tasted it. I'm thinking of making it a spring special and doing limited quantities, though, because it's a bear to make just right."

"I guarantee you'll sell out every time. In fact, I might have to stop in and get me a slice every time I have some spare cash." So maybe once, since she never really had spare cash.

Lilly gave a dismissive wave. "You can have whatever you want, whenever. Ruth already knows not to take a single cent from you."

"You don't have to do that, Lil. I'll pay for whatever I get."

"Nonsense. Family doesn't pay."

Family. A word so many people threw around without understanding the true gravity of it. But people like her and Lilly, people who never had family to speak of, understood just how much the word meant. Her smile felt bittersweet as her eyes burned with forming tears. "Thanks, sister."

Chapter 17

Chrissy

"There's no bird poop on the cars." Luke joked with Chrissy as she squinted at the mural.

She chuckled and spun around, sticking her hand on her hip in a dramatic flare. "I'm supposed to be painting the beauty of the city, and that happens to not include bird poop. For your information, I was trying to decide if the lighting is right on that car."

"I think it looks great, but what do I know? You're the artist." Luke handed Chrissy a large cup. "Here. I figured you might be thirsty."

Chrissy gulped down the ice-cold liquid and studied the plain white cup, searching for clues. "What is this? It's delicious."

"Gummy bear lemonade. I thought it sounded interesting."

She took another drink. "I think this is going on my favorites list. Where did you get it?"

"There's this park a couple of blocks down that has an area for food trucks. One of them sells nothing but lemonades. A Cup Full of Sunshine. Have you heard of it?"

Chrissy took another sip to disguise her gulp of uneasiness. She didn't like keeping secrets from Luke, but she also wasn't ready to tell him she had a crush on his friend. Who also happened to be her boss. "Yeah, I actually went there yesterday."

Luke's expression contorted in exaggerated surprise. "Oh, really? That's funny because Adam mentioned going there yesterday too."

She busied herself with brushing the loose gravel from the side-walk with her sneaker and decided to stick to the objective facts, leaving her feelings out of it. "I actually met him there."

"So why didn't you mention that when you called to cancel Sunday brunch? I thought you were taking it easy because you over-worked yourself."

Chrissy shrugged and kicked some more rocks with her toes, searching for a way out of her lie. "I was going to take it easy, but then Adam said he had something he needed to talk to me about. It was a business meeting, so I can't really say no to that. He's my boss."

Luke crossed his arms over his chest. "Man, I've been missing out. I've never had a business meeting that entailed lunch at a park followed by a stroll along the river while I eat ice cream."

Chrissy winced. "How did you find out?"

"I stopped by to finalize some things before I start working there, and I accidentally grabbed Adam's expense report off his desk along with some other paperwork. When I brought it back to him, he told me he'd taken you on a tour of some of the beautification projects. What I was wondering was why you didn't tell me. Why lie?" He gave Chrissy's arm a gentle nudge with his elbow.

She dragged her eyes to meet his, expecting judgment but finding hurt instead. "I'm sorry I didn't tell you the truth. Honestly, I'm not really sure why I didn't."

"Do you like him?"

The question caught her off guard. Sure, she'd had fantasies of a world where someone like Adam might choose to be with someone like her. She'd let herself fantasize about being good enough for him, but she might as well wish for a pet unicorn. "Even if I did, what difference would it make?"

"So you do?"

She threw her hands up in the air with a huff. "Yeah, okay, fine. I might like him a little. So what? It's not like anything will ever come from it, so I don't want to focus on it, okay? Yesterday was just a friendly business meeting. Nothing more."

Damien walked back through the fencing, returning from the dumpster. Luke took Chrissy by the elbow and led her around the corner, out of earshot.

"Why wouldn't anything ever come from it?" he asked.

"Do I really have to spell it out for you? Look at him, and look at me. One of his suits cost more than my entire wardrobe. He's so sophisticated and respectable. Why on earth would he even look at someone like me, let alone be interested?"

Chrissy turned away, but Luke ducked into her sight line. "You listen to me. You are a good person. Money doesn't make someone a good person. Trust me. I see horrible rich people every single day. You have a past, but so does everyone. Adam is a decent guy, but even he has some skeletons in his closet. He's not above you the way you think he is, and I'm confident he doesn't see himself as above you either. Only you do. But you shouldn't. You are a talented artist with a bright future ahead of you. More importantly, you are loyal to those who love you and you have a huge heart." He picked up her left arm and pulled up her sleeve, revealing her sobriety tattoo. "You are one of the strongest people I know and have overcome so much in your life. You're worth so much more than you think. Whoever you end up spending your life with will be a lucky man."

Chrissy dropped her head in her hands, humbled by Luke's kind words. She thought the world of her younger brother, so to hear him reciprocate the sentiment filled her heart with the hope that maybe his words were true.

Luke pulled her in for a hug. "I know I can come off a little harsh and overprotective sometimes, but I don't want you to be afraid of me. You can tell me anything, and I promise I'll try to keep my cool even if I'm freaking out on the inside. Ben is giving me lots of practice." He chuckled as he let go of her.

She wiped her cheeks and giggled. "Hopefully he's not as much of a handful as I was as a teen." She smiled down at the ground as she scuffed the toe of her shoe on the sidewalk. "And I guess I kind of do like Adam. The idea of a meaningful relationship seems so far-fetched, but it doesn't stop me from wishing for one. It's just hard for me to admit it, even to myself, because I still feel so damaged."

"But you're not broken beyond repair. You're on the right path now. Focus on that." His phone dinged in his pocket. "Dang, I lost track of time. I better get going. Are you good?"

She nodded and followed him around the corner and back to the jobsite. He was right. She needed to let go of the past and focus on her future.

Adam

Finally getting a break between meetings, Adam sank into his plush black leather chair. He typed in his password and pulled up his email, determined to accomplish something other than keeping his eyelids pried open. An email from Sheila, the photographer, caught his eye. His breath hitched as he clicked on the attachment and his screen lit up with a collage of Chrissy. She radiated pure joy as she painted the mural, the sun glistening off her golden hair. He clicked through the images, each one a masterpiece, until he reached one showing the two of them, arm in arm. He sat transfixed, overwhelmed by the sensations the image stirred deep within. They looked natural together, like they belonged in each other's arms. His thoughts wandered back to sitting at the riverfront. Before the boat had startled them both, she'd looked at him with those sparkling blue eyes that put the river to shame. He'd been so ready to throw caution to the wind and caress her lips with his.

"What's that?"

Adam jumped and looked over to find Luke filling his doorway. He knew he looked like a deer in headlights, but he was powerless to change it. "Wh-What's what?"

Luke nodded toward Adam's window. "Why am I seeing my sister reflected on your window?"

Heat traveled up Adam's neck and to his cheeks. "I... um... It's the pictures."

Luke cocked an eyebrow and waited.

Adam counted to five and took a deep breath. "I had Sheila come and take some pictures of the mural. Behind-the-scenes stuff. The tourism board wanted some for promotional purposes. Sheila just sent the proofs, so I was going through them."

Luke pushed off the doorway and rounded the desk, leaning down to see the screen. "By the look on your face when I walked in, you must like this one."

Adam stiffened, hyperaware of Luke inches from his shoulder. He slowly turned as Luke straightened. "I..."

"You like her, don't you?"

Oh no. "Y-You don't have to worry about me. Chrissy is an amazing woman, don't get me wrong, but you know I'm a bachelor for life now."

Luke leaned against the window frame, and Adam squirmed under his studious eye. "Does Chrissy know about Beth?"

At once Adam's stomach knotted and threatened to spill its contents. Though it played through his mind each and every day, he hadn't heard that name spoken out loud in probably a year. He gulped in air and sank back in his chair.

"I take that as a no," Luke said. "Look, Adam, I know that's all still raw for you, but I had to ask. I'm not the kind to beat around the bush, especially when it comes to family, so I'm going to give it to you straight. You like my sister. There's no doubt in my mind after seeing how you stared at that picture. You're my friend and a good guy, but Chrissy is my priority here. She's been through more in her thirty-one years than most people go through in ninety. Do both of you a favor and be upfront about your demons."

Adam scrubbed a hand over his face. "Is it that obvious?"

Luke nodded, one corner of his mouth twitching up.

"Shit." Adam groaned and propped up his forehead with his hand, his elbow on the desk. "I didn't mean to like her. Sorry. She's just so... I don't even know what to say without sounding corny. You know I swore off ever getting involved with anyone else, and I'm trying my best to stick to it, reminding myself constantly that I'm meant to be a lifelong bachelor. And I know Chrissy is the last person I should be interested in. She's your sister, and I'm her boss, for crying out loud. But it seems like no matter how many times I tell myself that, I just won't listen. I don't know what to do."

Adam waited for the wrath of a brother protecting his sister from a murderer, but instead a hand patted his shoulder. Where he expected to see fire in Luke's eyes, he found sympathy.

"I'm using one of Aria's lines here, but it sounds like the first thing you need to do is give yourself some grace. What happened with Beth wasn't your fault, and you have to stop blaming yourself. But one thing is for sure. Whatever you do, don't lie. If Chrissy gives you her trust, don't break it."

With one last pat on Adam's shoulder, Luke walked out of the office, leaving Adam reeling from their conversation. Adam wished he could believe Luke's confident claim that he wasn't to blame, but he'd never been able to shake off the guilt. Though he knew he should tell Chrissy, the idea petrified him. For once, he was glad he didn't have time for an end-of-the-day visit to the mural. Maybe he could grow some courage overnight.

Chapter 18

Adam

The gravel crunching under the tires didn't hold the welcoming tone Adam had grown accustomed to over the past two weeks. Instead, it rang sinister, announcing the end to his fantasy world where Chrissy might give him the time of day. Where his heart might get a second chance. After he told her the truth, she wouldn't want to see him ever again. But Luke was right. He had to tell her sooner or later, so he might as well do it now before either of them got in too deep.

The heat emitting from the sun-cooked gravel brought beads of sweat to Adam's forehead. His body melted, forgetting the blasting air conditioner from just seconds ago. He slipped his suit jacket off and draped it over his arm. As frigid as Chicago winters could be, the summer could be sweltering, and this was definitely a taste of summer.

He tugged at his tie and unbuttoned the collar of his shirt as he walked to the mural. Chrissy crouched under the scaffold, painting bright-purple flowers. Her smile when she saw him served as a punch in the gut. He didn't deserve that smile.

She sprang up from her seat on the sidewalk and closed the gap between them, her brows creasing as she drew near. "Hey. What's wrong? You look like someone stole your puppy."

Tell her, his brain screamed. "Just a tough day at the office looming over me. I'll survive." He glanced to the mural, unwilling to look in her beautiful, honest eyes. "Looks like it's coming along nicely."

Chrissy bit her lip. "I hope it's okay that I tweaked the design a little bit. The overall picture is still the same, but I kind of adjusted some of the details."

Adam scanned the painting for the differences but couldn't find them. "It depends on what the changes are."

Chrissy tipped her head toward the area she'd just been painting and motioned for him to follow. "These."

When he saw where she pointed, his heart skipped a beat. His brain abandoned its truth-telling mission at the sight of a patch of bright-yellow and white daisies painted front and center at the base of the mural. The bouquet he'd given her, immortalized in paint.

"Is it okay?" Chrissy asked, a mix of trepidation and hope on her face.

Adam blinked and nodded, collecting himself emotionally and mentally. He cleared his throat as he fought back a storm of emotions. "I-It's beautiful. Truly. You're an excellent artist. I'm sure there won't be any issues with a change this minor. If there are, I'll take care of it."

She rewarded him with a smile so bright it rivaled the sun. "Are you sure?"

Her joy sparked a smile on his own face. "I'm sure. Honestly, I doubt anyone will even notice except me."

"You're the only one that matters." Her cheeks blazed red, and she added a hurried explanation. "You know, since you're the one overseeing it and everything."

At that, his courage evaporated. He knew he had to lose her sooner or later, but he couldn't bring himself to pull the proverbial trigger. *Maybe tomorrow.*

"It sure is a hot one today, especially for spring," he said, changing the subject to take his mind off his inner turmoil.

She shot another smile his way before turning her attention back to the flowers. "Yeah, it's been pretty warm. Using the scaffold for shade helped a lot. I have to admit I'm not looking forward to standing on top of it later, though."

"Maybe you should wait and do that some other time." Sweat poured down his back, and his stomach twisted at the thought of her baking in the torturous heat.

Chrissy wiped her hands on her overalls. "Well, I would, but I'm running a little behind schedule. I underestimated the amount of time needed for flower details."

"I'm pretty sure you could sweet-talk the guy who made the schedule into giving you a few extra days." Adam hung his jacket on a scaffold rung and cuffed his sleeves.

"Wait. Aren't you the one who made the schedule?"

"Oh, yeah, I guess I am," he said, grinning. Her laugh was music to his ears, a rare sound he could never hear enough of. "On that note, I declare a long lunch break is in order. You can come back when it's cooler. I can order some flood lights if I need to so you can work in the evening."

Chrissy brushed the sleeve of her gauzy pink shirt over her red face. "That sounds amazing, actually. I'm trying to tough it out, but it's starting to get to me a little."

Adam turned to Damien, who'd been watching them from a distance. "Hey, Damien. Let's pack up and take a long lunch break. It's too hot."

"Whatever you say, boss man," Damien said, giving him a mock salute.

Adam clenched his jaw to keep his mouth shut. He had picked up a box of paint and started for the trailer when a sickening thud behind him stopped him in his tracks. He spun to see Chrissy sprawled on the sidewalk, not moving.

He dropped to his knees beside her and cradled her head in his hands. "Chrissy? Chrissy, can you hear me?" Then he turned and shouted over his shoulder. "Bring me some cold water!"

He snatched the cold water from Damien and poured it on Chrissy's forehead, pleading with the universe for her to be okay.

Chrissy

Chrissy's eyes fluttered open, and she blinked against the blazing sun. *Why am I waking up outside?* Her eyelids clamped closed against the light as the world spun around her.

"Chrissy? Can you hear me? You fainted."

That voice. She knew that voice. It soothed her for reasons she couldn't explain. And at that moment it pulled her back from the brink of darkness.

"Adam?" The word came out with a croak. "What happened?"

The visible relief in Adam's face when her eyes focused on him made her heart skip a beat.

"You fainted, probably from the heat. And you hit your head on the sidewalk. How do you feel?"

She took a conscious inventory of her ailing body. "I feel like I ran a marathon and got hit by a truck at the finish line."

"Do you think you can sit up? Maybe drink some water?"

"Water sounds good."

Adam slipped his hand under her back and helped her ease to a sitting position. Even in her woozy state, the fact that his uninvited touch didn't make her skin crawl stood out in her mind. She sipped the ice water he offered her and decided to mull over that oddity later.

Adam watched her, worry ever present in his features. "Forget the long lunch break. You just earned yourself the rest of the day off." He looked over his shoulder at Damien, who Chrissy hadn't even realized was there. "You get the rest of the day off too."

Damien stepped forward now, kneeling beside Adam. "Hey, Chrissy, I can take you home if you want."

Either Adam's nostrils flared as his jaw clenched, or Chrissy was imagining things. Either way, her gut answered for her. "No, that's okay. I'll be fine. It's just a quick bus ride."

Chrissy inched her way to standing, Adam's hand clutching her elbow as Damien crossed his arms over his chest. Chrissy wobbled, still weak from her spell.

"Damien, finish packing up all the supplies, and then you can head out," Adam said, then he turned to Chrissy. "And you need to get somewhere cooler. Pronto. Can you walk?"

Chrissy took a shaky step on legs like limp spaghetti. "I mean, technically I can, I guess."

Adam leaned in, making sure her eyes found his. "Is it okay if I put my arm around you to support you while we walk to my car? You need air conditioning."

She hadn't let a man be in control of touching her for two years. Too many had touched her for all the wrong, selfish reasons. Her chest tightened, and she gulped for air.

"On second thought, you sit here, and I'll run over and get my car. That way you only have to walk to the barricade." Adam held fast to her elbow as she sat, then he sprinted to the gravel lot beside the warehouse.

Chrissy stared after him, bewildered by his intuitiveness. Not only did he ask permission to touch her, he seemed to pick up on the stress triggered by the situation.

Damien's arm dropped around her shoulders as he plunked onto the sidewalk beside her. "You sure you trust this guy? I don't trust any of them suits."

Chrissy mustered all her strength but couldn't scrounge up enough to spring to her feet the way her brain screamed at her to do. Her skin itched like his arm was poison ivy draped over her shoulders, his unsolicited touch triggering such a flood of overwhelming sensations she was sure to explode.

Adam's BMW jerked to a stop by the gate, and unexplainable relief flooded her as he jumped out and jogged her way. He hesitated for a second when he noticed Damien, and she could almost see the words he fought back as he closed the distance.

Adam held out a hand for Chrissy. "Ready to go? I have the AC blasting."

"Yes, please," she said. *For several reasons,* she added in her head as she stood, Damien's arm falling away.

Chapter 19

Adam

For once in his life, Adam was grateful for crappy parking around a city project because it meant he had no choice but to move the car out of the street and away from Damien. Something about that guy rubbed him the wrong way, and not just because Damien clearly had the hots for Chrissy.

Adam cast a sideways glance at Chrissy, whose bangs rustled in the blasting air, the sleeves of her pink shirt still plastered to her skin. "Feeling any better?"

Chrissy sighed and sank back against the seat. "This air conditioning is glorious. I didn't realize I'd gotten so hot." Her stomach growled above the noise. "And apparently starving. Heat and hunger are not a good combo. I should've known better."

"How about lunch? Somewhere with AC. My treat." Adam's heart hammered in his chest at the thought of spending more time with this woman, even as his brain cursed him.

"I don't know..." Her words trailed off while she stared at her hot-pink nails.

"I'm sorry if I made you uncomfortable." The disappointment he felt earned him more internal cursing. He was supposed to be distancing himself, not getting flustered over a lunch proposal.

"No, it's not that. I just... Well, look at me. I'm in my painting overalls, and I'm dirty and sweaty. I'm not fit to go to any of the fancy places you'd go to."

"Who said I'm planning on anywhere fancy?"

"It's just that you dress so nice and your fancy car still has that new-car smell. I guess I figured everything about you was nice and fancy." She turned her face to the window. "I'm the farthest thing from that."

"I ate lunch from a food truck at the park, remember? I'm not stuck-up like Damien says I am," he said, an edge of defensiveness in his voice.

"I didn't mean anything bad. Lunch the other day was amazing, but I kind of assumed that was you slumming a little for my sake." She bowed her head and stared at her hands in her lap.

All traces of his raised temper vanished, and he gripped the wheel to keep from taking her hand in his. "I'm flattered, but I assure you the real me is far from fancy. I have to have these suits for the corporate world, but I'd much rather be in jeans and a T-shirt. And the car..." He paused, fighting to keep his voice in check. He knew he shouldn't let a prime opportunity to tell her the truth pass him by, but his courage was nowhere to be found. "Well, I had to get a new one two years ago, and I don't drive much, so it's easy to keep it nice." He paused again and snuck a glance at Chrissy, crossing his fingers he wasn't about to cross a line. "And for the record, I think you're perfectly fine, just the way you are."

Chrissy

Chrissy trained her gaze on the world beyond the window and cursed the emotions swirling in her chest. Those words. Those wonderful words that rolled so easily from Adam's mouth and straight to her heart meant more than he would ever know. Being fine just the way she was seemed as out of reach as being a renowned artist. But if he knew the truth about her past, perhaps he wouldn't think so positively of her. She'd been silent far too long, so she blinked away the tears and cleared her throat.

"Thank you. Also, for the record, I've never called you a suit. You've been nothing but nice and never stuck-up. Even when I ruined your pants and shoes." She examined his current pants and groaned. "And judging by the dirt on your knees, those pants are ruined too." She palmed her forehead and hazarded a look at him.

Adam glanced her way with a grin and a shrug. "It's just clothes. They sell more."

He brought the car to a stop in front of the City Club Café and pulled out his phone. He typed something and held the screen toward her. "Here's the menu. Just add whatever you want to the cart. They'll bring it out to us."

"You don't have to do this. I can buy my own food."

"I know you can, but I'd like to buy you lunch. It's the least I can do for working you half to death. Please. I'm starving, and I'd rather not sit here and argue all day."

His half smirk brought the long-dead butterflies in her stomach back to life again. *How did I not notice those adorable dimples before?* "Okay, fine. I'll let you pay this time."

Within minutes of ordering, a café worker brought their food to the car. "Here's your order, Mr. Rochester. Thank you for stopping by."

Chrissy watched in astonishment as Adam slipped the young boy a twenty-dollar tip.

He caught her gaping and gave her a sheepish shrug. "One of the perks of working for the city is good service everywhere you go."

"Or you get good service because you tip like a king. That tip was almost as much as our food, and all he did was walk it ten feet. I never got tipped that well when I was a waitress."

"Once upon a time I was in that kid's shoes. I try not to forget that." Adam pulled away from the curb. "Normally I'd say we could eat at the park, but you need to stay cool the rest of the day. I don't want you to take this the wrong way, but what do you think of eating lunch at my place? I need to change pants before I head back to the office, and you could freshen up if you want."

Chrissy waited for the tightness of panic to form in her chest, but it didn't come. She then uttered the last word she expected. "Okay."

Chrissy hugged her arms around herself, her paint-smeared denim sticking out like a sore thumb amongst the modern black-and-white marble décor in the lobby. If Adam noticed the hushed whispers and open stares, he hid it well.

"I'm on twenty-five," he said, nodding toward the elevator buttons.

Chrissy punched the twenty-five and let out her breath as the doors slid closed. "All those people are probably wondering why you went slumming for a charity case."

"Hey, don't talk about yourself like that." Adam's stern voice compelled her to look at him. "I guarantee you're a better person than ninety-five percent of those people. It would be a hundred if it wasn't for Winifred. She's basically my adopted grandma and a practical saint. No one could be a better person. But outside of her, who cares what any of those people think? I sure don't."

The doors dinged and opened, and Chrissy followed him down the hall, her sneakers squeaking on the shiny floor for every slap of his loafers.

"Can you hold the drinks so I can unlock the door?"

Chrissy took the drinks with a smirk. "I told you I could carry them the whole way, remember?"

"Yes, but that wouldn't be very gentlemanly of me, would it?" He fished the keys from his pocket.

Chrissy glanced nervously down the hall as he unlocked the door, praying no one saw them. The last thing she wanted was to ruin his reputation.

"Here we are," he announced, holding the door open wide.

Her jaw dropped as she drank in every detail, from the white marble floors to the sleek black cabinets. She all but sprinted to the wall of windows overlooking the city, unable to resist their beckoning call.

"Wow," she breathed. "This place is amazing."

Adam set the food on the coffee table behind her and took the drinks from her hands. "It's pretty nice. It's kind of sterile, but I'm not here enough to really personalize it."

Chrissy turned and surveyed the space again. She envisioned winter evenings spent in front of the black stone fireplace and movie nights lounging on the gray sofa. Her mind's eye pictured sitting on the acrylic barstools while eating expensive Italian food and talking about day-to-day life. She imagined a life worth living rather than just surviving.

She looked back to Adam, who watched her with curiosity in his eyes. "You say sterile, but I see clean. I think it's perfect. Why aren't you here all the time? I would be."

He shifted his focus to the glass coffee table and sat on the couch. "I spend most of my time at the office."

"Ah, so you're a workaholic."

"Not exactly," he said as he pulled the containers from the bag. "I wouldn't work all the time if I had something better to do. I figure if I'm going to be alone, I might as well be productive. It keeps my mind busy."

The hint of agony beneath his words tugged at her heart. Something somewhere along the way had wounded this man, and for some reason she longed to know more, to know what shaped him.

Chrissy started to join him but paused and scanned her clothes. "Do you have a towel or something to put down? I don't want to ruin your couch."

"It's okay."

Chrissy folded her arms across her chest. "I've already ruined two pairs of your pants and a pair of shoes. I refuse to risk ruining what I know is an expensive couch."

"Fair enough." Adam chuckled as he disappeared down the hallway. He came back moments later and laid a towel on the cushion next to his. "Better?"

"Yes." Chrissy took her seat.

Adam picked up his iced tea and held it toward her. "Cheers. Let's eat."

Chrissy bumped his cup with her lemonade. "Cheers."

She moaned as she bit into her barbecue-chicken sandwich. "Oh my gosh. This is amazing."

Adam licked mayonnaise from his lip. "That's always been one of my favorites. Their burgers are pretty awesome, too, but huge. I figured I earned it since I burned off a ton of calories between the heat and stress."

She swallowed her chicken with a side of guilt. "I'm really sorry about all this. I never meant to throw off the project schedule, let alone your whole day. And you have yet another ruined suit thanks to me. Now you're stress eating. I really made a mess of the day, huh?"

Adam laid his hand on her knee, a touch so light she wondered if she imagined it. His expression softened. "I didn't mean to make you feel bad. You really don't have to feel guilty. It's not like you wanted to pass out. Besides, I wouldn't count eating a delicious lunch in great company as a ruined day."

There he goes again, acting like a perfect guy, Chrissy thought. *How does he always know the exact right thing to say?* She saw his eyes flicker toward her mouth as he swallowed. Or maybe her mind kept conjuring up that scenario every time she came within three feet of him. She hated how being near Adam resurrected her desire from the deep, dark grave she'd buried it in. She couldn't just forget her past. But then again, her skin didn't crawl whenever he looked at her—or even when he touched her. That had to count for something.

"You got a little something..." Adam dabbed the corner of her mouth with a napkin, his eyes darkening.

Chrissy suppressed a groan and chastised herself. Of course he was just looking at sauce on her mouth. *How could I be so stupid?* No one like him would ever want damaged goods like her, and she'd benefit from remembering that. She self-consciously reached up to adjust her hair and sucked in a breath as her hand brushed a tender spot.

"Your head." Adam gasped. "With everything else going on, I forgot you hit your head. Here, let me see." She obliged, and he clicked his tongue. "I think it's stopped now, but you were bleeding. You need to get that checked out."

"No!" she said, almost shouting. She bit her lip then continued more quietly. "I mean, I don't have insurance. I can't really afford a big medical bill. I'll be fine."

"Then you can see my doctor." He pulled his phone from his pocket. "Hello, Dr. Bertrand. I was wondering if you could swing by and check on a friend of mine. She fainted in the heat and hit her head on the pavement. No, no vomiting. Some bleeding, but it's stopped and no open wound. Yeah, more like a scrape. Loss of consciousness happened prior to the fall. Coherent and alert. Eating and drinking fine. Okay. Thank you so much."

He hung up and laid the phone on the table. "He said he thinks since you're symptom-free now that you'll be fine, but if anything changes I can call him, and he'll be right over."

Chrissy raised a brow. "I didn't realize doctors still made house calls."

He stood and started gathering the trash. "They do for the right price."

Chrissy watched him, wondering how on earth a man like Adam had fallen into her path and how long she had before she woke up from the fairy tale. She watched the fabric of his pale-blue shirt stretch over his biceps as he reached for her trash, his cuffed sleeves exposing his forearm. *Who knew a forearm could be so sexy?* As he walked to the kitchen, she wondered if all of his pants fit so perfectly. She needed a breather before she outright swooned.

"Where's your restroom?"

"Down the hall on the right," he said.

In the bathroom, Chrissy splashed cold water on her face and peered at herself in the mirror. She'd definitely looked better. There was no way Adam was having the same thoughts about her as she was about him, and she'd do better to remember that.

"There," Chrissy breathed as she returned to the living room. "Who knew washing my face could make me human again? Once I change into some clean clothes, I might elevate to princess after all."

"I probably have a T-shirt from college that would work if you want to change. It might be more like a dress on you, though."

"Oh." Chrissy blinked. "I figured I better get going and let you get back to your important businessman stuff."

"I was thinking you should probably stick around so I can keep an eye on you. In case I need to call Dr. Bertrand."

"I have to leave by five anyway. It's Tuesday."

"You can't even make an exception for health reasons?"

She couldn't miss group therapy, but she couldn't tell Adam that. "Uh, not really. It's kind of important."

He studied her a moment, and she could tell he wanted to pry. Thankfully, he thought better of it. "That still gives you a few hours to stay here and rest."

"But what about your work?"

He shrugged. "The rest of the day is all meetings that should be emails. I can call in remotely and listen to them drone on and on. At least this way I can nod off without anyone seeing me."

"I don't know if I'm comfortable taking over your space like this." She shifted her weight from one foot to the other.

"We could go to your place instead."

"No." Her chest seized at the thought of him seeing where she lived. "I mean, that's okay. Here is fine." She forced herself to act calm even though the thought of him seeing where she lived had her on edge. If he had seen the panic in her eyes, he didn't let it show.

"It's settled, then. Make yourself comfortable."

"Only if you're one hundred percent sure."

"I promise. Relax. I want to make sure you're okay. That's more important than a couple of boring meetings." He picked up the remote and handed it to her. "You can watch TV if you want. I don't really have much else as far as entertainment, I'm afraid. I'm usually on my laptop or my phone. There're some books on the shelf in the corner, but mostly business stuff and coffee-table books people have bought me."

Chrissy took the remote. "Thanks. I don't need much. Heck, I could spend hours just looking out of these windows."

He laughed. "Be my guest. I'm going to get set up in my office."

Looking around the shiny, pristine apartment, Chrissy wondered just how hard she had hit her head, because surely she was hallucinating. All she had to do was make sure she didn't get too comfortable. It was just a temporary taste of the good life.

Chapter 20

Chrissy

Chrissy wasn't caught in another fantasy. Nope. Lounging on the world's comfiest couch and watching television with a great guy in the next room in a place fancy enough for an actual doorman was, in fact, her current reality. All that was missing was a magical fairy godmother. And if she had one, she needed to shake that woman's hand. The whole day was almost too good to be true. Other than the whole "passing out from the heat" thing, of course. But so far in her life, if things seemed too good to be true, it usually meant ulterior motives lurked beneath the surface.

Adam walked into the room, stretching his arms overhead in a way that made her mouth water. "Whew. I'm glad to be done with that meeting. I swear John should record his voice as a sleep aid for insomniacs."

"Why are you doing this?" Chrissy asked, the words leaving her mouth before she could stop them.

Adam froze and blinked. "Doing what?"

Chrissy tossed her hands in the air. "All of this. Buying me lunch. Giving me the rest of the day off. Having me stay here so you can call your rich-people doctor if anything happens to me. I was just wondering, why are you being so nice?"

He rubbed the back of his head. "I'm guessing 'just because I want to be nice' isn't going to be enough of an answer, is it?"

Chrissy shook her head and waited, afraid to hear his real answer.

He plopped down on the black leather chair across from her with a heavy sigh. "It's hard to explain because I don't fully know. I don't want to sound like a creeper or anything, but from your first day on the job there was just something that drew me to you, that made me want to help you. And it's not just because you're pretty. I don't know, I guess I see a little of myself in you. I haven't always lived like this, you know. I've had to fight my way above water too."

A dark cloud settled over Chrissy. *Poor, naïve Adam.* He'd never been as low as she had. "I hate to break it to you, but we're nothing alike. There's so much more to my sob story than what Luke told you. If you only knew how much of an underdog I really am, you wouldn't let me set foot in your fancy apartment building."

Adam leaned forward, his expression serious. "Actually, I never heard your 'sob story,' as you put it. Liam told me to hire you, so I did. He's a good judge of character, so I trust him. Well, as long as you forget about his ex-fiancé." When she didn't laugh at his joke, he continued. "I tend to prefer getting my information straight from the source."

Chrissy scoffed and crossed her arms over her chest. "I'm not going to tell you my sob story."

He leaned back with a one-shouldered shrug. "I don't want to hear a sob story. I just want to get to know you."

"If you don't want the sob story, then what do you want to know?"

"Well, for starters, I'm curious as to why you always wear pants and long sleeves, even when it makes you pass out from the heat. I don't buy the whole modesty thing, at least not completely."

Chrissy shrank into herself, willing herself to disappear into the cushions of the couch and become one with the fabric so no one would ever see her again.

Adam leaned forward again, concern etched in his features. "I'm sorry. I shouldn't have asked that. You don't have to tell me anything. Forget I ever said anything. It's none of my business."

With one look at him, she knew he meant every word. She had a choice. That was something Adam always gave her when no one else ever had. A choice. Her heart rate picked up speed until it raced like a steam train, roaring in her ears. Words formed in her mouth, ready to burst into the open for the first time in her life.

"It's so I can hide my past," she whispered.

"You don't have to tell me, Chrissy. I mean it. It's really none of my business."

She brought her tear-filled eyes to his. "No, it's okay. I want to."

"Are you sure? I don't want you to think you have to just because I helped you out. That's not why I did this."

"I know. I want you to know the truth." She pushed her sleeve up her left arm, inch by agonizing inch, her broken-chain tattoo being revealed first. "I don't know how much you know of Luke's story, but you'll recognize this tattoo. I copied it, and mine means the same thing. It marks when I broke free from my addiction. The day my life began again."

She glanced at Adam, searching for the judgment that comes from people hearing the word *addiction*. Instead, all she found was attentiveness and empathy, which gave her the strength to continue. She pushed her right sleeve up, revealing pale parallel scars marring her wrist and forearm. She let out a shaky breath. "And this... this is my permanent reminder of the day my life almost ended." She couldn't bring herself to look at Adam for fear she would lose the courage to continue. "I don't wear shorts because... because..."

She couldn't stop herself from glancing up at Adam any longer, and the pain in his features mirrored the pain in her heart. She choked back a sob, and he rushed to her side, putting a warm, comforting hand on her back. *Why is he not running away?*

She sucked in a ragged breath and forced herself to finish her confession. "To say I didn't exactly have the best of childhoods would be a huge understatement. I had a lot of trauma and pain, and no one ever really taught me how to handle it. So, I... I started sneaking into the bathroom with a razor and... and cutting myself. The sting of the metal slicing my skin took my mind off all the other shit in my life. All that existed in that moment was that pain, and the best part was that I controlled it. The only thing in my life I could control. I didn't think about scars that would last a lifetime. All I could think about was that release. Now I get to live with legs that serve as a roadmap of my pain."

She held her breath, waiting for the distance to grow between them. Waiting for the judgmental grimace and the breaking of all eye contact. She couldn't bring herself to look in his direction, to see the disgust on his face.

But none of it happened.

Instead, he not only stayed, but inched closer. "Can I hug you?"

She peered up at him, bewildered, and shocked herself with a nod. His strong arms slid around her, hesitant at first, as if she might break. After a moment, his grip on her became firm, bringing a comfort she never expected. For the first time in her life, having a man wrap his arms around her didn't make bile rise in her throat.

She closed her eyes and sank into his embrace, intoxicated by the security enveloping her. The gentle caress of his hand on her back relaxed her more than any touch ever had. The glorious feeling of safety she'd longed for her entire life washed over her. She snuggled her cheek against his chest, letting him hold her as her problems melted away.

His phone buzzed in his pocket, intruding on her perfect moment. When she reluctantly tried to pull away, he held fast.

"They can wait," he whispered. "This is more important."

Her throat constricted. "I don't deserve all this."

"No, you don't deserve your past. You didn't deserve any of the bad things that happened to you. But you do deserve the good things happening now. You deserve so much more. I haven't known you long, but it's long enough to know you're a good person, Chrissy. You're so much more than the bad things that happened to you."

A sob broke through, busting the dam wide open for a flood of tears. Adam's firm embrace encouraged the flow of emotions, and she let herself feel it all. She cried until his arms had wrung every ounce of grief from her, leaving her raw and exposed.

As the torrent of tears slowed, she gulped in a shaky breath. Like magic, Adam offered some tissues at the exact moment she began searching. He loosened his grip, letting her slip free to compose herself.

"Sorry about that. I don't know what came over me. I'm usually not such a disaster." She laughed in an attempt not to sound like the emotional mess she really was.

"Never apologize for your feelings. And you're far from a disaster."

She peeked at him through her wet lashes, and her heart ached to be the person he thought she was. She couldn't dare to hope for a life with someone like Adam, but she wanted to. She'd never wanted anything more. If souls could make love to one another, hers had just been ravished to the edge of oblivion. No matter what happened, this man had worked his way into the landscape of her heart and taken root, for better or worse.

One question still lingered. "Why aren't you running away? Why are you still here?"

His warm gaze held hers, unwavering. "I'll be here as long as you let me. You're worth it."

His words were so sincere, like he actually believed them. Like he truly felt she was worthy of such care. Maybe one day she would believe in her worth too.

Chapter 21

Adam

Settling into the booth across from Chrissy, Adam hoped he didn't look as uneasy as he felt. It had been two days since he'd seen her in person. Two days since her confessions and that embrace he couldn't get out of his mind. Meetings had kept him away from the worksite, and if he was being honest, he was okay with that. He'd needed the time to sort through his thoughts.

"This air conditioning is amazing," Chrissy said, leaning back against the booth.

"I hope you're making sure you don't get overheated again." He noticed her tattoo peeking out from under her cuffed sleeves.

"Yeah, I'm being extra careful. Taking lots of breaks in the shade and making sure to hydrate."

"Good." A silence stretched between them that bordered on awkward. "Sorry I haven't been able to make it out to check on you in person. We had some budgeting issues come up, so I've been swamped."

Hurt flashed in her eyes for a second, but she quickly put on a smile as the waitress came for their order.

When the waitress left again, Adam cleared his throat. "I, uh, thought we should clear the air about what happened the other day. I hope I didn't make you uncomfortable in any way." The way she'd left his condo shortly after their talk, like she couldn't get out of there fast enough, played through his mind.

She looked everywhere but at him. "Oh. No, I wasn't uncomfortable. I hope I didn't make *you* uncomfortable."

Adam clamped his hands together in his lap to keep from fidgeting. The last thing he wanted was for his body language to send the wrong message. "No. Not at all. Quite the opposite, actually." *Why did I say that?* It was true, but it sure didn't help his goal of keeping things professional. "But I think it might be best to keep it between us. Just so others don't get the impression that anything inappropriate is going on."

"Oh, for sure." Chrissy's nod was a little too enthusiastic, and he couldn't quite read how she truly felt.

"Not that anything that happened was inappropriate." The conversation wasn't going as smoothly as he'd practiced. "But I'd like to take an abundance of caution. I wouldn't want any rumors floating around that would put your job in jeopardy."

Chrissy's jaw dropped. "Do you really think I could get fired over a hug?"

Shit. He didn't mean to scare her. "It's very unlikely, but like I said, an abundance of caution. There is a pretty strict policy against any workplace romance."

"Oh."

"N-Not that there's a romance here or anything. But you can see how it might be twisted that way, right?" He tucked his hand under his leg to keep from smacking himself on the forehead. *I really just said all that? Smooth. Real smooth.*

"Right." Chrissy's tone was guarded, and she had one hell of a poker face.

Adam wished for a time machine so he could go back and try not to be such a bumbling idiot. But between his terrifying and confusing feelings for Chrissy and frayed nerves courtesy of an angry email from Mr. Lyones about the schedule, it was all he could do to even get words out. Even if they were clumsy and rambling.

Chrissy frowned. "But I have to admit that I kind of already told Luke that I went to your place. I didn't tell him all the details or anything, just that you took me there for an air-conditioned lunch after I fainted."

"I've already talked to him about it, so that's not a problem." He left out how Luke had lectured him yet again about coming clean before things went too far. "He would never say anything that would compromise either of our jobs."

"True." Chrissy's features softened. "He's a good guy."

Another stretch of silence hung between them until Chrissy eventually broke it. "So you said you had something to show me?"

"Oh. Yes." Adam pulled his laptop from its case and set it on the table, eternally grateful to have something to distract him from the rest of their conversation. "I finally got the official dimensions of the riverfront mural."

All awkwardness vanished as Chrissy leaned forward with excitement. "Really? That's great."

"It's a really large project, so they're going to have you do it in phases. You will have an assistant, like with the current mural. Assistants don't necessarily carry over from job to job, so you likely won't be working with Damien again." Adam would make sure of it.

"Speaking of that, I wanted to run an idea by you." Chrissy bit her lip, uncertainty etched in her features.

"I'm all ears." He hoped it didn't have anything to do with Damien.

"You remember Abilene, right?" When Adam nodded, she continued. "She sent me pictures of some of her work, and she's actually really good. I've been brainstorming ways I can help her, and I was wondering if I could maybe have her be an apprentice on the next mural. When she's not in school, of course."

Adam imagined himself pitching the idea to Mr. Lyones and had to suppress a shudder. "The budget for this is fairly tight, so I'm doubtful they would approve a paid apprenticeship. It would have to be a 'paid in experience' type of thing."

Chrissy nodded. "I kind of figured that's how it would be. I haven't mentioned it to her yet because I wanted to see what you thought first."

"I can run the idea by Mr. Lyones and let you know for sure."

"Thank you." Chrissy's fingers lifted like she was going to reach for his hand, but then she dropped her hands to her lap.

His heart ached at the awkwardness between them. He cleared his throat and returned to the slideshow of photos he'd been showing her. "They want to focus on the culture in the city. Art, music, famous people, and other stuff that makes Chicago, Chicago."

"That sounds fun. Although the idea of painting giant people is a little daunting."

Adam tilted his head. "Why? I saw the portraits you did of Luke, Aria, and Ben. And the others you added to your portfolio. They're amazing. That's one of the reasons they're so excited about having you on board for this project."

Chrissy leaned back in the booth. "It's different when you're doing something on such a large scale, though. It's harder to capture the little details that really make it great. If you took a magnifying glass to the portraits, they wouldn't look as good."

"I have every faith in your abilities."

"I'm glad one of us does."

Adam reached across the table and took her hand. The touch of her skin elicited the same feelings as when they hugged. He yanked his hand away as the waitress approached their table, but his skin clung to the memory of her hand in his just as his arms longed to pull her against him again. He was going to have to be more careful if he wanted to prevent people thinking there was something between them. And he would have to work even harder to convince himself.

Chrissy

Back at the mural, Chrissy's mind swam with dimensions and pictures of the people the city wanted to include in the giant riverfront mural. As much as she was honored to have been chosen for the job, the logistics of such a daunting task overwhelmed her. And if they approved Abilene's apprenticeship, Chrissy would have both of their reputations resting on her shoulders.

She stepped to her left and kicked over the can of blue paint she was using for the river. "Oh, shoot."

She set down her paint brush and scrambled to pick up the can, grumbling to herself.

"Here." Damien dropped some cloths beside the puddle of paint then knelt to help mop up the mess.

"Thanks."

"Where's your head today?"

Chrissy stopped swiping and looked up at him. "Excuse me?"

Damien started gathering the soiled cloths. "You've been distracted ever since lunch. First, you kept forgetting which supplies you needed. And you haven't been making much progress, spending half the time just staring at the wall. Now this."

"You're right." Chrissy handed him the last cleaning cloth with a sigh. "I just have a lot on my mind."

Damien didn't know about the future projects, and she was determined to keep it that way. She had decided long ago that she would be getting a new assistant for those jobs, but if Damien knew, she'd never hear the end of it. It was best for everyone if they just finished this mural and went their separate ways.

"It wouldn't have anything to do with the fact the boss man hasn't been around for a few days, would it?"

"That crap again? Seriously, Damien, just stop." She wished she could smack that stupid smirk off his face.

He held his hands up like he was ready to defend himself. "Don't get mad at me for calling it like I see it, princess."

"Then you need to get your eyes checked." Chrissy picked up the paint brush and focused her attention on the mural, something actually worth her energy. Damien was right, but she would never, ever let him know that. She'd shared such a special moment with Adam, and then for two whole days he'd avoided her. All she got was a couple of texts asking for updates on the mural. And when she finally saw him again, he said they needed to keep things professional. Talk about a cold dose of reality. She knew the whole workplace-romance thing was doomed from the start, but that hadn't kept her from getting her hopes up. And to top it off, she'd underestimated the commute from Adam's place to hers, so she had gotten in trouble for being late to group therapy. It was her first slipup, so the director had been lenient. At the time it felt worth it to have that moment with Adam, but after their meeting she wasn't so sure.

"If it's not the boss man, then who is it?"

She ground her teeth together to keep from screaming at him. "You do realize there is more to life than romance, don't you?"

"Who said anything about romance?"

"You did."

Damien scoffed. "People can have sex without romance."

Every cell in Chrissy's body screamed that their conversation needed to end. Pronto. "Well, that's definitely off the table. There's a whole world of things out there that could be distracting me that don't include a man. How about we get back to work? We're already two days behind schedule."

"Whatever you say." Damien stalked off to toss the rags in the bin they used for dirty rags and drop cloths.

Chrissy watched him go then tried her best to focus her attention on the job. She shook her arms, trying to shake off her nerves. As much as Adam's talk about being strictly professional had stung, he had been one hundred percent correct. If Damien found out she had gone to Adam's apartment, nothing would stop him from using it against her. She wouldn't put it past Damien to blackmail Adam if he knew how strict the "no workplace romance" policy was. No, Damien couldn't know the truth about any of it. She would just have to put on an award-worthy performance and act like her feelings for Adam didn't exist.

Chapter 22

Chrissy

Taking a sip of her strawberry-lemonade slushy, Chrissy couldn't wipe the goofy grin from her face. No one had to know her good mood stemmed more from who had gotten the food than from the food itself. As she sank her teeth into the burger, she leaned back and savored the flavors.

"City Club Café? Isn't that one of those snooty places downtown?" Damien plopped down beside her in the shade of the scaffold and popped open his lunchbox.

Chrissy held up a finger as she finished chewing. "It's surprisingly not snooty, and their food is delicious. Want some garlic fries?"

Damien popped a fry into his mouth and chewed. "Not bad, I guess. They must be paying you better than I thought if you can afford to have that delivered."

"I didn't, actually." She grimaced. In her haste to defend herself from Damien's incessant assumptions, she had stuck her foot in her mouth. Big time.

Damien raised a brow at her then made a show of slapping his forehead. "Oh, of course. The boss man ordered it for you, didn't he?"

Chrissy sipped her slushy again to buy herself some time to think. She and Adam had done so well keeping their distance the past couple days. It had helped that it was over the weekend and Chrissy hadn't worked, but it was still progress. And she had just blown it. Sure, he sent her lunch, but it was just a friendly gesture to make sure she was taking care of herself. To ensure the project stayed on track. That was what she told herself, at least. But Damien would never buy that. There had to be a professional reason for him to send her lunch. She just had to think of it. And quick. "With the mural getting closer to being done, they've started planning the reveal party. Since they were thinking about having City Club Café cater, Adam figured I needed to try some of their food."

"Uh-huh." Damien grunted and ripped the top off his beer. The one he wasn't supposed to drink while on the job, but Chrissy had let it slide each time. "Too bad the suit doesn't want to get in my pants. I'd put out to have someone buy me fancy food too."

Chrissy dropped the burger onto the wrapper and gaped at him. "What did you just say?"

"You heard me."

"How dare you. Not that it's any of your business whatsoever, but I haven't 'put out' for anyone. Like I said before, there's nothing going on between me and Adam. We're friends, but that's it."

Damien barked a humorless laugh. "No one is nice without expecting something in return, princess. And don't think I haven't noticed the way he looks at you, and you just fangirl right back. It's disgusting. I'm more man than he'll ever dream of being, but I don't have that plastic card to wave around so you don't even look my way. How about I run to that bakery the redhead works at and get you a cake? Can I sample what you're giving then?"

Chrissy stuffed her lunch back in the to-go bag and scrambled to her feet, eager to be as far away from Damien as possible. "You can pack up the stuff when you're done. If you're going to have that attitude, don't bother coming back." With a huff, she stomped away toward the bus stop.

"Where are you going, Miss High and Mighty?" Damien yelled after her.

She sank onto the bench, pulled out her phone, and sent a message to Adam. "Hey, something came up. I'm going to call it a day, if that's okay?"

Adam replied in an instant. "Are you okay? Do you need anything?"

Chrissy chewed her lip, not wanting to lie but not wanting to tell him the truth either. "I'm fine. Just some family stuff."

The hairs on the back of her neck stood up, and she scanned her surroundings for the cause, catching a glimpse of Damien as he ducked around the corner and out of sight. The downtown bus pulled to the curb, and she hopped on.

"Chrissy, what a nice surprise." Lilly shot around the counter and wiped her hands on a white towel hanging from her hot-pink apron.

Chrissy offered a sheepish grin as she held up the rest of her lunch. "Is it okay if I bring this in here?"

Lilly waved a hand in dismissal. "Oh, sure. I don't compete with them. Come on, let's go in the back where it's more private."

After settling Chrissy at a table in the back break room, Lilly slid her apron off. "Hey, Ruth, I'm taking a break. Yell if you need me." Then she sat down across from Chrissy. "Okay, girl. Spill it. What's going on?"

"Who says anything is going on?" Chrissy shrugged and looked everywhere but at Lilly.

"Come on, Chrissy. We shared a bedroom for almost a decade. We're basically sisters. Even after all these years apart, I can still tell when something is bothering you."

Chrissy gave a resigned sigh, but her mouth curled into a soft smile as she finally looked at Lilly. "I guess some things never change."

Lilly returned her grin. "Nope. So spill the beans before a baking disaster calls my name."

"All right, fine." Even though she acted annoyed, being able to run to her best friend after all these years healed a tiny piece of her heart. "You met Damien and pretty much knew he was bad news, right?"

Lilly's eyes grew wide. "Did you...?"

"No, no, no. I'm long past going for the bad boys. That led me barefoot down a road paved with shrapnel. I'm not going there again. No, the problem is he wants me to."

"Yeah, I picked up on that vibe, for sure." Lilly nodded. "Is he coming on too strong?"

Chrissy snorted. "That's an understatement. From the first time we met he flat-out told me he liked me, and I told him he was barking up the wrong tree. He says and does little suggestive things here and there every single day. I don't know, it all kind of makes my skin crawl." She shivered. "I brushed it off because I'm used to dealing with creeps and he really needed the job, but I think I made a mistake."

"Oh, sweetie, that's no way to spend your days. Is there anyone you can report him to? Surely you can get him fired." Lilly's face filled with sympathy.

Chrissy bit her lip and looked away.

"What are you not telling me?"

"The guy overseeing the project gave me his number the first day and told me to let him know about any and all issues I might have. He's almost fired Damien a couple of times already."

"So why hasn't he?" Lilly asked.

"I've told him not to." Chrissy winced, knowing how Lilly would react.

"And why on earth would you do that?"

Chrissy shrugged. "I don't know. He makes me uncomfortable, but what if I'm just being too sensitive? I don't want to be whiny and make someone else lose their job just because I'm a wimp. He really needs the work, and I think a lot of his attitude problem is a coping mechanism. It's not the best way to cope, but neither was mine. I know what it's like for no one to give you a chance, so I guess I've been determined to be the person to give him a chance. But I think I let it go too far."

Lilly eyed her for a moment then took her hand and gave it a squeeze. "You matter, too, Chrissy. You've always put yourself on the back burner. I don't know everything that's happened since you left the home, but one thing I do know is that no matter what it was, you matter. Your safety matters, and your comfort matters. I know you want to save the world, but it shouldn't have to be at your expense. No one should have to put up with being harassed."

Chrissy's eyes brimmed with tears, the lump in her throat making it impossible to reply.

Ruth popped her head through the doorway. "Excuse me, Lilly? Mrs. Vivian is out front again. Apparently, the ratio of red to yellow flowers isn't correct."

"I'll be right there," Lilly said then turned to Chrissy with a sigh. "Nothing is ever right the first time with that woman, yet she keeps coming back. This might take a bit, but I want you to stick around. I'm not done with this conversation."

Chrissy nodded and watched as Lilly slipped her apron over her head and disappeared. Then she blinked back her tears and inhaled a deep, shaky breath as she reached for her lunch sack.

She'd just finished the last of her fries when Lilly came through the doorway and plopped onto her chair. "A half dozen red flowers later, I'm back."

"Another satisfied customer?"

"For now," Lilly said with a shake of her head. "So, what are you going to do about Damien? You came halfway across town during the lunch rush to get away from him. Do you really think it's wise to go back and paint with the guy like nothing happened?"

"Oh, I'm not. I already told Adam I was taking the rest of the day off."

"Adam?"

Chrissy blushed. "Adam is the guy overseeing the project."

"I see." Lilly drummed her fingers on the table as if she sensed Chrissy was hiding something. "A first-name basis, huh? So, did you tell Adam why?"

Chrissy busied herself with gathering her trash. "No, I just told him something came up."

"Listen to me, Chrissy. You need to tell Adam the same things you told me. If you feel the need to run away from Damien, you shouldn't be working with him." She grabbed the trash from Chrissy and tossed it into a nearby trash can.

"Okay. You're right."

Lilly crossed her arms over her chest and waited.

Reluctantly, Chrissy dragged her phone from her overall bib.

Lilly watched as Chrissy typed. "Hey, I just wanted to let you know I'm not sure if I can keep working with Damien."

"And send," Chrissy said, laying her phone on the table. "There. It's done."

Lilly opened her mouth to speak, but Chrissy's phone buzzed to life with Adam's name on the screen.

"Put it on speaker," Lilly whispered, even though Adam couldn't hear them.

Chrissy nodded as she accepted the call. "Hello?"

Adam's voice rushed through the phone. "Chrissy? Are you okay? What happened? Where are you?"

"Adam, slow down. I'm fine, I promise. I'm with a friend."

A sigh of relief whooshed through the speaker. "Okay, good. What happened?"

"Nothing big happened, really. There've just been little things here and there. Today he came up while I was eating lunch and started saying some things that really made me uncomfortable."

"What did he say?" Adam's tone became defensive.

"Uh, I... just some suggestive stuff I'd rather not repeat."

The line was silent for a beat before Adam's low tone came through. "Say no more. He won't be a bother to you starting now. I'll have a replacement in the morning, and this time I will personally select them."

The amount of relief Chrissy felt surprised her, her shoulders relaxing and her head throbbing from the adrenaline crash. "Okay. Thanks."

Adam cleared his throat. "And, Chrissy... I'm sorry. I had a bad feeling about him from the start. You never should've had to go through that."

Yet again, the genuine concern in his tone made her throat tighten with emotion. "Thanks, but it's not your fault. I told you not to fire him."

"But I'm the one in charge and the one that let him keep working. Either way, you won't have to worry about it anymore. And please, call me if you need anything. Day or night. I mean it. Okay?"

"Okay." Chrissy hung up the phone but kept her eyes focused on the screen as she relished having a protector.

"Wow." Lilly's voice snapped Chrissy out of her reverie.

Chrissy blinked at her. "What?"

"Forget Damien. Let's talk about Adam."

Chrissy picked at her cobalt-blue fingernail polish. "What about him?"

Lilly leaned back in her chair. "Well, for starters, how about the massive crush he has on you?"

Chrissy tried her best to act shocked at the suggestion. "What? That's crazy. We're just friends."

"Uh-huh. Sure." Lilly pursed her lips.

"I swear nothing has happened between us."

Lilly just sat there, waiting.

Chrissy squirmed under Lilly's knowing stare, amazed once more at how well Lilly still read her after all these years. Then again, Chrissy was learning maybe she wasn't as good an actress as she originally thought. "Okay, fine. We've hugged. But that's it."

Lilly finally broke her silence. "What kind of hug? And who initiated?"

"I hugged him when he told me about another job I might get. And he hugged me the other day when I was upset." Chrissy peeked at Lilly and could tell that answer didn't satisfy her.

"And?"

"And it was the most amazing hug ever, okay?" Chrissy flopped back in the seat with a sigh, resigning herself to spilling the proverbial beans. "I passed out from the heat, and Adam took me to his car to cool off. He picked up lunch at City Club Café, and we went to his condo." She saw the shock on Lilly's face and put her palm up. "All we did was have lunch. Since I hit my head when I fell, he had me stay for a few hours while he worked in his home office. We talked about some kind of heavy stuff, and he held me while I cried. Then I went home. It was nothing."

"It doesn't sound like nothing." Lilly leaned forward, a conspiratorial grin curling her lips. "If I didn't know any better, I'd say you have a crush on him too."

Chrissy gasped. "I do not. Besides, he's my boss. Liking him is basically illegal."

"Yeah, okay. Whatever you need to tell yourself." Lilly's eyes twinkled as she smirked at Chrissy.

Two oven timers started beeping in offset rhythms, making both women jump. Lilly giggled at herself and gave Chrissy a regretful look. "Those are some of my evening orders. I'm afraid the lull between the lunch and evening rushes is officially over. You can stay back here or hang out up front if you want."

Chrissy rose to her feet and slung her purse on her shoulder. "Thanks, but I think I'll head home and get some rest."

"Text me when you make it home!" Lilly called out as she headed for the ovens.

Chrissy pulled the stop cord, thankful to be almost home at last. As her feet hit the sidewalk, alarm bells went off in her head. She swiveled as she scanned the area for whatever danger her instincts were picking up. A shadow ducked into an alleyway as the bus moved from view, sending chills cascading down her back.

"You've got to get ahold of yourself," she mumbled as she shook her head. She hugged her purse tighter as she walked the final two blocks to the Path of Hope Sober Living facility, which had once been her sanctuary and beacon of hope. Chrissy now looked at the lackluster building with disdain and determination.

After she'd left the halfway house and the reality of her situation had punched her in the gut, the crowded town house lived up to its name and gave her a path of hope. Without it... Well, she couldn't let herself go down that particular road of what-ifs.

But in that moment, as she climbed the concrete steps and pulled open the creaking door, she wanted more. The shared bedroom became too small, too crowded. She sank onto her bed, the springs protesting beneath her, and longed for the crisp, clean lines of Adam's apartment. All her confusion about what she wanted in life evaporated into thin air. Without meaning to, Adam had shown her the future of her dreams. All she had to do now was go after it.

Chapter 23

Chrissy

Chrissy pulled the trailer door open and surveyed the contents. She found the five-gallon bucket of blue paint and grunted as she carried it to the foot of the scaffold.

She swiped her hands across the front of her overalls. "Whew. Who needs a man?"

"I sure don't."

Chrissy spun around to find a woman with cropped black hair approaching, her hand outstretched. "Hi. I'm Liz. It's short for Elizabeth, but don't you dare call me by my grandma's name."

Liz's smile lit up her previously stern face. Her black muscle tank boasted a heavy metal band and sat in stark juxtaposition to the bright rainbow leggings underneath. She towered over Chrissy by at least a foot and boasted curves Chrissy could only dream about.

Chrissy shook her hand with a smile. "Hi, Liz. I'm Chrissy. It's short for Christine, but I've never gone by that."

Liz clapped her hands together. "How about we get to work? A project is always behind schedule if they're getting a new assistant this late in the game." She headed for the trailer but paused and looked at Chrissy over her shoulder. "And don't worry. I'm not an oversexed jackass like the last guy."

"So you heard about that?"

"A little birdie told me," Liz said then disappeared into the trailer.

Chrissy giggled and climbed up the scaffold. She liked Liz already.

"That's a wrap," Liz said as she snapped the padlock shut. "See you tomorrow."

"Thanks for your help." Chrissy waved goodbye and started for the bus stop.

She squinted against the setting sun and reached into her bag. Both Lilly and Adam had made her promise to text them when she got home, so running an hour late probably had them both chewing their nails. But she couldn't stop long enough to text them yet. She would barely be making it home in time for group therapy as it was, so she would have to wait and text them on the bus.

The scuff of a footstep behind her drew her attention, every cell of her body going into high alert. She turned and saw nothing, but her senses still tingled. A person didn't live the life Chrissy had and not question every person trailing them. She increased her speed, and so did the steps behind her, kicking her adrenaline into overdrive. Reaching the bus stop shelter, she ducked inside but was dismayed to find it devoid of the usual crowd.

Her heart thundered in her ears, almost drowning out the approaching footsteps as they slowed and a shadow approached the side of the shelter. Chrissy's fight-or-flight response kicked in, and it screamed for her to flee.

She gripped her bag and darted out of the shelter, but something solid collided with her ankle. Her body slammed into the concrete, her left arm catching the brunt of her fall. The metallic crunch of her phone on the concrete shot waves of panic through her. Someone grabbed her overall straps and lifted her from the ground. Two rough, tanned hands gripped her arms and pulled her toward the darkened alleyway.

"No!" Chrissy shouted. She tugged at her arms but couldn't budge from the tightening grip. "Let go of me. You can have everything in my purse. Just let me go!"

"I don't want your purse."

The air was sucked out of Chrissy's lungs as Damien's hot breath met her ear. "Damien? What are you doing?"

In one quick motion, he spun her around and shoved her against the brick wall. "I figured I'd come teach you a lesson, princess. Maybe knock you down a few pegs."

"I'm not a princess. I swear, I don't think I'm better than you. Please, believe me. I don't think I'm better than anyone."

Danger danced in his eyes. "Sure you do. Bossing me around like I'm a dog. Not giving me the time of day and looking down your nose at me. All the while getting cozy with the boss man. Giving the suit a chance since he has the almighty dollar." His hand slipped under the neckline of her shirt and fished out her necklace. He yanked on the pendant, snapping the chain from around her neck, and tossed the necklace to the ground. "A saint doesn't belong on a money-hungry little slut like you."

"No, it's not like that. You've got it all wrong. It's not just you. I don't want to date anyone until I've got my life back on the right track. Adam is just a friend." Chrissy's neck burned, and she despised the desperation in her voice.

Damien tossed his head back with a humorless laugh. "You expect me to believe that? You're just sleeping your way to the top. Well, buckle up, baby. I'm gonna show you what a real man is like. After I'm done, you'll never go back to the suit."

Chrissy strained to free herself from his grip as she screamed at the top of her lungs. "No! Stop it! Get off me!"

He pinned her arms with one hand and covered her mouth with the other. "The harder you make this, the harder it'll be for you."

In a flash, Chrissy felt something rip Damien backward, his hands letting go of Chrissy as he grappled at his attacker.

"Get in the car." Adam's voice came from behind Damien.

Chrissy stood frozen in shock as she watched the two men wrestle, Damien landing several blows to Adam's ribs.

"Chrissy! Get in the car and call the cops!" Adam said as he struggled to maintain his grip on Damien.

Chrissy sprang into action and sprinted to Adam's car, grabbing his phone from the console. "Hello? Police? I'm at the bus stop at Broadview and Clark. I was attacked, and now the guy is attacking someone else. Please hurry."

The operator's voice fell away as Chrissy watched Damien break free of Adam's choke hold.

Damien spun on Adam, his face full of rage. "You uptight son of a—"

Adam's fist collided with Damien's mouth before he could complete the insult.

In the faint glow of the low sun, a flash of silver sliding from Damien's pocket made Chrissy's heart stop. She jumped from the car, searching for a way to help. She couldn't let him hurt Adam.

Damien massaged his jaw as he stepped toward Adam, holding the pocketknife in plain view. "Let's see how much of a hotshot you are now, pretty boy."

Sirens rang in the distance, growing closer by the second. Adam hooked his thumb toward the sound. "Let's see how much of a hotshot you are when the police get here."

Damien stepped back, his eyes taking on the look of a caged animal as they darted around. Taking advantage of Damien's distraction, Chrissy rushed forward and kicked him solidly in his groin.

The knife tumbled from Damien's hand and onto the sidewalk as he grabbed his crotch. "You bitch!"

Hatred raged in Damien's features as he reached for the knife, but Adam lunged forward and kicked the blade out of reach. Damien and Adam collided in a blur of fists, but as the sirens grew nearer, Damien pulled free from Adam's grip and bolted away.

With the threat gone, Chrissy ran to Adam, throwing her arms around his chest. His arms wrapped around her, and he caressed her head.

"Are you okay?" Adam's panting breath rustled through her hair.

Words failed her, so she settled for a nod against his chest as tears of relief flooded her cheeks.

Adam

A police car screeched to a halt next to Adam's car.

Adam let go of Chrissy with one arm and pointed in the direction Damien had fled. "He just ran off that way. Caucasian male but tanned. Gray tank top and jeans. Buzzed dark hair."

One car sped off as another pulled up. Two officers climbed out of the second car and rushed to Chrissy and Adam.

The tall male officer's brows rose when he reached them. "Mr. Rochester. Are you two okay? Do you need medical?"

Adam peeled Chrissy off and held her at arm's length. "Did he hurt you? Do you need an ambulance?"

Chrissy choked back a sob and shook her head. "You got here just in time."

Adam pulled her back into his arms, wanting nothing more than to kiss away the pain etched in her features. *How could I let this happen?* He should've looked into Damien's history more rather than trust a friend. And he should've fired him that very first day like he'd wanted to.

The shorter officer cleared his throat. "We're going to need to take your statements. Separately."

Adam nodded, but his arms refused to listen. He didn't want to let her out of his sight ever again, especially with Damien on the run.

It was Chrissy who pushed away, forcing his arms to loosen. She peered up at him with appreciation in her red-rimmed eyes. "It's okay, Adam." She turned to the officer and squared her shoulders. "I'm ready."

Adam couldn't keep his attention from darting over to Chrissy as he gave his statement. His mind tortured him with thoughts of what might've happened if he'd been just minutes later. He could've lost her. He'd spent so much time trying to protect her from his own messed-up world, but all he'd done was waste time he could've had with her. He wouldn't make that mistake again.

Chrissy joined Adam by the car as he finished his statement.

One officer talked into his radio and approached them with a grim expression. "They haven't apprehended the suspect yet, but rest assured every cop will be on the lookout. We promise we'll catch the guy, Mr. Rochester."

Adam nodded, and the officer turned to Chrissy and gave her broken phone to her. "Do you have a safe place to stay tonight? Maybe with a friend? Can we call someone for you?"

"She can stay with me." The words flew out of Adam's mouth before he could even think. His cheeks flushed as he turned to Chrissy. "You can stay with me, if you want. I'll alert building security. You'll be safe. I promise."

Hesitation flashed across her face, but then a tiny smile curled her lips. "Okay. Thanks."

The officer nodded. "All right, then. You two can be on your way. I'll let you know of any developments, Mr. Rochester."

Chapter 24

Adam

As the door to Adam's condo shut behind him, Chrissy sank to the floor and buried her face in her hands. Adam dropped to his knees and draped an arm over her shoulders.

"It's okay. I'm here for you. You're safe now," he said, his heart breaking all over again.

"How could I be so stupid?"

Adam recoiled. "What are you talking about?"

"All of this is my fault."

"What? No. You did nothing wrong. He attacked you. The blame is solidly at the feet of that monster."

Chrissy shook her head and shrugged Adam's arm from her shoulders. "If I would've let you fire him in the beginning, none of this would've happened. I shouldn't have worried about whether or not he needed the job, and I shouldn't have fallen for his act. I should've known better. But no. Instead, I was stupid and not only put myself in danger, but you too. I'm so sorry."

Adam's heart couldn't have been more crushed if it had been smashed by a steamroller. He put a gentle finger under Chrissy's chin and nudged her face upward. Her tear-soaked lashes caused his chest to squeeze. "Listen to me. You have nothing to be sorry about. I'm fine. And you didn't do anything wrong. It's not stupid to have a big heart. If anyone is to blame, it's me. I'm the one in charge, remember? I could've fired him at any time, with or without your blessing, but I hesitated because, well, honestly, I didn't want it to look like I was jealous. So how's that for stupid?"

Adam hung his head, shame and regret coursing through him.

Chrissy's hand gripped his. "I appreciate the fact that you actually listened to me, though. And thank you for saving me. If you hadn't shown up..."

Adam wrapped his arms around her as his brain refused to entertain the what-ifs. She sucked in her breath as he gave her a squeeze. "What's wrong? Did that hurt?"

Chrissy winced as she pushed herself away. "My left arm really hurts. I guess with all the adrenaline going I didn't notice it before. I landed on it pretty hard when he knocked me down."

Adam pulled his phone from his pocket. "I'll text Dr. Bertrand that we need to see him immediately. We'll have to go to him so you can get an X-ray."

"You don't have to do all that. I'll be fine."

"Already done. Let's go ahead and head there. I'll help you up." Adam grimaced as he pulled her to her feet, a sharp pain stabbing in his ribs.

Alarm filled Chrissy's eyes. "Are you hurt too?"

Adam brushed off her concern with the wave of a hand. "I'm fine."

Chrissy pursed her lips. "Fine just like me?"

Adam chuckled, so glad to see her spunk returning. "Okay, fine. I must've pulled a muscle or something."

"I saw Damien punching you pretty hard. If I'm going to get checked, so are you, mister."

Adam turned and grabbed his keys to hide his grin. "Yes, ma'am."

Chrissy

Back in the apartment with her arm in a sling, Chrissy breathed a sigh of relief. She let Adam guide her to the couch, and she bit back a grin as he built a bed of pillows under her arm.

"Thank you for taking care of me yet again. I promise I'm not usually such a damsel in distress. Typically, I can take care of myself. I have all my life."

Adam took the seat beside her. "I've never been happier to be in the right place at the right time."

"Why were you there?"

Redness crept into his cheeks as he cleared his throat. "When you didn't text me, I jumped in the car to come check on you."

If her heart could talk, it would've just said, "Awww." She took a moment to bask in the glow of his thoughtfulness, then she gasped as her brain made a connection. "Oh no. I forgot to text Lilly. She's probably losing her mind right now." The image of her phone smacking the concrete popped into her head. "My phone is shattered. Can I use yours? I have to let her know I'm okay."

"Of course." Adam dug his phone from his pocket and handed it over.

Lilly answered on the first ring. "Hello? Who is this?"

"It's me, Chrissy. I'm okay."

A rush of breath whooshed through the phone. "Chrissy? Oh, thank God. I thought you were dead. Where are you? What happened? Whose phone are you calling from? I didn't recognize the number."

Chrissy smiled at the barrage of questions. "This is Adam's phone. I'm at his place."

Lilly was silent for a beat. "Oh. So are you two finally...?"

Chrissy peeked over at Adam, who rose to his feet and busied himself in the kitchen. She cupped her hand over her mouth and whispered into the phone. "No, it's not that. Get your mind out of the gutter." She removed her hand and returned her voice to its normal volume. "I don't have the energy for the long version right now, but the short version is that Damien... He, uh... he followed me to the bus stop and attacked me. Thankfully, Adam had been headed to the mural to check on me and swooped in to the rescue. All I ended up with was a partially dislocated shoulder, thankfully. It could've been so much worse if Adam hadn't shown up." Her voice hitched at thoughts of what could've been.

Lilly's gasp rang through the phone. "Oh my gosh. Are you okay? Mentally, I mean. That must've been horrible. Is there anything I can do?"

Chrissy's heart swelled with gratitude that she'd been reconnected with Lilly, her friendship a soothing balm for Chrissy's battered soul. "I'm a little shaken up, but I'll be okay. Adam is letting me stay here until they catch Damien. The cops didn't really want me going home, just in case he might show up there. He shouldn't know where I live, but you never know. I had a funny feeling the other day like someone was following me when I was going home."

"Definitely can't be too careful. I'm glad you're safe," Lilly said. "You sound exhausted, so I won't keep you. I'm always here to talk if you need me, no matter the time. I'll add Adam's number to my contacts so I'll know it's you. Keep me updated."

"Thanks, Lilly. I'll call you in the morning to let you know what's going on."

Chrissy said her goodbyes and laid Adam's phone on the coffee table. He came back to the couch, confirming her suspicions that he'd been giving her privacy.

"I put a pizza in the oven for dinner. I hope that's okay," Adam said as he sat down.

"That sounds perfect."

Adam gestured toward his phone. "Do you need to call anyone else?"

Chrissy leaned back against the cushions with a groan. "I should call Luke, but I'm too drained to deal with that right now."

Adam's brows shot up.

"Don't get me wrong, it's not that he's a bad guy or anything. It's just that... Well, we had a rocky start, and I haven't always had the best judgment since he's known me. I'm not ready to hear what he has to say about this. He's not going to be very happy."

Adam's hand rested on hers with a gentle squeeze. "I'm sure he will be upset about what Damien did, but he'll be relieved to know you're okay. He won't be mad at you."

"Maybe you're right." She stared at the phone, considering Adam's words, then shook her head. "I think I need to rest some first."

Adam gave her hand another squeeze and rose to his feet. "How about we get started on your room while we wait for the pizza?" He motioned for her to follow and disappeared into his office.

Chrissy stopped in the doorway and watched as he shoved his desk to the far side of the room. He then went to the black leather love seat by the door and pulled the cushions off. With one tug, he freed a hide-a-bed from its resting place.

He spread his arms out wide. "Ta-da."

Before Chrissy could react, he went to the closet and pulled out the bedding.

"Let me help you with that," she said, finally stepping into the room.

"With one arm out of commission?" He shot her a wry grin.

She froze and peered down at her arm, internally cussing its uselessness. "Oh. Right."

She stood helplessly and watched as he made the bed with surprising deftness for a man with so much money. She'd assumed he would have a housekeeper do such a mundane task. Just as he finished, the oven timer beeped.

"Let's go eat." Adam brushed his hands together and ushered her to the kitchen.

Every time Chrissy thought she knew exactly who Adam was, he surprised her. She'd grown accustomed to people throwing her for a loop, but ninety-nine percent of the time that was a bad thing. Adam was different. He kept exceeding her expectations in ways she didn't know were possible in real life. Even the little surprises like his ability to make a bed like a regular person felt like hope. Good surprises were refreshing and something she wanted to get used to. She was going to have to work double time to protect her heart from devastation when it all went away.

Chapter 25

Chrissy

Chrissy finger-combed her hair and gave her reflection a once-over, wishing she hadn't left her brush in the guest bathroom. She slipped her arm out of the sling and pulled her messy waves into a ponytail in an attempt to tame them. She wanted to look somewhat nice, but she didn't want it to be obvious that she wanted to look nice. It needed to be a middle ground between looking like a zombie and looking like she'd spent hours stressing over her appearance.

"This will have to do." She knew it was silly to care so much, but that fact didn't stop her. Besides, it was just common courtesy. She didn't want to scare the poor guy.

As she opened the bedroom door, Adam began sputtering and choking in the kitchen. He set his coffee cup on the counter as he struggled to breathe.

"Are you okay?" she asked. Maybe she had scared him with her bedhead after all.

He managed to take in a breath without coughing and nodded. "Just drinking coffee. Well, trying to, at least."

Chrissy giggled. "I hate when it goes down the wrong pipe." She tilted her head toward the coffeepot. "Mind if I have some?"

"Of course not." Adam grabbed a mug and handed it to her. "Just don't drown yourself like I did. There's cream in the fridge and sugar in that box beside the pot."

She filled her cup to the brim. "That's okay. I'm used to drinking it black. It's cheaper that way."

"I would've ordered breakfast already, but I didn't know if you were a sweet or savory kind of person," he said as she slid onto the stool across from him.

She shrugged her uninjured shoulder. "I can just make a piece of toast or something."

"Nonsense. You barely ate yesterday and went through a lot of trauma. I'm sure you're starving, so a good breakfast is in order." He slid his phone across the counter, a breakfast menu cued up on the screen.

As if on command, her stomach growled. A small laugh escaped her as she peeked up at him. "I guess my stomach agrees. And I'm guessing you won't let me pay?"

Adam winked as he turned for more coffee. "You're a fast learner."

An hour later, Chrissy pushed her plate away and patted her stomach. "Man, you know all the good places for food."

"I'll be honest, I don't cook a whole lot. After trying out pretty much every place in town, I've homed in on the best." Adam stood and gathered the dishes.

Chrissy jumped down from her stool. "Here, let me do the dishes."

"No need," Adam said then turned and began loading the dishwasher.

Chrissy palmed her forehead. "Of course. No fancy place like this would be without a dishwasher."

Adam's phone buzzed beside her, Luke's name on the screen.

Adam answered it. "Hello? Oh. There was an issue yesterday. No, everything is fine. Um, yeah, actually. She's here. Uh, sure. Just a second."

He turned toward Chrissy with an apologetic grimace. "Before my coffee woke up my brain, I sent out an email alerting everyone I was taking a personal day. And I sent an email letting people know the mural was on hold for an undetermined amount of time. I might've forgotten that Luke received both of those emails." He held the phone out toward her. "I'm sorry."

Chrissy groaned as she took it, her natural high from the amazing breakfast vanishing. "Hello?"

Luke's voice boomed through the phone. "Chrissy? What happened? Why is the mural postponed? I've been calling your phone for an hour. Why are you with Adam?"

Chrissy filled him in with the same brief recap she'd given Lilly, wincing every time a growl met her ear.

When she finished and Luke finally got to speak, she could hear the fire behind his voice. "I knew that guy was bad news. Something about him rubbed me the wrong way. Have they caught him?"

"No, I don't think we've had any updates from the cops." She looked over at Adam, who shook his head and gave her a thumbs-down. "Nope. No updates yet."

"Well, if they can't find him, I will," Luke said.

Chrissy's heart warmed to hear how much he cared. "Thanks, but you have too good of a life going for you to screw it up over a loser like Damien. Besides, you're my little brother. I'm supposed to be protecting you, not the other way around."

"It doesn't matter who's younger. We're family. We all protect each other, no matter what."

Tears sprang to Chrissy's eyes. Family. What she'd longed for her entire life.

"Do you need me to come get you? You can stay with us if you want. I don't think you should be alone until they catch that asshole," Luke said, his voice rife with concern.

She forced words around the lump forming in her throat. "Thanks for the offer. I'm not really sure what I'm going to do, but I'll let you know. I'll have to get a new phone since mine won't even turn on, but I'll try to keep you updated the best I can. Adam said I can use his phone whenever I need to for now, so you can call this number."

"I'm really glad Adam was in the right place at the right time. Speaking of Adam, can I talk to him again?"

"Of course." Chrissy handed the phone to Adam.

She watched as Adam glanced her way and answered Luke with a hushed tone. He hung up and laid the phone on the counter. "Well, that wasn't so bad, was it?"

"No, it actually wasn't."

Adam's eyes filled with something she couldn't quite decipher. "So, Luke mentioned you might be staying with him for a while until they catch Damien."

Chrissy gasped. "Oh no. I totally forgot to call and check in with the—with my roommate." Her heart hammered at her near slipup as she grabbed the phone. "I need to make another call. Sorry."

She dashed to her temporary room and shut the door as her trembling fingers punched in the number for the halfway house.

"Hello?" Mrs. Chaufin, the director, answered in a flat tone.

"Hi. This is Chrissy Hardin. I'm so sorry I didn't check in last night. My phone got smashed, and I was attacked, so I stayed with someone, and I totally forgot to call." Chrissy's knuckles ached as she gripped the phone.

"Ah, yes, Miss Hardin. As you are aware, one of the stipulations for your stay here is that you follow the guidelines set by the program. We overlooked the fact you missed half of group therapy last week due to supposed heat exhaustion. However, we cannot overlook your failure to meet curfew. You also missed your check-in with your sponsor along with your weekly drug test."

Chrissy's heart seized. The director couldn't possibly be saying what she thought she was saying. "But all those things should count as one strike. They all happened within twelve hours and for the same reason. I swear I'm not doing anything bad."

Mrs. Chaufin remained unfazed. "Be that as it may, each offense counts separately. You know the demand for a placement in this house. I simply cannot bend the rules for you when a hundred other women wait in the streets. I'm sorry, but I'm going to need you to come pick up your things by noon. Goodbye and good luck."

Chrissy sank to the floor, the oxygen evacuating her lungs and her legs losing the strength to support her weight. *This can't be happening.* Not only had Damien stolen her sense of security and injured her body, but the aftermath of his attack had stripped away her path to a better life. He took away her hope, her future.

She pushed her sleeve up her right arm, past the scars that told her history. Trailing her fingers along the raised lines, her thoughts turned dark. Maybe it was a mistake to survive and try again. Being born was her first mistake, and surviving her suicide attempt was the second. No. She gripped her arm, squeezing until pain radiated outward like a burst of light, bringing a calm control back into her world. She let go, running her hands along her thighs and picturing a razor between her fingers. She slammed her palms onto the floor, not caring that the action sent pain shooting through her hurt shoulder as a primal growl raged from her throat.

Adam

Adam burst through the door, his adrenaline racing. Seeing Chrissy distraught on the floor, he sank to his knees beside her. "I heard you yell. What's wrong?"

Chrissy flung her arms around his neck, clinging to him as if he was her sole source of oxygen. "It's over."

He caressed her hair, his mind racing. "What's over?"

"My life."

Adam stiffened, his mind going to her scars. "What do you mean? What happened?"

Chrissy let go, wiping her face on her sleeve. "I got kicked out for not going home last night, and I have to get my stuff by noon. I'm homeless again."

Again. Another heartbreaking window into her past. "Homeless? But why? How can your roommate kick you out for that? You're an adult."

She hung her head and turned away from him. "Because sober-living facilities have a lot of rules and long waiting lists."

Adam bit his lip to stifle a gasp. He knew her life was no picnic, but he never would've guessed she lived in a sober-living situation. This magnificent woman had been through so much. More than he could ever imagine. Dozens of questions filled his mind, but it was not the right time to ask any of them. Maybe someday. Even though he knew she shared Luke's tattoo, he hadn't realized her sobriety was so new. He also knew enough about addiction to know a life-upending event like she was experiencing could bring all her progress to a screeching halt. And he couldn't let something that was out of her control throw her off track. "Stay here."

"What?"

"You're already here, so stay here." He made it sound so easy, but deep down he knew the risks. His boss would demand answers as to why the project was delayed, and Adam would have to tell him the truth about the attack. It was the only way to keep Mr. Lyones from going ballistic at another setback. But his boss would likely have more questions than Adam had answers for. At least answers he would want to share. Maybe Adam could tell his boss he found

Chrissy some temporary housing and leave it at that, but she would need to change her address on file. Surely Luke would let her use his address, especially if Adam filled him in on the risks. Adam couldn't be certain any of it would work out, but he had to try.

She turned around, her expression hesitant and questioning. "Stay here as in live here? I can't do that to you. Luke said I can stay with him. It's not ideal, but it'll work until I can find something else."

"No offense to Luke, but I'm pretty sure his house is at max capacity. Why sleep on his couch when you can have your own room here? Plus, you'd be a lot closer to the mural. You mentioned before how much you'd love to live in a place like this. Well, here's your chance." He watched the wheels turning behind her eyes as she picked at her fingernail. "Plus, this way I can ensure your safety. It's the least I can do after hiring that monster."

"I told you it wasn't your fault. You don't have to apologize or make up for it somehow, especially not like this."

He put his hand on her knee, even though his heart yearned to pull her into his arms. "I know, but I want to. This room is already set up as a guest room now. So how about we go get your stuff?"

Chapter 26
Chrissy

Chrissy's stomach knotted as they edged closer to her former home, trading the shiny buildings of downtown for lackluster townhomes. "You can stop here, and I'll walk the rest of the way."

Adam shook his head and glanced down at the GPS. "Not a chance."

Her chest constricted as they neared Path of Hope. No one that mattered in her life had ever seen where she lived, and Adam was the last person she wanted to break that streak. She knew in her heart that getting the help she needed was nothing to be embarrassed about, but once people saw that part of someone, it tended to be *all* they saw. The last thing she wanted was for people to see everything she did through the lens of "recovering addict." The fact that Adam even looked at her after hearing about her accommodations left her in shock, yet there he was driving her to pick up her belongings.

The car came to a stop, and she peered up at the four-story building that had been her home for the past few months.

She spun at the sound of Adam's door opening. "No," she said, her voice louder than she'd intended. "Please, stay here."

"But what about your arm? Won't you need help carrying stuff?"

"I promise I'll come get you if I need help." She took a shaky breath and looked at the front door of her former home. "I need to do this alone."

Adam nodded and pulled his door shut. "Okay. I'll wait here."

She gave him a smile of gratitude before climbing out of the car. With a deep inhale for courage, she dragged herself up the concrete steps. Two cardboard boxes with her name scrawled on them in black marker greeted her just inside the entrance.

Mrs. Chaufin nodded her welcome from her heavy oak desk. "I'm sorry. It's protocol."

"Can I say bye to Donna?"

"I'm afraid that's not for the best." The director's features softened a tiny bit. "I'll let her know you said goodbye."

Without a word, Chrissy slid her arm out of its sling and scooped up the boxes, balancing them in her arms and bracing them with her chin. She shoved the door open with her butt and stepped over the threshold. The finality of the moment brought her a fresh wave of grief. As much as she'd resented needing to live there, this wasn't the way she'd wanted to leave.

Adam leaned against the side of the car with the trunk open. When he saw Chrissy, he rushed to take the boxes from her. "What are you doing? You said you'd come get me if you needed help. You shouldn't be carrying boxes with your shoulder being hurt."

"It's fine. They're not heavy." She slid her arm back in the sling as she observed the two pathetic boxes resting in Adam's trunk. Her whole life fit in two boxes.

They got back in the car without a word and drove back to Adam's building.

They rode in silence, and Chrissy fought to rein in her storm of emotions. The bitterness of Damien attacking her and costing her so much mixed with the sting of her cold interaction with Mrs. Chaufin and the fact that Chrissy couldn't even say goodbye to those she left behind. While the prospect of living in a swanky condo with Adam brought some excitement, apprehension and feeling like a fish out of water in that fancy world kept her from enjoying any of it.

Back in Adam's place, Chrissy patted the still-taped boxes sitting on the bed. "Are you sure about this? It's not too late to back out. I can call Luke back and tell him I changed my mind and that I'll stay with him."

Adam grunted as he moved things around in the closet then popped his head out. "I'm sure." One last shuffle and he came out into the room. "There. Now you should have plenty of room for your stuff. I didn't realize I had so much junk in there."

His gray T-shirt hugged his muscles as he swiped his arm across his brow, resurrecting feelings Chrissy hadn't felt in ages. As eye-catching as Adam was in his suits, something about a simple T-shirt and jeans ramped up his sex appeal in ways she didn't quite understand. Maybe it was the window into his softer, more vulnerable side. A peek behind the curtain, so to speak. And it melted her.

"Everything okay?"

Chrissy jumped, her cheeks blazing at being caught ogling him. "Oh, yeah. Sorry. I was lost in thought." She busied herself with trying to pull open the boxes one-handed.

"Here, let me open those for you." Adam grabbed some scissors from the desk and made quick work of the tape. He scanned the room. "Sorry there's no dresser in here. I never really expected to have anyone actually use this as a guest room."

"Don't be sorry. This place is more than I could ask for. I don't have much stuff anyway."

"We can figure out something better for long-term." Adam froze. "I mean, if you end up wanting to stay for a while." He cleared his throat and pointed behind him. "Anyway, I'll get my work stuff out of the desk."

Chrissy grinned. Adam was absolutely adorable when he got flustered.

She inhaled and opened the first box, her hands shaking. Unpacking meant it was official. She was moving in with Adam. Whether she was emotionally ready or not.

Adam turned as she lifted a silver urn from the box.

"What's that?" he asked.

"It's my mom's ashes." She walked over and set the urn on the desk, tucking it to one side against the wall so it wouldn't get bumped. "Luke gave them to me."

Adam stopped digging in the lower drawer but said nothing.

"I never got to meet her." Chrissy slid her fingers over the urn and felt her heart open. For once, she wanted to talk about it. "While I was in the children's home, I snuck into the office and read my files once. I didn't remember my parents, so it felt like I was reading about some other poor kid's crappy life. Even now when I stop and think about the fact that all that stuff was about me, it seems surreal. But at the time it helped me cope with the fact I was taken away from them."

"That's a lot to deal with." Adam's voice was gruff, and Chrissy figured if she could bring herself to look at him, she might see that he was ready to shed some tears on her behalf.

She nodded. "It is. But at least I was able to learn my parents' names. I would keep tabs on them over the years through legal filings. All those years, I could've contacted them, but I was too scared. I was terrified of getting hurt or being rejected, so I avoided it. Then when I saw her obituary, it was like the wind had been knocked out of me. I waited too long, and now I'll never get to meet her. But I saw Luke's name. Until then, I never knew I had a sibling. He's been the best thing to come out of it all. He gave me her ashes so I could maybe get some kind of closure about never meeting her."

"Did you ever meet your dad?"

She shook her head then finally looked at Adam. "No. Luke warned me not to go alone because our dad wasn't exactly a good guy. But I felt like I had to go see him because I didn't want the same kind of regrets I had about not seeing Mom. I never told Luke, but I actually did try to go meet our dad once. He wanted to meet at a bar, but I was in recovery so I talked him into meeting at the park across from the bar. When I got there, he was drunk and ranting at everyone who walked past. I pretended like I didn't know him."

Adam rounded the desk and pulled her in for a quick hug. "I'm so sorry."

Chrissy let out a shaky breath. "Luke was right. We were better off without our dad."

"Still, it had to be hard to not have a relationship with your parents."

"It is. I think I'll always have a little piece of my heart empty." A question that had been stirring in her mind for weeks worked its way to the surface and out of her mouth before she could stop it. "What about your parents?"

Adam stiffened. "What about them?"

"Are you close?" She hadn't ever seen him call them, and there were no family pictures in his apartment, so she could guess the answer to her question. But she wanted to hear it from him.

"Uh, we used to be." Adam returned to the half-empty desk drawer, concentrating like it was the most important task in the world.

"What happened?"

"It's complicated."

With as much as she'd shared with him, she wished he would open up a little to her.

Well, duh. Family is complicated. It was obvious he wasn't going to give any more information, so she switched tactics.

She walked over to the bed and began pulling her clothes from the boxes. "You know, therapists are great at helping you work through complicated stuff."

Adam stood up straight. "Who says I need to work through anything?"

Chrissy shrugged, trying to keep herself cool and casual against his defensiveness. "It's not a bad thing. I think every single person could benefit from some therapy. And I can tell whatever happened with your parents still bothers you. A good therapist could help you repair that relationship if you want or help you get over the loss of it.”

“I doubt that.” By Adam’s clipped tone, Chrissy knew she’d struck a nerve.

“Well, you never know if you don’t try. And for what it’s worth, I would do anything to have a good relationship with even one of my parents, but I’ll never get that chance. The fear of pain got in the way, but I got hurt in the end just the same. It just ended up being a different kind of pain. Don’t let fear get in the way of talking to your parents. Either way there’s pain, but by letting fear win, you become the one to blame. Don’t wait until you no longer have a chance.”

Adam surveyed the stuff he’d piled on the desk then headed for the door. “I’m going to go get a box for all this.”

Chrissy watched him go, crossing her fingers she hadn’t hit a nerve so deep it cost her the use of his guest room.

“So how did Luke take the news of you living here?” Adam asked as he breezed back into the room like their heavy conversation hadn’t just happened.

So that’s how he wants to play it. Okay. Chrissy sat on the bed with a groan and massaged her shoulder. “I think he was a little insulted I didn’t want to stay with him, honestly, though he wouldn’t admit it. But ultimately, he knows I’ll have a lot more space this way and I’m closer to work.” No need to tell Adam about the lecture Luke had given her about not letting her crush on Adam affect her decisions.

A knock at the door made her jump, her brain still on high alert.

“Just in time.” Adam flashed her a conspiratorial grin before going to the front door and receiving a package.

Chrissy stood in her bedroom doorway.

He tipped the delivery man and shut the door, then he held the box out for her. "Here. This is for you."

Chrissy's brows knit together. "What?"

"Open it."

She couldn't believe her eyes when she opened the box and found a brand-new phone nestled inside. "You got me a phone?"

"I figured you were tired of having to ask to use mine. Plus, you need one before you go back to work on the mural on Monday." He lifted the phone from the box and pulled out an envelope from underneath. "I hope you like it."

Chrissy ripped open the envelope, and out slid a glittery pink phone case with yellow and white daisies painted on the back. Her heart swooned at the sentimental gesture. "This is perfect."

Adam grinned, clearly pleased with himself, and slid the phone into the case with a click. "It was supposed to come set up, so all you should have to do is set your passwords and go."

She clicked the screen to life, her hand flying to her mouth when she saw the home screen. Staring back at her was an image of herself, her hair glowing in the sunshine as she painted a bright-green tree.

Adam leaned over to look at the screen. "It's one of the pictures Sheila took for promotions. I had the lady who set up your phone put that as your home screen so you can see it every time you open your phone. That way you have a constant reminder of how amazing you are."

"Adam, it's..." Words failed her as she gaped at the image.

"The rest of the album Sheila sent is loaded on there too. They're pictures of you and your work, so I felt you should have them. They're all great, but I really liked your smile in that one." Pink filled Adam's cheeks, and he cleared his throat. "I also had them preload some contacts in there to save you some time."

"I don't know what to say." The thoughtfulness behind such a gift shook her to the core. From the phone to the daisies to having it set up for her, Adam had thought of every possible way to make her feel special. For once, through the image on her screen, she saw herself the way she'd always wanted to be seen. The way she wanted Adam to see her.

"No need to say anything. But you'd better text Luke and Lilly your new number. I'll go order some food for dinner." With a wink, Adam went to the kitchen.

An hour later, Chrissy waltzed out of her room into the kitchen, clutching her new phone. "All done, finally. Lilly was talkative." She stopped dead in her tracks. "What's that?"

Adam looked up from the sparkling liquid he was pouring into two glasses. "It's sparkling cider. Nonalcoholic. A celebratory drink. I don't really drink alcohol either."

Her muscles relaxed, and she slid into her seat at the counter. She took the glass he offered and clinked it with his.

"Here's to putting the past where it belongs." Adam took a swig and set his glass down, but something flashed in his eyes Chrissy couldn't quite read.

Though curious, she brushed it off. She didn't need to pry any more than she already had. "What's that mouthwatering smell?"

Adam began pulling containers from a black bag. "I ordered from Maggiano's tonight. We've got chicken Parmesan, fettuccini Alfredo, and lasagna. Oh, and an order of their garlic cheese bread. You can have your pick because I'm good with whatever. These are all my favorites."

"How about a sampling of each?"

"I like the way you think." He pointed two finger guns at her then began scooping a little of each dish onto two plates.

Chrissy stared down at the plate as he slid it in front of her, her mind flashing to the first time she'd come to his condo. Her picturesque daydream of eating fancy Italian food in his kitchen had become reality down to the tiniest detail, with her perched in the very same seat.

Adam rounded the counter and took the seat next to her, frowning with concern. "Why aren't you eating? Is something wrong?"

Chrissy shook her head to clear the daydream, only this time it wasn't a daydream. It was real. "No. Nothing wrong at all."

She scooped a forkful of the best fettuccini she'd ever tasted into her mouth and savored the flavors. Absolutely nothing was wrong with anything in that very moment, when she was sitting in a swanky condo with a gorgeous and kind man, eating yet another best meal of her life. It was a taste of bright possibilities, and she was hell-bent on savoring every single morsel.

Chapter 27
Chrissy

Another sleepless night. Worries about the future coursed through Chrissy's mind. With a sigh, she flopped onto her back and grabbed her phone from the nightstand. The corner of her mouth ticked upward as the image of her on her lock screen glowed bright.

"Let's see if all the pictures are this good." She clicked on her photo album. A vibrant rainbow of pictures filled her screen, and she marveled at how effortlessly normal she appeared. The woman in the pictures didn't have a dark cloud hovering overhead. Absent was the neon sign with an arrow pointing to her, screaming "damaged goods." From the outside, she appeared on par with all the regular people she watched on her lunch breaks. She'd even venture so far as saying she looked pretty. She marveled at how the outsider perspective could be so vastly different from how she felt on the inside.

The next swipe brought a picture of her and Adam, his arm looped behind her back. Their faces beamed at her, both joyful and full of life. The richness of emotion captured on the screen gave her pause. By all accounts, the Chrissy in that picture was happy.

Laying her phone on her chest, she closed her eyes and traveled back to that moment. The sun's rays beat down, sweat beading on her forehead and pooling on her lower back. Her stomach knotted with every click and whir of the camera. Delicious smells and raucous sounds drifted over from the farmer's market as she dabbed details over the broad swatches of base color.

And there was Adam, standing on the sidelines and cheering her on, spouting compliments and words of encouragement with ease. She giggled at his face when the photographer suggested he join in the pictures. When he'd slipped his arm around her, all the bothersome heat and noise had evaporated.

She looked happy in the picture because she *was* happy. Actually happy. And with that thought, she drifted off to sleep.

With a yawn, Chrissy felt on her nightstand for her phone to quiet the incessant alarm. Coming up empty, she pried her eyelids open, finding her phone tangled in the covers beside her. *What the—?* Oh yeah.

Flashbacks of falling asleep while ogling Adam's picture made her palm her forehead. She was as bad as a teenager with a crush. She rubbed her face and plodded toward the guest bathroom with a groan.

"Well, hello."

Her hands dropped to her sides, and her eyes flew open and were greeted with the sight of Adam's bare chest blocking the doorway. "Oh my gosh. I'm sorry. I didn't see you there."

"So I noticed." His mouth twisted in a bemused, lopsided grin, the one that showcased his adorable dimple.

That grin froze her in her tracks and kicked her pulse up a notch. Powerless to stop them, Chrissy let her eyes rake over his muscular frame, her hands itching to trail along his broad shoulders. The plush white towel around his waist hung low and tantalizing, as if one movement would send it falling.

Adam's chuckle reached her ears, stopping her swoon just in time. Her ears burned red-hot as she pulled her gaze back to his face.

The smirk she found there only fueled her mortified flames. "Sorry, I zoned out. I guess I'm not all the way awake yet."

The excuse sounded lame even to her, and she watched Adam struggle to suppress his self-satisfied grin.

"It looks like your bruises are healing well," Chrissy said, hoping that was a believable excuse for her wandering eyes. He hadn't mentioned having bruises on his ribs, but with all the punches Damien had landed it wasn't surprising. Still, seeing the proof of what Adam had endured in order to save her stirred guilt and gratefulness in her all at once.

"They're fine. Anyway, I ran out of soap in my bathroom, so I was just grabbing some from here. This bathroom is all yours." He gripped his towel with one hand and sauntered past her, oozing swagger.

Alone in the bathroom, Chrissy leaned against the sink and fanned herself. If she'd known what lurked underneath those three-piece suits, she never would've let herself move in. Her whole body awoke from its dormant slumber and hummed with desire. She needed a shower to snap herself out of it, and she'd better make it a cold one.

Adam

The light-gray tie constricted around Adam's neck like a noose as he slipped on his navy suit jacket. For the first time in years, he didn't want to go to work. For the first time since Beth, he had something to be home for. He glanced over at the picture face down on his dresser then brought his attention back to his reflection and cursed himself. He should've just let Chrissy stay with Luke. He should've known he wouldn't be able to keep his emotions in check. A cardinal rule of bachelorhood was to not play house with a woman you had a crush on. Yet there he was, proving himself to be an idiot, once again.

Luke's words echoed in his head. "If she gives you her trust, don't break it." But he had already let it go too far. Even if he told Chrissy the truth that very minute, she would feel betrayed, especially after everything she had shared with him. And there was no doubt in his mind that she wouldn't want anything to do with him. Adam turned his back to the mirror, unable to stomach the sight of such a fool any longer. Pasting a neutral look on his face, he pulled open his bedroom door and stepped out into the mess he'd created.

He stopped short when he caught Chrissy rubbing a dark line on her neck. "What's that?"

Chrissy's head shot up, and she pulled her hair forward to cover her neck. "Oh. I didn't notice you were over there."

He took a step closer, concern overriding all his other thoughts. "What's that mark on your neck?"

"It's nothing." She waved a dismissive hand but wouldn't look his way.

He eased down onto the couch beside her, his stomach knotting. "I can tell it's something or you wouldn't be hiding it. Did you... Did you do something?"

She turned toward him and shook her head. "No. No, it's nothing like that. When Damien attacked me, he ripped my necklace off. I was so concerned about my arm that I didn't tell Dr. Bertrand about my neck. Or tell you." She offered up a sheepish, apologetic grin then pulled her hair to one side.

The deep-purple line across the back of her neck served as a stronger sucker punch to his ribs than Damien's blows. His hands clenched into tight fists, and he cursed under his breath.

"I figured it would go away on its own, so it wasn't really worth bothering anyone over. From what I can see, it's just a bruise, right?"

"Can I touch it?" Adam asked. Chrissy nodded, so he gingerly ran a finger along the bruise. He prodded a few places along the line. "Is it sore?"

"Yeah, but not as bad as it was."

Adam bit his lip, resisting the urge to kiss her neck along the marking. He pulled his hands away before he lost control, then he cleared his throat. "There're a couple of places with scabs where it looks like the chain scraped the skin, but other than that it's just bruising. I wish you would've told me, though. We need to tell the police."

Chrissy let her hair fall around her shoulders. "I told them when I gave my statement. They took pictures of my neck and took the necklace as evidence. I'm sorry I didn't tell you. I promise I wasn't trying to lie to you. You'd just gone so above and beyond, I didn't want to dump anything else on you."

Even following an assault, this woman put others above herself. Adam laid his hand on her knee. "I'm not mad at you for not telling me. You don't owe me anything, no confessions or explanations. My frown was only because of my concern. I just want to make sure you're okay."

She smiled up at him. "Thanks."

The buzz of his phone made him flinch. "Starting the day off with a bang. I better get going to the office. Are you sure you'll be okay here?"

Chrissy shot him a smirk. "I'm pretty sure I can manage a day of lounging in a palace."

He chuckled as he grabbed his wallet and pulled out some cash. He held up a finger to staunch the inevitable protest. "I'm leaving this here just in case. I know you plan to eat the leftovers and watch TV, but if you get bored, I'm also leaving an extra key and directions to the various amenities. I informed management of your presence, so if anyone questions you, just tell them you're my guest." He opened the door but turned back around. "Oh, and of course you can call me if you need anything. I put all my info into your contact list."

He hesitated, unable to shake all the worries and stress of the last two days, then forced himself to leave. As much as he told himself anyone would share his concern for Chrissy given her traumas, he knew it was more than that. And as much as he fought it, his feelings for her were growing every day, and they were definitely not staying platonic. Or professional. He was in trouble. And he had no idea what he was going to do about it.

Chapter 28
Chrissy

The door clicked shut behind Adam, leaving Chrissy free to collapse on the couch and fan herself. She'd barely managed to hold herself together when he'd inspected her injury. His fingertips gliding across the back of her neck had sent fireworks shooting to her core. Maybe she should've taken Luke up on his offer. Or Lilly on hers. Either would've been safe choices, but no. Instead of sleeping on her brother's couch or in her best friend's guest room, she'd chosen to take over the home office of Prince Charming himself. With each glance, she fell deeper under his spell, and each touch, no matter how mundane, awakened her body from the dead piece by piece.

Her eyes flitted over to the pile of money, keys, and paper Adam had left for her, and she huffed. Like she'd ever have the nerve to mingle with the rich people. She sat up and grabbed the remote, determined to get Adam and romantic fantasies out of her brain with some mind-numbing reality television.

After four hours of watching botched surgery repairs, Chrissy climbed off the couch and stretched. Sliding her arm from the sling, she gave her shoulder a gentle stretch and decided to let her arm have some time out of it. Staying in the condo made it easy to follow Dr. Bertrand's order not to do anything too strenuous.

She padded across the cool marble tile, pulled open the refrigerator, and surveyed its contents. She marveled at the well-organized space, realizing that in all her time there so far, this was the first time she'd actually gotten her own food or drink. Ever the gentleman, Adam always got whatever she needed. She swooned as she pulled the leftover lasagna and cheesy bread from the shelf. While it warmed in the microwave, her mind wandered to Adam yet again. She pictured him sitting in a swanky office and eating lunch while checking emails. Or perhaps he was eating at a restaurant with some clients.

The microwave beeped, and she grumbled at herself. So much for keeping her mind off Adam. She carried her plate over to her favorite spot—the wall of windows—and sat on the floor. Another "this can't be real" moment smacked her upside the head. She chewed the delectable pasta and looked out over the hustle and bustle of the city. The people below went about their day, oblivious to the woman twenty-five stories up watching them like a kid watching ants.

From her perspective high above it all, it dawned on her just how minuscule an individual was in the grand scheme of things. The actions of one person rarely changed the world. Instead of depressing her, the thought liberated her. Maybe her screwups weren't as huge a deal as she perceived them to be.

Maybe instead of worrying about what society thought of her, Chrissy should just focus on the people close to her. She couldn't control society, but she could control who she let into her little corner of the world. Only the opinions of those close to her mattered, and if they thought she deserved better, then maybe it was true.

Armed with a box of art supplies, the condo key, her phone, and the directions Adam had written out, Chrissy stepped into the hallway. Her instinct was to shrink into herself, but she forced her body tall and proud. This was her home now for the near future, so she'd better start acting like she belonged.

She stepped into the elevator, glanced at the paper, then pushed the R button. When the doors opened again, wind and sunlight blasted her. Regretting not grabbing her sunglasses, she squinted and stepped out onto the tile walkway on the roof. To the left, brilliant turquoise water sparkled as the wind sent ripples across the pool's surface. Maybe one day Chrissy would feel comfortable in a swimsuit. *Today is not that day.*

She turned her focus to the right and zeroed in on what she'd come for. Two massive concrete planters filled with purple and pink blooms marked the entrance to the rooftop garden. Crossing the threshold, she stepped into a green oasis amongst the grays and blues of buildings tickling the sky. Inching her way to the edge, she peeked over the concrete wall at the streets below.

An ornate bench nestled amongst the planters on one end of the garden, its sleek white finish gleaming in the sunlight. The opposite end of the garden boasted a matching bistro set. Chrissy settled into one of the chairs and dug a notebook and colored pencils from her box. She needed to buy some canvases pronto, but for now her sketch pad would have to do.

Turning the page to start her fourth sketch, Chrissy paused to stretch her hand. The last time she'd sketched that much, she'd been doing individual portraits for a family of six at the park near Luke's house. That was months ago. She took a sip of water and admired the skyline, giving her hand a rest.

Rippling water reached her ear, and she turned toward the sound. Stuffing her sketchpad into her box, she stood and peeked over the garden wall.

An elderly woman bobbing toward the deep end of the pool waved hello. "I hope I'm not disturbing you, dear."

Chrissy pointed to herself. "Me? No, not at all."

"Good. There usually isn't anyone else up here when I do my water aerobics." The slender woman continued her leisurely stroll toward the deep end, a blue foam tube held firmly in front of her. A silver swim cap with black roses printed all over it covered her hair. From what Chrissy could see through the water, the woman's one-piece swimsuit coordinated perfectly with the cap.

"I can leave, if you'd like privacy," Chrissy said, taking a step backward.

"I don't monopolize the roof, dear." When the water reached the woman's shoulders, she turned and headed in the other direction. "Forgive me for not shaking your hand. My name is Winifred Smythe. I don't believe I've seen you here before."

Winifred was the name of the woman Adam considered to be like a grandma.

Chrissy neared the edge of the pool and fidgeted with her purple fingernails. "My name is Chrissy Hardin. Well, technically I'm Christine, but I go by Chrissy. I'm new to the building, and I'm staying with Adam Rochester."

Winifred halted for a beat then continued the last few feet to the end of the pool and gripped the silver handrail as she climbed the steps. She crossed to a gray lounge chair and wrapped a fluffy white robe around herself, a black filigree monogram splaying across the chest.

Chrissy's anxiety skyrocketed as she watched the woman wordlessly move about, hoping she hadn't offended her in some way. But when Winifred turned her way, a smile graced her face.

"Mind if I join you in the garden?" Winifred asked as she lifted her swim cap and revealed silver shoulder-length waves.

"Oh, uh, not at all," Chrissy stammered, then she stepped aside to let the older woman pass. "I hope I didn't bother you."

Winifred tutted and waved a hand as she slid into the other seat at the bistro set. "I always take a rest mid-workout. I've been in the pool for a while now, but I suspected you didn't notice. You seemed very engrossed in whatever you were doing."

Chrissy's cheeks flushed at the thought of someone watching her sketch. "I guess I did get a little carried away."

"Might I ask what held your interest?"

"Oh. Sure." Chrissy pulled her sketch pad from the box, whose well-worn cardboard and fraying tape looked pathetic against the rooftop's finery. Wishing she had found something nicer to carry her supplies in, she set the sketch pad in front of her new acquaintance. "I was just working on some sketches of the beautiful views."

Winifred slipped some delicate silver-framed glasses from the pocket of her robe and set them on her nose.

Chrissy sat on her hands to keep from picking at her fingernail polish as she watched Winifred flip through the pages. Winifred was the only person of importance in Adam's life that Chrissy had met so far, and she wanted to make the best impression possible. So far all she'd managed was being aloof.

Winifred peered over the rims of her glasses and studied Chrissy. "You drew these just now?"

"Yes…" Chrissy meant it as a statement, but it came out as more of a question.

Winifred pursed her lips as she scanned over the pages again. "Well, these are fantastic. No wonder you didn't notice an old lady like me paddling about."

So much pent-up air rushed out of Chrissy she imagined she might fly off like a runaway balloon. "Thanks. I'm working on some ideas for future projects, so these are just the rough sketches."

"If these are the rough ideas, I can't wait to see the real thing when you're done." Winifred handed the sketch pad back to her with a smile. "Did I hear you correctly that you're staying with Adam Rochester?"

Chrissy busied herself with putting her sketch pad away so Winifred wouldn't see her panic as she sent a silent plea to the universe to make this woman like her. She secured a calm smile on her face before she straightened. "Yes, that's the one. I'm assuming you're the Winifred he mentioned."

"All good things, I hope."

Chrissy looked around and leaned toward the woman with a conspiratorial look. "He might've said something along the lines of you being a better person than everyone in the entire building."

Winifred chuckled, a sound that loosened a few of the knots in Chrissy's shoulders. "That sounds like my Adam. So, Chrissy, tell me. How do you two know each other?"

Winifred's voice held an investigative tone that twisted the knot back into Chrissy's muscles. Her brain scrambled for a way to explain the convoluted path that led her to being Adam's roommate without baring her secrets to a woman she'd just met and craved approval from. "Well, um, it's kind of complicated."

"I'm retired, dear. I have all the time you need, and my mind is still sharp despite my advanced age." Winifred reclined against the chair and crossed her arms over her chest, waiting.

A nervous chuckle burst out of Chrissy, and she swallowed, feeling very much like she stood in front of a firing squad. *Focus on the facts.* "Okay. I'm not really sure where to start. Let's see. Um, I don't know if you've heard about the mural being painted down by the farmer's market, but I'm the artist they hired. Adam is the one overseeing the project, and we've become friends over the past month. Due to a series of unfortunate events, I was left without a place to stay, so Adam offered to let me stay here with him."

"As a roommate?"

"Yes. He turned his home office into a guest room."

Winifred nodded. "Adam has always been such a nice young man, so it's no surprise he would help you. Did he tell you how we met?"

"No, he didn't. He doesn't talk about himself much." Chrissy leaned forward on her elbows, eager for a glimpse into Adam's past.

A look flickered across Winifred's face that was at once both wistful and guarded. "As the longest-term resident in the building, I take it upon myself to meet everyone who moves in. A self-made welcoming committee of sorts. When he moved in two years ago, I could tell he could use some companionship. He resisted me at first." She paused to chuckle. "Oh boy, did he resist me. Left to his own devices, he would've become a hermit. In my sixty-plus years, I've learned persistence is key. I paid him a visit every Wednesday night and Saturday morning like clockwork, and he continued to shut me out. After a couple of months, I fell ill and missed our Wednesday-night meeting. On Thursday, he came to check on me and seemed genuinely upset to hear I was under the weather. Friday, soup was delivered to my door for lunch, and he stopped by again that night. Instead of our usual quick conversation, he asked to come in for a visit. Saturday morning, he showed up again and visited all day, helping with whatever I needed. Now here we are."

Chrissy blinked away some tears as her heart swooned full force. "That's a lovely story. Thank you for telling me."

A gleam sparkled in the older woman's eyes as she gave Chrissy a soft smile. "A lovely story about a lovely young man."

"Yeah, he's a really nice guy." Chrissy shifted in her seat.

"It's a pity for such a nice man to go to waste. He would make a wonderful husband to some lucky woman, don't you think?" She gave Chrissy a sidelong look.

Chrissy begged the earth to open up and swallow her before she had to answer that question. Of course Adam was amazing and would undoubtedly do everything in his power to make the woman blessed enough to marry him as happy as he possibly could. That exact scenario played out in Chrissy's head almost nightly when she needed soothing thoughts to lull herself to sleep. But there was no way she could confess any of that to his honorary grandma.

The awkward silence stretching, Chrissy cleared her throat and forced herself to form words. "Whoever she is will be very lucky."

"Indeed." Winifred's gaze bored into Chrissy for a second before she patted the table and stood. "Well, I'd best be getting back to the second half of my regimen. It was nice chatting with you, dear."

Chrissy blinked, thrown for a loop by the sudden departure. "Oh, okay. It was nice meeting you."

At the garden entrance, Winifred turned back. "We all have pasts, and if I learned anything from my six husbands, it's that we're never promised a future. The only thing that truly matters is the present, so we must let go of fear and make the most of it." She turned back to the pool and tossed her parting words over her shoulder. "Don't be a stranger, dear."

The wind rustled through the flowers and tugged at Chrissy's hair as she gaped at the insightful woman tucking her hair back into the swim cap. After a delicate wiggle of her fingers in Chrissy's direction, Winifred retrieved her float and slipped back into the water.

The way Winifred seemed to read between the lines left Chrissy reeling, her chest ripped open and her heart revealed for all to see. The once-relaxing sunshine now beat down with relentless fury. Her hair whipping in the wind irritated her to no end. Retrieving her unsightly box from the ground, she made a beeline for her new safe haven, Adam's apartment.

Chapter 29

Adam

Drumming his fingers on the railing, Adam watched the numbers tick by as the elevator climbed higher and brought him closer and closer to a place he'd never been excited to be. His condo. Until then, the condo had served as his prison, the place he went to hide away from the world when the grief and guilt became too much. It was the place where his past couldn't find him.

But everything had changed. His prison had transformed into a home from the moment a certain blonde filled the monochromatic space with her color. Chrissy not only painted with her brush but also with her presence, bringing sunshine back to the dreary, barren landscape of his life. She awoke a part of him he'd written off as dead, a part he'd long thought buried alongside Beth.

Being around Chrissy made him want what he didn't deserve. A second chance. His brain knew he deserved nothing more than to sit alone in his prison, watching the world slip by as it left him behind. Try as he might, he couldn't get his heart to listen.

By the time the elevator dinged, his stomach was fluttering and twisting. The mix of hope and despair left both his heart and head aching and confused. He sucked air in through his nose and let it out through his mouth as he reached for the door.

As soon as he stepped inside, he was greeted by the sight of Chrissy seated by the windows with art supplies strewn about her. "It looks like you found something to keep yourself busy."

She turned a bright face in his direction. "Yeah. Having a bird's-eye view is perfect inspiration for murals of the city."

He tossed his satchel on the entryway table then tugged at his tie as he strolled over. Cityscapes from various angles and in different colorations littered the floor. "Wow. You've been really busy. I can't believe you can churn out this many sketches in a day."

She sprang to her feet and grabbed a stack of papers from the coffee table. "These are the rest." She laid them all out along with the others and then stood back, hands on her hips. "What do you think? Anything catch your eye? Some are duplicates with just a different color palette, but it's crazy how much the colors change as the day goes on."

Adam snuck a sidelong glance at her, his heart soaring at seeing her exhilaration. Tearing his eyes from her, he scanned over the sketches, his sight snagging on the set she'd just laid down. "Where did you draw these? That's not the view from my windows."

"I ventured to the roof after lunch."

He couldn't help but nod in approval. "Good. I'm glad you're making yourself at home." He picked up a picture drawn as if looking through the rooftop flowers and let out a low whistle. "I like this one a lot. It looks like the roof was good inspiration."

"It was. I also ran into Winifred while I was up there." Her voice held an odd edge that piqued his curiosity.

He raised a brow. "Oh yeah?"

Chrissy nodded and began gathering her sketches. "She's definitely a big fan of yours."

Adam chuckled at that statement. "Is that so? Well, I'm a bigger fan of hers. What all did she tell you?" Though he trusted Winifred, his pulse elevated at the thought of her spilling his secrets.

"She told me about you taking care of her while she was sick. Also that you were standoffish at first."

He tried to keep his expression neutral as he studied Chrissy's features for hints about whether she knew his history. "Yeah, I'm a little slow to warm up to people and usually prefer to stay in the shadows. I'm glad she didn't give up on me, though."

It was Chrissy's turn to raise an eyebrow at him. "I never pegged you as shy or a loner. You've always seemed so confident and friendly."

He panicked, searching for a way to reconcile his statement with her perception. Both were true, but he couldn't tell her the reason. Though typically a shy loner, he crawled from his shell whenever Chrissy was around. Her presence brought out all his better qualities, and her smile made him feel invincible.

Blinking away his panic, he mustered a nonchalant shrug. "You're easy to talk to, and you're friendly. It puts me at ease. Most people in this building look like they just smelled a fart or something."

A loud guffaw burst from Chrissy. "Oh my gosh. It's true. I thought they just didn't like me or something. Now I'm going to have to hold in giggles when I see the grumpy faces."

"You're welcome. It helps me keep from letting their bad mood in." He wondered if she could see his chest puff with pride from making her laugh.

"You'd think being rich, they'd be in better moods."

"Honestly, a lot of them worry too much about their image. Always worrying about what everyone thinks and constantly being on guard must be draining."

Chrissy propped a hand on her hip. "Huh. I never thought about that, but it makes sense. That would be miserable. I must say, Winifred seems pretty comfortable in her skin. She didn't strike me as the type to care too much about what other people think."

Adam smiled at the thought of the older woman. "Yeah, she's a gem. And a spitfire. She's somewhat of a black sheep in the building thanks to her no-nonsense attitude, but she's been here forever, so people have to play nice. She won't talk about it, but she's loaded, so people automatically respect her. And they're probably trying to stay on her good side in hopes of maybe getting their hands in the honeypot."

She crinkled her nose. "That's a horrible reason to be friends with someone."

"And because you think like that, I'm sure Winifred likes you. She's pretty good at reading people, from what I've seen." He gave her a playful wink.

"I don't know. Sometimes it seemed like she liked me, but other times I was in the hot seat." Chrissy toyed with her fingernail, a nervous habit Adam found endearing.

"She puts everyone in the hot seat. I'm sure you have nothing to worry about." He was secretly dying to know what the two women had talked about but reminded himself it wasn't any of his business. "Hey, how about a change of scenery? Do you want to venture out to eat tonight instead of getting delivery?"

Her eyes widened with trepidation as her hand flew to her messy bun. "Are you sure you want to be seen with me?"

He made sure he exuded confidence so she wouldn't find any reason to doubt herself. "I wouldn't ask if I wasn't okay with it. And stop putting yourself beneath me like that. You're not beneath me or anyone else in this building. I'm proud to be seen with you. Okay? I don't care what other people say, anyway. Besides, it's just a meal. Everyone has to eat. Right? So let's go out. I'm going to change out of this suit first, though."

Chrissy

Slamming the hangers to one side of the closet, Chrissy scowled at her pitiful collection of clothes. Having had no intention of ever looking at a man romantically again as long as she lived, she lacked any clothing with even an ounce of sex appeal. Damien was right when he called her a nun. Long sleeves and high necklines stared at her mockingly. *But would I dare wear anything showy if I had it?* After giving up her former lifestyle, she'd sworn off anything appealing to the opposite sex.

The white garment bag she'd hung in the very back of the closet caught her eye. An image of the dress Aria had given her for Luke and Aria's wedding popped into her head. She hadn't opened the bag since and had never considered wearing the dress ever again. It had felt like a symbol of a life she couldn't have. Out of sight, out of mind had been her strategy.

With an inhale for courage, she unzipped the bag and ran her fingers over the cornflower-blue fabric adorned with delicate white flowers. She chewed her lip as she slipped the soft, silky dress from the hanger.

When Aria had first given Chrissy the dress, Chrissy had balked at the idea of wearing something so eye-catching. The last thing she'd wanted was to draw attention to herself. But it was Luke and Aria's special day, and she would've done anything to be a part of it, even if it meant climbing out of her comfort zone. And she did. She'd worn the dress, though she'd avoided her reflection like the plague, not wanting to see how out of place she was in something so gorgeous. The rightful owner of such a gorgeous dress should've been someone who would do its beauty justice. But as she held the garment in front of herself in the mirror, she wondered for the first time if maybe that someone could be her.

Without thinking a second longer, she shucked her long-sleeved green T-shirt and jeans, averting her eyes from the mirror. She slid into the luxurious, silky material and tied the wrap-style waistline. She started at the bottom of the mirror, the ruffle of the high-low hemline tickling the back of her ankles. The front of the hem kissed her knees, keeping her scars hidden. The V-neck and wrapping accentuated her waistline and enhanced her modest bust. Her eyes cut over to the loose, flowing fabric that gathered into a ruffle between her wrist and elbow. Not quite a long sleeve, but long enough to mostly hide her scars, even though her tattoo played peekaboo when she moved.

Closing her eyes, she took a few steps back and steeled herself for the full view. Her eyelids crept open at first then flew open as her jaw dropped. Staring back at her was a pretty woman. She looked... normal. Long gone were the ghosts of her past, and the hateful words she told herself were no longer etched into her flesh. Instead of worthless and ugly, she felt pretty and worthwhile. Maybe that person, the stranger in the mirror, was what Adam could see all along.

A mix of nerves and excitement came out in a chuckle as she twirled the skirt around herself. She dashed to the closet and dug out her one pair of nice shoes, the brown leather sandals she'd worn on their walk in the park. Tugging her hair tie out, she combed her fingers through her waves. Her hand dropped to her neck, reaching for her missing necklace by instinct. A necklace would've been the final touch, but she'd have to go without.

Before she could change her mind, she yanked open her bedroom door.

Adam, mouthwatering in his white shirt, blue blazer, and dark jeans, spun at the sound of her door opening. His mouth hung agape as his eyes drank her in from head to toe. "Wow. You look amazing."

Chrissy's heart leapt at the pure adoration on his face, and she spun around for the full effect. "Thanks. I actually feel amazing. And to think I've had this hidden in a bag for over a year."

Adam took two eager steps forward as if he were about to scoop her into his arms, but he screeched to a halt and cleared his throat. "I'm glad you took it out of hiding. It suits you."

Conversation halted, and the air grew thick between them, alive with tension and energy in the best way possible. The pause was anything but awkward, and Chrissy felt herself getting lightheaded from the hum of electricity. Reluctant to break the spell, she also wanted to protect whatever this was between them. It was all still so early, nothing beyond an attraction, and she wasn't sure she could ever go beyond that. For now, she would just savor the fantasies.

"Are you ready to go to dinner?" she asked.

He blinked as her words broke his trance. "Oh. Yeah. I'm ready if you are."

She nodded then followed him out of the condo. She didn't feel ready for any of the things happening in her life. Dinner out with Adam, her growing attraction to him, her career taking off. It all seemed to be forging ahead, and while it was everything she'd ever wanted, she still couldn't help but feel overwhelmed by it all. But if she waited until she thought she was ready, that day might never come. So she would just take a deep breath and put one foot in front of the other, ready or not.

Chapter 30
Chrissy

As much confidence as the amazing dress gave her, Chrissy shrank back as Adam ushered her through the doors of Lounge 312, one of the trendy restaurants in the heart of downtown.

"What's wrong?" he asked.

She lowered her voice as she scanned the posh room. "I can't go in a place like this."

"Why not? A dress like that deserves to be shown off." He took her hand and hooked it around his arm. "For bravery. Trust me, you belong here just as much as everyone else in the room."

She looked down at her arm looped through his like it belonged there. Maybe it did. And maybe she belonged there too. She straightened her shoulders and smiled up at him. "Okay. Let's do this."

He gave the hostess his name, and with a nod she motioned for them to follow. *He made reservations?* She snuck a sideways glance at Adam, who she suspected was pretending not to notice as they wove between the dark wood tables. The hostess stopped at a table tucked in a quiet corner, and Adam held a chair out for Chrissy.

Seated on the green velvet cushion, she couldn't stop her eyes from exploring. Never in a million years would she have guessed she'd eat in a place this nice. The ivory walls boasted sconces with actual candles, not the fake electric kind. A vase with real gardenias nestled in the middle of their table, surrounded by a half dozen votives.

"Like it so far?" Adam asked.

"This place is beautiful. I've never seen anything like it except in movies." When she tore her gaze away from the scenery and looked at Adam, the world froze. His sandy hair and warm eyes glowed in the candlelight, and his skin took on a sun-kissed hue. If the restaurant looked like a movie set, Adam fit right in with his "leading man" good looks. The moment was better than any of her fantasies, and the best part was that it was real.

"Yes. It's very beautiful indeed." His voice came out huskier than she'd heard before, giving her the impression that he wasn't just talking about the restaurant.

The waiter picked that very moment to stride up to their table for their drink order, his shoulders slouching when they failed to order expensive wine.

Adam scanned the menu. "I've heard the steak is fantastic. The chicken cordon bleu as well."

"You haven't been here before?" Chrissy asked.

"They don't deliver, and I haven't ever had a good reason to come." He peeked at her over the menu, a crooked grin gracing his face. "And I figured it would be fun to try something new together."

A blush crept up Chrissy's neck as all the things she'd love to try with Adam rushed through her mind.

The waiter, with impeccable timing, returned with their drinks and asked for their orders.

Adam gave a nod. "Thank you. I'll have the steak. Medium rare. And the scallops."

"And for you, miss?" the waiter asked.

"I'll go with the chicken cordon bleu and roasted potatoes. Thank you." Chrissy handed him the menu and waited for him to leave. Just as she opened her mouth to speak to Adam, a woman approached their table.

"Oh my gosh. It's you. Are you all right?" The woman rested her bejeweled hand on her chest.

Chrissy blinked at her, unsure who she was or what she was talking about.

Adam cleared his throat. "Excuse me, ma'am, but I think you have her confused with someone else."

She shook her head, her brown bob swishing back and forth. "No, I thought so at first until I saw she was with you, Mr. Rochester. And I must say, how brave of you to step in."

All color drained from Adam's face, and Chrissy could see his struggle to maintain his composure. "I just did what anyone would've done. Could you excuse us, please?"

"Oh. Yes, of course." The woman patted her hair, appearing flustered by Adam's not-so-subtle suggestion that she leave. "I just wanted to let you know I'm so relieved you're okay. Enjoy your dinner."

Chrissy stared after the woman with a million questions popping into her mind. Turning back to the table, she found Adam clicking furiously on his phone.

"Damn it," he muttered.

She craned her neck in an attempt to see his screen. "What's wrong? What was that all about?"

He grimaced and turned the phone for her to see. "Looks like the tabloids caught wind of my name being attached to your assault."

The room swirled around Chrissy as she read the words on the screen aloud. "'Adam Rochester rescues woman from attacker, resulting in altercation.' It's true, but how? Why?"

Adam set his phone on the table and dropped his forehead to his palm. "Those tabloids have people on their payroll whose sole job is to listen to police scanners and scour public records, so that's how. As for the why, I'm so sorry. One of the huge disadvantages of having a job like mine is being stalked by tabloids. As someone working for the city in a relatively high position, I'm a target for people who want to dig up the dirt. I'm sorry I didn't warn you. They haven't had anything on me in years, so I didn't think about it. Usually they're focused on Liam, with him being the most eligible bachelor and all. With his spotlight so bright, I'm usually left in the shadows in peace."

"So, everyone in Chicago will know?" At the nod of his head, her eyes darted around the room, taking note of the number of eyes that met hers. "But if they got the info from public records, how do they know what I look like?"

Adam opened his mouth then closed it with a frown. He grabbed his phone and searched some more, then he groaned at the screen. "Either a cop or a passerby apparently snapped pictures."

She took the phone and scrolled through the images. *How did I not notice someone snapping half a dozen pictures?* One picture showed her during her police interview, her face distraught as she hugged her arms around her waist. Another showed Adam during his interview, fists balled at his sides as if ready to make contact with Damien's face again. A series of images showcased them getting into Adam's BMW together. But her breath caught at the final image, the beauty of the captured moment searing a permanent home for itself into her heart forever. In it, her petite frame nestled against Adam's broad body, his muscular arms wrapped around her as if he would never let go. His chin rested atop her messy bun, and his face held so much relief and compassion it made her heart swell. The whole scene elicited an emotion she'd never felt for anyone but Luke, Aria, Ben, and Lilly. Love. And from the look Adam was giving her when she raised her eyes to his, he felt it too.

Adam

The sincerity and gratitude in Chrissy's eyes melted Adam's heart. He'd been holding his breath as she scrolled through the pictures, counting down the swipes until she reached the last one. He'd wondered if she would be able to see his emotions written as clearly as he had, but the way she stared at the picture answered his question. His secret was out, not only to her but all of Chicago and beyond. No one could look at that picture and not see a protective, lovesick fool. But now that everyone knew, it meant so did Mr. Lyones. Adam would have some major damage control to do with his boss, for both of their sakes. And it was only a matter of time before someone mentioned Beth to Chrissy. He couldn't run from his past any longer. Chrissy needed the truth from him before someone blindsided her with it.

Flash.

Adam and Chrissy both startled and turned in the direction of the camera that had gone off.

"It looks like they found us," Adam said, groaning as he jabbed a thumb toward the window.

"Who?" Chrissy asked as she turned to look.

"The paparazzi. I should've known better. We should probably leave." He never should have been so naïve as to think he could have a private life.

Chrissy looked from the window to the phone, then to Adam. "I think we should stay."

"What?"

Her attention moved back to the phone. "They've already taken pictures and shared them with the world, so does it really matter if they do it again? At least this time it'll be happy pictures instead of them exploiting a horrible event. And it's just a meal. Like you said, everyone has to eat, right?"

Adam leaned in and lowered his voice. "But more pictures means more interest in you. And that means digging up old skeletons."

Fear flashed in her eyes as they darted to the window, but she straightened her spine. "The people in my life have been telling me that my past doesn't define me and that I have nothing to be ashamed of. I'm trying to start listening to them more."

"That's very brave and admirable. And I'm glad you're starting to listen to the positives." He reached across the table and took her hand, knowing full well he shouldn't.

Flash.

Images of the headlines that would accompany the picture the paparazzi had just snapped popped into Adam's mind, and he pulled his hand away. The other pictures could be explained away for the most part, as he had stepped in to help her during a horrible event, as he would for anyone. People might see their embrace and be suspicious, but they couldn't really prove anything. Holding hands across a candlelit table was a different story. The paparazzi would latch on to the narrative and dig up dirt about Chrissy. It would not only hurt her but also put their jobs at risk. Mr. Lyones would have Adam's head for creating such a scandal, especially so close to the completion of the mural. All the publicity would be shifted onto Adam and Chrissy's "sordid love affair" rather than showcasing the city's efforts to improve.

"I'm sorry, but we need to leave." Adam took a sip of his tea and motioned for the waiter.

"What? Why? I promise it's okay."

"I wish it was, but there's just too much at stake right now. Who knows what crazy stories they'll make up about us?" Giving up on the waiter, Adam laid some cash on the table and stood. "The last thing we need is for people to think we are dating."

"Oh." Chrissy rose to her feet, her crestfallen expression like a dagger to his heart.

He led her to the door, only to find a sea of paparazzi waiting for them just beyond the entrance. He froze. One look at Chrissy's pale face made him curse under his breath. *Why did I have to be so stupid?* He'd gone from keeping a hug a secret to taking her to a fancy restaurant faster than he could say "I'm an idiot."

"Hold on." He shrugged off his blazer, slipped his arm around her shoulder, and held the blazer up in front of her like a veil.

"What are you doing?"

"Blocking some of the chaos."

"Won't it look bad if you have your arm around me like that?"

Adam shrugged. The candlelit dinner pictures were going to cause more trouble than pictures of him shielding her from the paparazzi. "Right now all I'm worried about is getting to the car. Are you ready?"

Chrissy blinked at the world beyond the door and nodded.

Adam pushed open the door and led Chrissy through the clicks and flashes of a half dozen cameras, wishing he had more than a blazer to protect her. He had to be more careful going forward. Letting his guard down again could cost him everything. He'd already done that once with Beth. He couldn't let himself go down that road again.

Chapter 31

Chrissy

"Giiiiiirl." Lilly's drawn-out word filled the bakery as soon as Chrissy crossed the threshold.

Chrissy faked being aloof, looking around the room, now empty after the lunch rush. "Who? Me?"

Lilly gave Chrissy's arm a playful swat. "Don't you play dumb with me, girl. I've seen the pictures."

"What pictures?" Chrissy asked, continuing her charade.

Lilly shot her a smirk and quirked her head toward the display case. "Pick out something to snack on because you'll need the energy. You've got a lot of explaining to do."

With a giggle, Chrissy grabbed a blueberry crumble muffin and followed Lilly to the break room.

"Where is Adam?" Lilly asked over her shoulder.

"He dropped me off, saying he needed to go to the dry cleaner and stop by another worksite. Honestly, I think he knew I needed some girl time."

"Smart man." Slipping her apron over her head, Lilly dropped into the chair across from Chrissy and leaned forward on her elbows, obviously eager. "Spill it. And don't spare any detail."

"I honestly don't even know where to start."

"How about with the picture of you two after the incident? When that popped onto my screen I just about choked on my brownie."

Warmth enveloped Chrissy as the image filled her mind's eye. "Me, too, honestly. We were out at Lounge 312 last night when some random lady came up asking if I was okay. Adam connected the dots and found the story in the tabloids. When I got to that picture…"

"If a picture is worth a thousand words, that one wrote a love letter." Lilly fanned herself for maximum effect.

"I want to deny it, but I can't. And the way he was looking at me after showing me the picture, it just adds to the craziness."

Lilly held up a hand. "Wait. Why do you want to deny it?"

A sigh came from deep within her soul. "Because if things seem too good to be true… I mean, look at him. He's rich and gorgeous and thoughtful and just all around amazing in every way. It's too much. As much as I want it to be true, this isn't a fairy tale. Things like this don't happen in real life."

Lilly reached across the table and squeezed Chrissy's hand. "Oh, honey. I know life hasn't been easy, but that doesn't mean it has to stay hard. You're not used to good things, so it's understandable that you're cautious. You know I understand that more than anyone. But sometimes you have to trust your heart and go with how something makes you feel. Judging by that picture and the ones from last night, I'm pretty sure I know how Adam makes you feel."

"But you weren't there last night." Chrissy pulled her hand away and hugged herself.

"What do you mean?"

"Things were going great at first. It felt like a scene from a movie. But when the paparazzi showed up, Adam started acting completely different. I mean, yeah, it was weird for me to think people were taking our picture, but he seemed genuinely terrified. He insisted we leave, even after I said I was okay with staying."

"He was probably just trying to protect you from it all."

"Maybe." Chrissy shifted in her seat and picked at her muffin. "After we left, he said it was all because of the rules against workplace romance and he didn't want anyone getting the wrong idea about us."

Lilly nodded like it explained everything. "You two have talked about that before, haven't you? That seems pretty reasonable to me. The pictures of him reaching across the table and of you two running to the car definitely have romantic vibes."

"I know." Chrissy threw her hands up, frustrated with herself. "I know the no-romance rule, and I know how the pictures look. But I can't help feeling like there was more to it. It kind of felt like he was hiding something."

"How so?"

"I can't really explain it." Chrissy shook her head then forced herself to say the words she didn't want to admit to herself. "I think he's embarrassed to be seen with me."

"Oh, honey. Don't think like that."

"I can't help it. And when we were running out, he covered my face with the blazer, but not his. He was trying to hide *me*."

Lilly's face was gentle and understanding. "Your insecurities are clouding your judgment right now. You see him shielding you from the cameras as him hiding you out of embarrassment. Have you considered it might actually be because he wanted to protect you more than himself?"

"Embarrassment seems more logical to me."

"Look at those pictures. All of them. Do you see any inkling of embarrassment in any of them? Because I sure don't. But I'll tell you what I do see. Adoration, caring, and protectiveness. So much protectiveness."

Lilly was right. Chrissy knew Lilly was right, but she couldn't make her heart accept it. Whenever she was with Adam, he made her feel as if the only thing in the world that mattered was their little bubble. Her past didn't matter, only her future. With him, the weight of the world lifted off her shoulders and allowed her to stand tall for the first time in ages. Instead of cringing at his touch, she craved it with unnerving desire. The way his eyes dove into hers, like he could see her soul and loved every ounce of her, turned her knees into jelly.

"Earth to Chrissy. Where'd you just go?" Lilly waved her hand in front of Chrissy's face.

Chrissy blinked and gave Lilly a sheepish grin. "Sorry. I was letting myself feel."

"Judging by your wistful glow, I'm assuming it felt good?"

With a sigh, Chrissy propped her chin in her hand. "If I went by feelings alone, I'd marry him this afternoon."

"Whoa." Lilly put her hands in front of her, palms out. "I knew you had it bad, but I wasn't expecting that."

"But I can't just go by my feelings." Chrissy's elated high from love fizzled as reality took over. "I have to be rational too. Thinking things through is part of my therapy. No more instant gratification."

Lilly pursed her lips and studied Chrissy, which Chrissy knew meant she was cooking up a plan. "Open that album of the pictures they took of you at the mural."

Chrissy took out her phone and did as she was told.

"Now go to the ones of you and Adam." Lilly slid her phone beside Chrissy's, the paparazzi shots of Chrissy and Adam on the screen. "Look at all these. You look the happiest I've ever seen you in those pictures. How about instead of thinking years in the future, you just enjoy the moment? You don't have to marry Adam today, but you can appreciate the fact that he makes you want to. For once in your life, let yourself live in moment."

A smile tugged at Chrissy's mouth as Lilly echoed the sentiment Winifred had left Chrissy with on the rooftop. "You're actually not the first person to tell me that in the past twenty-four hours."

"Then maybe you should listen." Lilly winked, then she turned serious. "I just want you to be happy."

"I want me to be happy too." Happiness with her life was the ultimate goal, no matter how unachievable it seemed.

Adam

Standing on Luke's doorstep, Adam counted his breathing to rein in his panic. On an inhale, he rapped his knuckles on the freshly painted navy-blue door. Footsteps on the other side made his stomach knot.

Aria's initial smile turned hesitant as she saw him, a harbinger of how his meeting with Luke would go. "Adam. Nice to see you."

"Y-You too. Is Luke home?" Try as he might, Adam knew his nervousness shone through his attempt at a calm demeanor.

"Just finishing up with some yard work. Come on in." Aria stepped aside.

Following Aria to the backyard felt akin to walking into a lion's den. All the deep breaths and counting in the world couldn't calm his storm of nerves. As he stepped onto the patio, Luke stood and locked eyes with him.

"I'll go make some lemonade," Aria said before slipping back into the house, leaving Adam to face the fire alone.

"H-Hey, Luke. Looks like your garden is coming along nicely." Adam cringed at his pathetic attempt at small talk.

Luke set down the tomato cage he'd been holding and brushed the dirt from his hands. "I'm pretty sure you didn't come to talk about my garden."

Any hopes that Luke hadn't seen the tabloids vanished, and Adam ran his hand through his hair. "Look, I... Well, honestly, I don't have any excuses for myself. I'm sorry, man. It's just that..." Adam stood with his mouth open and his hands to his sides, racking his brain for ways to explain his behavior. Alas, he came up empty.

So Luke finished the sentence for him. "It's just that you and Chrissy are becoming more than either of you will admit."

Adam's brain woke up at last. "I'll admit I like her, but nothing has happened between us."

Luke strolled over to a metal glider on the patio and motioned for Adam to join him. "The sooner you two stop lying to yourselves, the better. I've seen all the pictures. I'm forever grateful for you being there at the right time, but the look on your face after you stopped Damien shows the truth neither of you will admit to yourselves. Then the dinner pictures with you reaching across the table. Sure, maybe nothing physical has happened between you two, but something emotional sure as hell has. I don't care what your mouth says, man."

Adam rested his elbows on his knees and cradled his head in his hands. "You're right. I'm trying so hard to ignore it, but damn it, you're right. I don't know what to do."

"Have you told her the truth?" Luke's challenge hit the nail right on the head.

Adam's head hung lower. "Not really."

"Then listen to me, and listen carefully. Everyone in Chicago knows you two are smitten with each other. You both know it, too, though you're both solidly in denial. Whatever is between you two is happening regardless of how much you resist it. I know it's scary, but you have to just rip off the bandage and tell her the truth. All of it. Before you both get hurt."

Adam sank back into the glider. "I told her that I don't drink, but I didn't tell her why."

"The why is the most important part, though. Just telling her you don't drink doesn't mean anything without the backstory."

"I know you're right. I've almost told her so many times, but I keep chickening out at the last second. Honestly, I'm surprised you haven't told her."

Luke cocked his head to the side. "I've wanted to, and I've come close, but ultimately it's not my place. It's your past, and it coming from anyone but you will hurt her. She needs to hear it from the source. She needs your honesty."

The gravity of Luke's words sank in Adam's stomach like a brick. Adam told himself all the time that Chrissy deserved more from her life, and he longed to provide it for her, yet all the while he'd been denying her the most fundamental element of any relationship. Honesty.

"You're right. It's time for me to man up." Adam stood to leave.

"Good luck," Luke said before returning to his gardening.

The entire drive back to the Gilded Lilly, Adam rehearsed the conversation in his head. No matter how many variations he tried, the imagined scenarios ended with Chrissy leaving him to wallow in his bed of lies. Even as panic seized his chest, he knew he had no other choice. The alternative to confessing the entire truth was having his skeletons grow larger and larger until they burst from the closet he held shut tight. And Luke was right. It was only a matter of time before Chrissy learned the truth anyway, and it would be best coming from Adam. He knew all of this, but it was still so hard to follow through.

He pulled to the curb in front of the bakery and gulped in air as if it could feed him courage. But before he could gather enough from the universe to go in, Chrissy rapped her knuckles on the car window. He was jolted back to reality and unlocked the car.

"I was just about to come in," he said as Chrissy slipped into the seat beside him.

"Lilly is slammed with orders today, so I was sitting at a table and watching her work. I saw you pull up, so I just said my goodbyes and ducked out so she could concentrate." She stopped and frowned at him, then she reached across the console and laid her hand on his knee. "Are you okay?"

Tell her now, his brain screamed, but he noticed the edge of her sobriety tattoo peeking from underneath her sleeve and lost any resolve he had mustered. He couldn't bring himself to chase her away. Not yet. "Just tired, I guess."

She gave his knee a squeeze, sending electricity to his core. "You've been so busy, you need to stop and take care of yourself. How about this weekend we make it our mission to do nothing?"

Hearing her make plans for their time together and say "we" intensified that electrical spark, rendering his brain useless. "That sounds perfect."

Chapter 32

Adam

Walking down the hall to Mr. Lyones's office felt like walking to the gallows. Adam tried to swallow, but despite chugging half a water bottle before leaving his office, his throat was as dry as a desert. He knew exactly what the impromptu meeting was going to be about, and he had a pretty good idea of how it was going to go.

He sucked in a deep breath before knocking on the frosted glass door.

"Come in."

Adam opened the door and stepped in.

"Mr. Rochester. Have a seat," said Mr. Lyones, his face set in his usual scowl.

A formal greeting. Not a great sign.

Before Adam could say a word, his boss swiveled the computer monitor so Adam could see the tabloid articles littering the screen.

Adam swallowed hard. "Sir, I—"

"Let me guess, you can explain."

"Y-Yes, sir. I happened to be driving to check on the mural when I saw her being attacked and stopped to help."

Mr. Lyones leaned back in his seat with a huff. "And was she in need of help at the restaurant as well?"

"N-No, sir."

"You are aware of the no-dating policy we have in place, are you not?"

Adam started to count to five so he could answer, but before he could finish, Mr. Lyones continued.

"Interoffice dalliances have caused major scandals in the past. Scandals that have ended up ruining projects and costing people their jobs. Things with the city take long enough to get done without all the drama added by ongoing or failed office relationships. We take it very seriously when people cross certain lines."

"I promise there's nothing going on between us, sir. I haven't crossed any lines." Adam could think of several rumored "dalliances" involving people much higher up than himself, but apparently the bigger your name, the more people looked the other way. He wasn't high enough on the list to have the same privileges.

Mr. Lyones leaned forward, his features set in hard lines. "Whether that's true or not, what matters here is perception. Look at those articles. If those were written about someone else, what would you think was going on?"

Adam scanned the computer screen, his shoulders slouching in defeat.

"Exactly." Mr. Lyones moved the screen back to its original position and laced his fingers together on his desk. "Look, Adam, you're an excellent employee, and I would hate to see something like this jeopardize your position here."

"Thank you, sir. I'm sorry to let you down. It won't happen again." At least he'd moved from "Mr. Rochester" back to "Adam" again.

"No. It won't."

Is he firing me?

"As it stands, I believe we can manage the damage control on the situation. We can use the 'hero saving the day' spin and hope people forget about the restaurant bit. The mural has been delayed by a week thanks to this mess, which I'm not happy about, but in this case, it could help let all of this blow over before the unveiling party."

Air filled Adam's lungs for the first time in what felt like an eternity. His job was safe.

"But absolutely no more delays. And absolutely zero chances for more tabloid fodder. If anything else goes wrong, that little blonde can kiss any more contracts with the city goodbye." Mr. Lyones shuffled some papers on his desk then handed Adam one. "This is the new timeline. The party is scheduled, and services are being booked. Everything from here on out needs to be perfect or she's out. And you might not be far behind."

Adam took the paper and tried to keep his hands from shaking. "Understood, sir."

"Good. I'm counting on you to not let me or the city down." Mr. Lyones turned away from Adam and began clicking away on his keyboard.

Adam took that as his cue and scrambled out of his boss's office as fast as possible without it being too obvious that he'd rather be anywhere else in the world.

The meeting had been bad, but not as bad as it could have been. As it almost was. As much as he felt relieved, he also realized just how close he and Chrissy had come to losing everything. It was one thing to cause problems for himself, but he had almost cost her the future she'd worked so hard for thanks to his carelessness. He couldn't let that happen again.

Chapter 33

Chrissy

"Excuse me. I'm gonna need you to stop right there, mister. No one comes through the gate without permission from the city." Liz's authoritative tone rang loud and clear across the jobsite.

Chrissy's heart seized as she spun in the direction of the gate, but relief flooded her upon seeing Luke standing by the gate with his hands up in surrender. Scurrying down the scaffold ladder, Chrissy called out to Liz, "It's okay. He's my brother."

"Your brother?" Liz's balled fists loosened, and she jerked her chin upward. "All right, come on in."

Luke eased the gate open and slipped through, then he extended his hand to Liz. "I'm Luke. You must be her new assistant."

"That I am," Liz said, shaking his hand. "I would say sorry for the rude welcome, but I'd be lying. After what happened with my predecessor, everyone is guilty until proven innocent as far as I'm concerned."

"No harm. I completely respect and support that stance. I'm glad to see my sister is in good hands." He turned to Chrissy, his features softening with empathy. "Speaking of which, how are you doing with your first day back?"

Chrissy rocked her hand back and forth. "Meh. I had some anxiety when I first got here, but once I got started painting, it honestly just felt so good being back at it. I know I only took a couple days off, but I missed it. Plus, Liz here puts me at ease."

She wasn't about to tell Luke about the panic attack she'd had after Adam dropped her off. She wasn't going to tell Adam either, for that matter. Both of them worried about her enough as it was. No, the panic attack would be her and Liz's little secret. Well, until Chrissy told her new therapist at their next session.

"Are you sure you're okay?" Luke asked, butting in on her thoughts.

"Yeah, as okay as I can be." At least that was the truth. "Liz taught me some self-defense moves earlier, and that really helped."

"Good. I'm really glad to hear that." Luke's features softened, signaling to Chrissy how much he'd been worried about her. "I came to see what you wanted for lunch. And before you protest, I insist. It's my way of showing support for my sister."

She'd never grow tired of hearing him call her that. "Thank you. I'm not too picky. You know what I like."

"I think the Tex-Mex truck is at the park," Luke said.

"That sounds perfect. Whatever their special is today is okay. I haven't found a single thing I don't like."

He turned to Liz. "What would you like?"

Liz looked around and pointed to her chest. "Me?"

"Yep. I'm going to buy you lunch as my thank-you for not being a..." He swiveled toward Chrissy. "How did she put it? An oversexed jackass?"

Liz tossed her head back with a laugh. "Yeah, that sounds like me. But I don't need thanks for being a decent human instead of a scumbag."

"I'm sure I don't have to tell you about the lack of human decency nowadays. Lunch is a small price to pay for the assurance there's someone here watching Chrissy's back with that asshole still on the loose. So, tacos, the special, or cheesy chicken and rice?"

Liz crossed her arms over her chest, but a grin tugged up at the corner of her mouth. "I like surprises, so I'll go with the special. Extra hot salsa if they have it."

"Great. I'll be back soon."

As they watched Luke walk away, Liz chuckled. "You know, I never thought I'd say this about a member of the opposite sex, but he seems like he's a pretty decent person." Liz nudged Chrissy with her elbow and winked before turning for the trailer.

Chrissy giggled and joined Liz to get cleaned up for lunch.

Wiping her hands on the legs of her overalls, Chrissy squared her shoulders as she peered up at her progress for the day.

Liz sidled up beside her and nodded her approval. "You work pretty fast. How long until it's done, do you think?"

Chrissy scanned over the image, taking stock of all the missing elements. "My best guess is I'll be done in under two weeks. I could've been done by the end of this week if it wasn't for all the setbacks."

"Hello, ladies."

Just the sound of Adam's voice brought a smile to Chrissy's face and sped up her heart rate. She spun around, trying but failing to rein in her giddiness at seeing him.

His face mirrored hers. "How was your first day back?"

"Uneventful in the best way. It felt good to get back to it."

"I don't know. I'm kind of bummed I didn't have to kick anyone's ass," Liz joked.

Adam chuckled. "There's always tomorrow, but hopefully it doesn't come to that. I'm glad to know you're ready if the time comes." Then he turned to Chrissy. "Are you ready to get going?"

"Yep. Liz and I just got done locking everything up."

After goodbyes with Liz, Chrissy and Adam strolled over to the gravel lot, and Chrissy imagined reaching over and taking his hand. The idea felt so natural and comfortable it almost stopped her in her tracks. Comfortable and natural could describe everything about her life at that moment. And nothing of her past. The stark contrast of her current life versus just a few months ago gave her pause, her past having taught her that when things seemed too good to be true, it likely meant something *wasn't* true. If her life had taught her anything, it was that the better things were going, the more she could get hurt when things inevitably went wrong.

"Something wrong?" Adam's voice broke into her thoughts as he opened the back passenger door for her.

She frowned. "Why can't I ride in the front?"

Adam paled. "I-It's just so the paparazzi can't get any more pictures of you. The back windows are more tinted."

"Oh." It sounded logical enough, but she had a sneaking suspicion there was more to the story. Not trusting her voice, she silently sank into the back seat and let him close the door.

He took his place in the driver's seat and made eye contact with her in the rearview mirror. "Are you upset?"

She forced a smile. "No. I'm just tired."

"Are you sure?" Adam asked as he drove away from the worksite. "I promise the only reason I'm having you sit in the back is so people can't take your picture. After the past two instances, I've noticed more paparazzi following me, just waiting for something else to take pictures of."

"Really?" Chrissy shivered at the thought that people might have been watching her too.

Adam nodded as he turned a corner. "I actually think it would be a good idea to have a car service bring you back and forth instead of me driving you. If we give them nothing, eventually they'll go away."

"That makes sense." It did make sense, but that didn't stop it from stinging. Adam picking her up in the afternoon had become one of Chrissy's favorite moments of the day.

"I'm tired too. Want to order some food and have a lazy night in?"

"Yes, please," Chrissy said. He talked like they had a choice. If she couldn't even sit in the front seat of the car, it wasn't like they could go out to a restaurant. They couldn't ever repeat that disaster. The only way she could ever be with Adam was in secrecy. *And what kind of life is that?*

Chapter 34

Chrissy

Chrissy thanked the driver then nodded at the doorman as she entered the lobby of Adam's building. It was the second day of having a driver, but it all still felt so surreal. She had gotten used to entering with Adam, so walking in alone allowed her self-consciousness to spiral. Just when she had begun to feel okay in his world, the tabloids had to invade and steal it all away.

As she approached the seclusion of the elevator, Adam appeared from somewhere off to the side and joined her inside. But instead of going to their floor, he pushed the button for the roof.

"What are you doing?" she asked.

"It's a surprise."

"What kind of surprise?" Her relief at seeing him gave way to curiosity.

He sighed and studied the closed elevator doors. "An apologetic one."

"Why are you apologizing?" She gulped, hoping he didn't have bad news to deliver. Maybe Adam's boss had changed his mind and decided to fire her.

He finally looked at her. "Because I can tell you've been upset ever since the restaurant debacle. I should've thought about the paparazzi and how it might look to my boss. Now because of my lack of forethought, you have to hide from the world. It's not fair, and I wanted to cheer you up."

"You don't have to do that." Even so, it didn't stop her from appreciating the gesture.

"I know, but I wanted to." A conspiratorial grin spread across his face.

As much as she studied him, all she could read was mischief. When the doors dinged and opened, Adam all but skipped from the elevator.

Chrissy's breath caught, Adam's cryptic giddiness momentarily forgotten as the sun set behind the cityscape, brilliant oranges, reds, and purples blazing in a dazzling light show. "Wow. It's pretty up here during the day, but this... this is breathtakingly gorgeous."

"Yes, it is."

Adam's thick voice brought her out of her awe, but the look in his eyes took her breath just the same. With his back to the sunset, he looked admiringly at her as if she was the beauty to behold.

"This is only half of the surprise." He held his hand out and cocked his head toward the garden. "It's this way, but close your eyes."

With zero hesitation, she slid her hand into his and let her eyes close, trusting him to guide her. Flowers tickled her arm as he led her through the garden. She traced their path in her mind's eye and knew they should be reaching the bistro set any second.

Adam let go of her hand. "Okay. Open them."

She opened her eyes to find Adam standing beside the table, his arms outstretched to showcase the surprise. A lantern illuminated the to-go containers on the table, but her gaze snagged on a large gift box tucked behind Adam.

"What's all this about? And what's that behind you?"

"Well, remember when I came home, and you had all those sketches lying all over the floor? You mentioned you'd love to get some canvases so you could paint instead of just doing sketches." He stepped aside and pulled the lid off the box. "Ta-da."

Chrissy rushed forward, giddy like a kid at Christmas, and ran her hands over the edges of the canvases. "Seriously? You didn't have to do this."

"I wasn't sure what you liked best, so I got a variety of sizes. There should be a dozen in there, and I have another box in the condo."

Without hesitation, Chrissy rose on her tiptoes and threw her arms around his neck. "Thank you so much. This means so much to me."

The warmth of his arms enveloped her in return, the tension from the past few days melting away. "So, you like it?"

She pulled back and looked over at the canvases again. "Like it? Are you kidding? I love it. It's perfect. I'm so happy I could kiss you." As the words left her mouth, she froze. "I mean... uh, I just... It's not..."

Words failed her, and she inched her gaze upward, afraid to see his reaction but also needing to see it. His lips curled into a grin so kissable it took every ounce of self-control for her not to lick her own. When her eyes met his, the intensity she found there made her heart skip a beat. Those eyes belonged to a man filled with desire, and their heat was aimed at her.

Adam's hand brushed her arm as his lips parted ever so slightly, sending fireworks of anticipation ricocheting throughout her body.

At that very moment, the universe turned against her and her body's cravings and sent the signature Chicago wind in as a cock-block. A gust took hold of the box lid and threw it across the garden, breaking the spell. Adam lunged for the lid, snagging it with two fingers just as it rose for another tumble.

"Whew, that was close." Adam went over to the box and secured the lid. "Could you imagine being a pedestrian and getting taken out by a box lid?"

Nervous laughter bounced between them as they regained their bearings. Chrissy couldn't help but mourn the moment lost and turned her attention to the table to distract herself. "I'm assuming this is for us."

Adam turned to the table as if he'd forgotten its existence. "Oh, yeah. It's not a restaurant, but better than another night stuck in the condo. I picked up some food from City Club Café and brought it up here so you'd have fuel for painting."

"That's nice, but I don't have any supplies with me."

Another crooked grin graced his handsome face as he reached behind the box of canvases. "I'm no artist, so I had the woman at the art store put this together. It should be everything you need."

Chrissy peered into the box and found an overabundance of supplies like she'd never seen before. "Oh, Adam, this is too much. It must've cost a fortune."

He carried on as if he hadn't heard her. "Did you want to set the easel up now, or wait until after we eat?"

Adam

W*oo, boy, am I in trouble,* Adam thought as he watched Chrissy set up her easel. He'd barely tasted his food thanks to his mind wandering off into imagined scenarios where his mouth was otherwise occupied. Every word, every glance, fueled his ever-growing desires. No matter how many times he reminded himself of the reprimands from his boss, he couldn't make himself listen.

Seeing her in her element, watching her let go of her problems and just be her true self, turned out to be a much bigger turn-on than he'd anticipated. The intimacy of being welcomed into her passion left him intoxicated.

"I'm glad you brought that lantern. It's perfect lighting." Chrissy tossed the words over her shoulder as her brush glided over the canvas.

Adam adjusted himself and cleared his throat. "I couldn't bring candles up here with all the wind, so a lantern seemed like a good workaround. Not exactly pretty, but it works."

Chrissy threw her head back with a laugh. "I could use 'not exactly pretty, but it works' to describe so many things in my life. I think you just coined my new motto."

"Don't talk about yourself that way." The thick emotion in his voice shocked him, and judging by the way Chrissy spun around, she heard it too. He cleared his throat and blinked. "Sorry, it's just hard to hear you put yourself down like that. You deserve better."

She studied him for a moment before speaking. "I'm sorry. You're right. I'll try to be nicer to myself." She turned back toward her painting but paused. "Thank you."

Adam's phone buzzed, and he pulled it from his pocket, sucking in a breath when he saw the screen. "It's the police."

Chrissy spun around, her knuckles turning white as she gripped her paintbrush.

He answered it. "Hello? Yes, this is he. You did? I see. Okay. We'll be there as soon as possible."

He hung up and gave her a triumphant smile. "They caught Damien."

Chrissy set down her brush and palette. "Really?"

Adam nodded as he rose to his feet. "Yes. We have to go to the station and confirm it's him, but they're ninety-nine percent sure they got the right guy."

Her lip trembled as she peered up at him. "I didn't realize how much it bothered me that he was still out there until just now. I'm so relieved."

Adam pulled her in for a hug, lingering just a few seconds longer than he should have, then he pulled away and surveyed the area. "I guess we better get this stuff packed away and head to the station."

Chrissy nodded. "The sooner we get this over with, the better."

Two hours later, Adam's hand itched to touch Chrissy's lower back and guide her as they walked through his building's lobby to the elevators.

As the elevator doors closed, Chrissy leaned against the railing. "I feel like I can finally breathe."

Adam punched the button and joined her against the wall. "I never thought I'd say I was glad to see Damien, yet here I am. The arresting officer said he put up quite a fight so he earned himself some more charges. I hope it's not overstepping, but I plan to use some of my clout to make sure he doesn't get out anytime soon."

"That sounds like the perfect use of your clout."

The elevator doors opened, and they walked in silence to the condo. Adam figured Chrissy needed some time to process everything, so he didn't want to push her with too much discussion.

After locking the door behind him, he turned to find Chrissy watching him and picking at her fingernail. "Want to talk about it?"

She shied away as if ashamed of what she was about to say. Or maybe she was scared. "I guess this means I don't have to stay here anymore. You don't need to keep an eye on me now that Damien has been caught."

Adam stepped forward and took Chrissy's hand in his. "You know me better than that by now, I hope. I'm not going to throw you out just because they caught your attacker. Plus, I kind of like having you here."

I shouldn't have said that.

The worried lines on her forehead finally softened. "Thank you. I like being here."

The thought of Chrissy's other living arrangement options made Adam realize they needed to spread the good news. "I guess we need to let Luke and Lilly know they caught Damien now that it's con-firmed."

Chrissy gasped. "You're right. I can't believe I didn't think of that. They're both going to be so relieved." She dug her phone out of her purse. "I'm going to go call them."

As Adam watched her pace in front of the wall of windows as she talked, he wished he could enjoy the moment. But even though one danger was crossed off the list, others still lurked. With the paparazzi still sniffing around, they would no doubt discover Damien's arrest and have renewed interest in Chrissy. And they loved nothing more than digging up old skeletons. No. He couldn't let that happen to Chrissy. And he knew just who to ask for help.

Chapter 35

Adam

"To what do I owe this pleasure?" Winifred asked as she air-kissed Adam's cheeks.

"Uh. Well, I was hoping you could help me with something." Adam's nerves frayed one by one as those steel-blue eyes bored into his.

"All right, then. This way." She led him to her lavish study. Wooden bookcases lined three walls, with the fourth being a wall of windows. Instead of the black metal framing of Adam's wall of windows, a rich wood matching the floor trimmed Winifred's. By the windows, a set of green velvet chairs and a gold bench were gathered around a gold filigree table sparkling in the sunlight. She motioned for him to join her at the table. "I sense this might not be pleasant, so let's have some tea, shall we? I was just about to have some anyway."

A nervous chuckle escaped him as he sat. "Sounds good." In all honesty, it would take something a hell of a lot stronger to calm his nerves. Ever since Damien had been caught, all he could think about was how to broach such a touchy subject with Winifred, and the only strategy he could come up with was straight honesty. Winifred wasn't one for games.

She kept a guarded face as she poured the tea and offered sugar. She took a sip then set her cup down, turning an expectant look his way. "Let's get on with it, then."

Adam's cup rattled as he set it back down and gulped. "Right. Okay. So, I'm sure you've guessed that Chrissy has a not-so-clean past." He scanned her for any hint of shock or surprise and found nothing. "And as you know, the paparazzi have taken an interest in her now that we've been spotted together." Good grief, Winifred had one hell of a poker face. "I'm dreading the day they dig up something that will hurt her."

Winifred quirked one of her brows. "And what does this have to do with me?"

She was really going to make him say it out loud. He drew in a breath and counted to five, but his nerves still rattled. "W-Well, I've looked you up on the internet. I'm sorry, I know it's kind of sneaky, but I was just curious."

Something flashed across her eyes for a millisecond before she blinked it away. She sipped her tea and waited.

Another gulp, and he continued. "One thing I noticed is that there's zero information about you prior to the eighties. Nothing about your childhood or early adult years. It's like the internet has been wiped clean."

Her hardened, guarded exterior cracked, an ounce of fear peeking through as she shifted in her seat.

Adam pushed aside his heightened curiosity and zeroed in on his reason for having this painful conversation. "I'm not asking about your skeletons, Winifred. I'm asking how you buried them."

Chrissy

Scroll after scroll, all the results came up the same. No matter how many ways Chrissy searched, nothing from her past appeared. Almost a week after her night out with Adam, and the paparazzi hadn't dug up any dirt. She had been waiting for the sensational headlines everyone warned her about, but none had popped up.

She clicked on her messages with Lilly. "Find anything?"

Lilly's reply came a couple minutes later. "Nope. Weird. Usually they're super fast with this stuff. What's crazy is that I can't find anything about you anywhere—other than mural stuff. I thought you had a record?"

"I do. You couldn't find it?"

"Nope."

Odd. Maybe Lilly just wasn't looking in the right places. Thirty minutes later, Chrissy still couldn't dig up any trace of the skeletons in her past.

The front door clicked open, and Adam rushed through. "Hey, sorry I'm late."

"It's fine. I've just been watching some TV and texting Lilly." Chrissy set her phone on the coffee table and shifted toward Adam as he joined her on the couch.

He tugged at his tie and unbuttoned his collar. "I hate the nights when I work late. But right now, the city is really trying to lock in some donors for some major projects, which of course means wining and dining."

When he threw his head back and closed his eyes, Chrissy took full advantage of the opportunity to drink it all in. With him lying on the couch with his fancy suit tousled, she envisioned climbing onto his lap and using that loosened tie to pull his mouth to hers.

"Did you eat?" He chose that moment to open his eyes, and she almost swallowed her tongue.

She twisted away from him and grabbed the remote, trying to make herself and her actions seem normal and hide the fact she'd just been ogling him. Again. "Considering you had food delivered, you should know I did."

He straightened, lifting away from the back of the couch, and turned toward her. "Is something wrong?"

Nothing was wrong, which was exactly what bothered her. "Kind of? I don't know. It's just that I've been waiting and waiting for headlines to pop up about me, but the only things I find are articles calling me your mystery woman. Then when I tried to find my old records, I couldn't find any of them either. It's like my past was erased."

"Huh. That's odd." He stiffened and averted his eyes, his tone cautious.

She studied his features. Either the coffee table was the most interesting thing in the world, or he was avoiding her seeing the truth on his face.

"Thank you," she said, her voice soft.

He shrugged. "For what?"

"For protecting me." Even if he wouldn't admit it, she knew beyond a doubt he was the reason her past was staying buried. And she knew Lilly was right. All the secrecy and separation was so he could protect her, not because he was embarrassed. He truly cared.

Adam finally looked at her. "I don't want to be the reason you get hurt."

No words existed to convey her gratitude, so instead she scooted closer until her thigh butted against his. She waited for him to relax beside her then laced her fingers through his. Without a word, she clicked the television back to life and settled in, allowing herself to snuggle against her real-life knight in shining armor.

Chapter 36
Chrissy

With the morning sun warming her skin and the rooftop wind tugging at her messy bun, Chrissy chewed the end of her paintbrush and squinted at the rough skyline on her canvas. The forecasted rain had given her a day off from the mural, but it wouldn't keep her from her art altogether. She took the chance to work on some "easy to move out of the rain" paintings instead. Except she wasn't getting very far.

The scuff of a shoe drew her away from her painting.

"I hope I'm not disturbing you." Winifred entered the garden space, her bright-white robe blinding in the midday sun.

"Not at all." Chrissy set her palette and brush inside her box so they wouldn't blow away and turned her full attention to Winifred. "Did you need something?"

"No, I just saw you over here and thought we might chat. But I see you're in the middle of something, so I'll leave you to it." She turned toward the pool area.

"It's fine. We can talk now. I need a break anyway. No matter how I look at this painting, I can't seem to find the spark."

"The spark?"

Chrissy slid into one of the chairs and pulled out the seat next to her. "That's what I call it, anyway. It's basically the spirit of the piece. Each painting has a story to tell, and it's my job to find it."

"How so?" Winifred set her bag beside the chair and took a seat.

"You know how you can look at a painting and it brings up unexpected emotions? That's the spark or spirit. Some paintings, like the mural, are supposed to make you happy. They're all bright colors and pretty images, typically. Cool colors go along with sadness, and reds with blacks can represent danger and bring out fear. That's the basics, and then you build from there. Usually, I can just feel it once I get to a certain point, but I'm stuck on this one. Maybe I've just done too many skylines." Chrissy propped her chin in her hand, elbow on the table.

"May I see what you have so far?"

With a nod, Chrissy fished her phone from her overall bib and brought her painting album to the screen. "I have pictures of everything I've done recently." She handed the phone to Winifred and returned her attention to the infuriating painting.

"Is this of you?"

"What?" Chrissy's eyes jerked to the screen, and she cringed. "Oh, that. I forgot that was on there. I meant to delete it." She reached for the phone, but Winifred held up a hand. All other sounds came second to Chrissy's heartbeat thundering in her ears as she watched Winifred study the portrait.

"This is quite good. It would be a shame to throw it away."

"It was just an experiment with a different style." Her cheeks flamed, and her hand itched to snatch her phone back.

"The experiment proved successful. Of all the pieces, this one has the most vivid spark." Winifred tapped a manicured finger on the screen.

"You really think so?" Chrissy shifted to look over Winifred's shoulder, curious and eager to see the portrait through a fresh perspective.

A raw version of herself stared back at her. Her light hair contrasted with the dark blues and purples of the background, but her golden locks lacked their sunny luster, instead shining platinum like the moon. Purple lines and bruises marred her pale skin, a dark-maroon cut prominent on her muted pink lips. Everything screamed depression and defeat. Everything except the eyes. The sky-blue irises shone like beacons in the dark, little pools of hope and light. Amid the bright blue, the irises also contained little flecks of yellow as if they reflected firelight from beyond the painting. Or perhaps the light came from within. Squared shoulders and the hard set of the mouth exuded a determination matching the fire in the eyes.

Chrissy sniffed and turned away from the screen.

"Now you see what I mean," Winifred said, laying the phone on the table.

Chrissy slid the phone back into her overalls and blinked back her tears. "I painted that one night when I couldn't sleep. All of this… crap was just swirling in my brain, and I got this overwhelming urge to do a self-portrait. When I was done, I snapped a picture and hid it in the closet so Adam wouldn't see it. Since it was two in the morning when I got done, I didn't even bother stepping back to really look at it. I never went back to it."

"Perhaps your heart knew you needed some time in order to fully appreciate it."

"Maybe."

"And perhaps this painting"—Winifred nodded toward the easel—"is demanding a similar spark."

"What do you mean?"

"All of your landscapes and skylines so far showcase beauty and happiness. Perhaps this painting longs to be grittier and less polished."

Chrissy frowned at the canvas, the Chicago of her childhood flashing in her mind's eye. Her therapist's words ran through her thoughts. After learning she was an artist, every therapist had encouraged her to explore all of her emotions through her work, not just the happy ones. They'd warned her against ignoring the unpleasant feelings. There were no bad emotions, and she needed to allow herself to feel them all in order to move forward. Maybe she was finally ready to let herself go down that road. "I think you might be on to something."

"Well, then." Winifred patted Chrissy's knee and stood. "I best be off to my water aerobics. You're welcome to join me anytime."

"Oh, uh, thanks for the offer. Maybe someday."

"Scars are things of beauty and remind us of our tremendous strength. Ta-ta." With a wiggle of her fingers, she slipped from the garden as if she hadn't just dropped another emotional bomb in Chrissy's lap.

How does that woman seem to know everything? Chrissy shook her hands at her sides, but she couldn't shake off the funk left in Winifred's all-knowing wake. She retrieved her palette and brush and rolled her shoulders like she was getting ready for a fist fight. Instead of the bright sky blue, she dipped her brush into charcoal gray. If this painting wanted grit, then grit it would have.

Adam

The elevator chimed with each passing floor, bringing Adam closer to home. And closer to the woman who made it feel like home. He massaged the back of his aching neck and leaned against the handrail.

The door slid open, and he made his way to the condo. A burst of renewed energy filled him when he opened the door and saw Chrissy. A drop cloth covered the floor by the windows. Chrissy and her easel stood in the center with various supplies scattered about.

"Another day full of inspiration?"

She turned a megawatt smile his way. "I hope you don't mind me taking over the living room. I started out on the rooftop this morning, but I got rained out. I have to say, though, I've never been happier for a rainy afternoon. It was just the mood I needed."

"Let's see what you've got." He strode over and scanned the half dozen paintings as she studied his features. "These are great, but they're a lot different from your other stuff."

The light in her face dulled. "Different good or different bad?"

"Just different." He took in the subdued colors. Gone were the vibrant, full-of-life images he'd come to expect from her. "I guess I'm just used to you painting happy stuff. These are more... I don't know. Sad? Gloomy?"

One glance at her downtrodden expression and he could've punched himself. He rushed over and took her hand. "I didn't mean to upset you. They're still great paintings. Hauntingly beautiful. It's just, well, it scares me a little."

"Scares you? Why?" Her eyes darted to her paintings.

Adam swallowed against what felt like cotton in his throat. "Are you feeling depressed? I can get you some help."

Understanding dawned on her features, and one hand went to her heart. "You were afraid I was mentally struggling? I'm so sorry to scare you like that. I promise, I'm fine."

He wasn't convinced. "Then why the sad paintings?"

"Before the rain started, I went up to the roof for some fresh air and inspiration." She let go of his hands and picked up a gloomy skyline picture. "I was having a hard time figuring out the direction I wanted for this one when Winifred showed up. She asked to see some of my other work, and then she saw— Uh, she mentioned maybe I could try a different emotion for this one. After thinking about it, I wanted to try tackling some of the darker stuff."

"And how did that make you feel?"

She set the canvas down and stepped beside him, looking over the paintings again. "It felt good. At first it hurt to let myself go there, but once I got started, it just flowed. Heck, I think this is just as good as if not better than my therapy. Now I see why my therapist kept suggesting I do it."

He could breathe at last. "That's great. I'm glad it helps." Now that his panic was subdued, he studied the paintings from an objective viewpoint. "These are so raw. It's like I can see the pain from your past." He blinked hard. "It takes me back to... uh, times that weren't so great for me."

"I'm sorry."

He ran a hand through his hair. "No, it's fine. I just haven't let myself go there mentally in a while."

"Does it have to do with why you don't speak to your parents?"

He froze, torn between baring his soul and keeping things bottled up like he had for years. "It's complicated."

Such a clichéd and lame cop-out, yet again, but it was the best he could manage. He just hoped Chrissy would read between the lines and not press him further.

"Anytime you want to talk about it, I'm here to listen," she said.

"Thanks." He couldn't tell her about the issue with his parents without telling her about Beth, and he couldn't talk about Beth without bringing up his complicated past with alcohol. He could come clean about everything all at once, but he had been hiding it for so long, he wasn't even sure where to start. He found himself genuinely wishing he could pry the words from his mouth so he could really start moving on. Maybe Chrissy was right. Maybe he did need a therapist to help him untangle his thoughts.

Beside him, Chrissy stared at the paintings in silence for a moment, then she put her hand on his forearm. "Wait here. There's another one I want to show you."

She disappeared into the guest room then came out several minutes later, holding a painting toward her body. "I painted this one night when I couldn't sleep. It's a self-portrait."

When she turned the painting around, the image knocked the air from his lungs. A tattered and lonely Chrissy graced the canvas, her eyes filled with a determination to not only endure but rise above. "It's not just a self-portrait. It's your soul, immortalized in paint."

"You like it?"

His heart both shattered and filled with pride as he studied the painting again. "It's hard to explain. I love it and think it's a masterpiece, but it's also heartbreaking to look at."

"That makes perfect sense to me. It was painful the first time I really stopped to look at it, but it really helped to get it all out into the open."

He knew she was talking about her journey, but he could also take the hint about his own. He had some serious work to do on himself. Especially if he ever truly wanted to move forward.

Chapter 37

Adam

Absolute perfection. Nothing in all of Chicago could compete with being curled up on the couch with Chrissy on a Friday night. He could tolerate any bad day at work if he had this to look forward to. Pulling his arm from under the blanket, he massaged his neck again.

"Is your neck bothering you?" Chrissy asked.

"Yeah. There was a scheduling error with some people from the state, so I spent all day hunched over my keyboard and on the phone, trying to fix it all. Even a high-dollar ergonomic chair couldn't help me today." With a heavy sigh, he let his hand slide from his neck.

"I can try to massage it for you." She reached over and paused the television.

"Nah, I'll be fine." *And I don't think I can handle that.*

"I don't mind. Turn." She shifted to face him.

He did as he was told and moved so his back was toward her. The first touch of her hands on his neck sent shivers and shockwaves careening through his system. He caught a moan a millisecond before it would have escaped his mouth.

"Wow, you weren't kidding. There's a ton of tension in your neck." Her hands slid to his shoulder blade.

"What are you doing?"

"All your muscles are connected. Just massaging your neck won't help if everything else is knotted up." She dug her thumb into a tight muscle just below his right shoulder blade. "Like this knot here. It would just pull everything back out of whack."

This time he did moan before he could stop himself as the muscle under his shoulder blade released.

"See? That feels better, doesn't it?"

You have no idea, he thought. "You seem to know what you're doing."

"At one point I thought about being a massage therapist. It seemed like something that could be fun, and it didn't involve a bunch of numbers. I used the school computers to watch tutorials and taught myself."

His eyelids slid closed as she worked her way back to his neck. "What happened?"

"Life." Her hands shifted as she shrugged. "I found out you had to go to school and get certified to be a legitimate massage therapist. That's a problem when you don't have money and your grades are too crappy for scholarships."

"That's so unfair. And for what it's worth, you're a natural."

"Thanks." She patted the tops of his shoulders. "All done. Feel better?"

He rolled his neck around, and his bones cracked, able to move with the muscle tension alleviated. Twisting back around, he settled against the couch with a sigh. "I don't remember the last time I felt so relaxed. Your hands are magic."

"At your service anytime."

He couldn't help but think about other things her hands might be capable of. *Snap out of it.*

Chrissy sat up straight. "I forgot to tell you. I made social media accounts to showcase my art."

"Oh really? That's awesome."

She opened her phone and turned the screen so he could see. "I just started with the three main platforms that well-known artists seem to have. So far I've only posted a couple of my sketches and paintings. I didn't want to flood them all at once. And I wasn't sure if I could post anything about the mural or not."

Adam thought for a moment, trying to remember the exact wording in her contract. He hadn't really paid attention to that portion before since she hadn't had social media at the time. "I'll have to check and get back to you on that."

"Okay." Chrissy didn't seem fazed by the uncertainty. "I also think I'm going to get a portfolio together to submit to some art galleries."

"That's amazing, Chrissy."

She tucked her hair behind her ear. "The amazing part would be if someone accepts. If I'm going to be Abilene's mentor and help her achieve her dreams, I figure I need to follow my own advice and put myself out there more. It's hypocritical for me to tell her to be brave unless I'm being brave, too, so I created the accounts before I could talk myself out it. I read that having followers on social media can help persuade galleries to showcase an artist because there's a proven interest. I don't have many followers yet, but I just started the accounts a few hours ago."

"Either way, I'm proud of you for taking the initiative and trying to make it happen. That takes a lot of courage." He remembered a jewelry box he'd left sitting on his dresser for days. "I have something for you to celebrate."

"But you just found out about it. And I haven't really accomplished anything yet."

He got up and retrieved the box from his bedroom then sat down, holding it behind his back. "I was going to give this to you at the restaurant that night before the whole paparazzi thing." With an inhale, he held the box out toward her.

"What's this?"

"Open it and see."

She quirked a brow at him and lifted the lid, her hand covering her gasp as the light glistened on silver. "My necklace."

"Not the exact one, but a replica. The police still have the original. I knew it was a saint, but I had to do some detective work to figure out which one. Saint Jude, the patron saint of lost causes, huh?"

Gratitude poured from her as she held the necklace toward him. "Would you put it on me, please?"

Adam took the delicate silver chain and reached across the space between them as she pulled her hair over her shoulder. His mouth watered again at her creamy skin as he fastened the necklace.

She beamed at him as she picked up the pendant. "Thank you so much. This means the world to me. I don't think I can ever repay you."

"You're more than welcome. Seeing you happy is payment enough." He surprised himself with how much that rang true.

"I've never really been a religious person, but when I first started rehab, one of the ladies gave this to me. Something about it really spoke to me. The fact that there was a saint whose sole purpose was to look after lost causes was oddly comforting. I'd always felt like people like me, a lost cause if there ever was one, were ignored and forgotten about. But not by Saint Jude. At least one person out there cared. I spent a lot of time clutching this necklace for dear life."

"Thank you for trusting me with that." Adam reached for her hand, and they sat for a moment, their fingers intertwined. The silence between them filled with more understanding and appreciation than he had ever experienced. He wanted nothing more than to bare his soul to her the way she had bared hers to him. It was high time he sought the help he needed to make that happen.

Chapter 38

Adam

Adam plopped down on the couch, grateful for the end of a stressful week at work. Every day had stretched into the evening as he dealt with investors, eating away at his time with Chrissy. It hadn't been easy, but he'd managed to finagle his schedule to end his Friday night of schmoozing early.

Chrissy came into the living room, her golden hair cascading around her shoulders as she freed it from the confines of her signature messy bun. God, she was gorgeous.

She sank onto the couch beside him and fidgeted with her violet fingernails. "Before we start our movie, we need to talk. I've been trying to figure out how to say this because the guilt is eating me alive."

Her statement served as a bucket of ice water on the fire growing inside him. The same words could come from his mouth just as easily. In fact, they should have already. But at least he was finally working toward that goal. "What are you feeling guilty about?"

"I feel like I've been lying to you by not telling you about my past. There're things you should know."

He shrugged. "We all have a past." He definitely did.

Chrissy averted her eyes to the window. "Some of us have pretty dark pasts, though."

"True, but we can't let the past define us." *Hypocrite,* he thought.

"I guess..." She sat picking at her fingernails, and he waited as she formed the words for whatever she needed to say. "Look, I... you've been amazing to me and maybe I'm wrong, but I sense there might be something between us."

She peeked at him, her face questioning, and he answered her with a grin and the understatement of the year. "I won't argue there."

Instead of the smile he'd expected and hoped for, her features twisted with remorse. "I was afraid of that. No offense, I promise. It just makes me feel evil, like I've led you on."

"Are you saying you don't feel anything?" His heart dropped like a lead balloon.

"No, that's the problem. I do feel something."

"How is that a problem?"

"It's a problem because nothing can ever happen between us, and I don't want to see you get hurt."

"Why can't anything ever happen between us?" His heart hammered in his chest as his past flashed through his mind. As much as he knew he shouldn't, he wanted her to want him.

"I'm damaged goods. You don't want me. Trust me. If you only knew..." Her words trailed off as a tear fell down her cheek.

He moved closer and took her hand in his, inhaling as he prepared to bare his soul. Well, at least the part of it he had finally come to terms with. "Everyone is damaged in some way. Your past made you who you are today, which is an amazingly strong and beautiful woman. I assure you that I most certainly do want you. Sometimes I can barely breathe when I'm around you because I want you so badly."

"I was a prostitute," she blurted, throwing his hand back to him as she shot to her feet. "I used to sell my body to the highest bidder so I could buy drugs to feed my demons. Dozens of men have touched me and done unspeakable things to my body, and I let them. So, how's that for damage? Nothing about me is good. Every part of me is dirty and unworthy. How could anyone want me?"

He'd suspected something along those lines had happened in her past, but to hear it point-blank left him reeling. The thought of her going through such pain, both physically and mentally, stirred an anger in him he hadn't expected. Not an anger toward her but toward the circumstances that led her there. In the past, as much as he hated to admit it, he would've judged someone in her shoes harshly without ever bothering to know their story. But he found himself wanting nothing more than to comfort her and convince her she was more than her past. He had gotten to know the true Chrissy, and none of the messiness in her life could ever dull the light she had found within.

He willed his body to move, the initial shock rendering it useless. After several agonizing moments, his joints creaked back to life, and he climbed to his feet. He took slow, deliberate steps toward her and wrapped his arms around her. She stiffened, undoubtedly surprised by his embrace.

He kissed the top of her head and nuzzled her ear. "I don't care about any of that. None of it makes me want you less. It's in the past. All I've seen from the moment I met you is the beautiful, funny, quick-witted, caring, and talented woman you are right now. The woman who clawed her way out of hell with her heart of gold intact. That's the woman I want."

"What on earth could you want with me?"

He kissed the top of her head again. "What I want..." He paused to kiss her temple. "Is to kiss every inch of you until the only touch your body remembers is mine." He trailed kisses down her cheek to her neck, and she trembled in his arms. "I want you to show me your scars so I can kiss them until they lose their power over you." His mouth traveled across her collarbone and to her other earlobe. "I want to kiss you until you see how truly beautiful you are." He brushed his lips against her soft mouth and paused, resting his forehead on hers. "Now the question is, what do you want?"

Her eyes shimmered as she looked into his and breathed, "I want to let you."

At that he pressed his mouth to hers, lacing his fingers through her blond waves. His lips caressed hers with an urgency he'd never experienced before, his pent-up desire spilling over all at once. She melted against him as he slid a hand to her lower back, pressing her closer, needing her touch more than air.

He let go for only a second to pull his shirt over his head, and the hunger in her features at seeing his chest fueled his desire. He gave a low growl as she ran her hands along his skin, her eyes dancing with delight as she caressed his body.

"I want to see you," he said.

Hesitation flitted across her face for a second, but then she lifted her shirt over her head.

He took her hand and pressed his lips to her wrist then worked his way up her arm, kissing each and every scar. His mouth traveled back to hers, and he eased her down onto the couch. Pulling back, he curled his fingers under the waistline of her lavender lounge pants.

His heart broke at the insecurities swimming in her bright-blue eyes. "You're safe with me," he said, assuring her before caressing her lips with his.

She cradled his cheek in her hand, and a soft smile curled her mouth. "I've known that from day one."

His heart surged, and he leaned down, kissing that beautiful smile. His lips trailed down her chest and past her belly button, stopping at where his fingers still gripped soft fabric. He gently slid the pants down, checking her eyes with every inch.

Tears swam in her eyes as her thighs were exposed. The enormous amount of pain expressed in the marked flesh took his breath away and seized his heart. He tossed her pants aside and took in the magnificent woman before him.

"My God, you're beautiful," he said with a moan.

She nibbled her lip, her eyes letting him know her heart didn't believe his words yet. He lowered his mouth to her thighs, caressing the marked skin with his lips. Inch by inch, he would prove to her how much her past didn't define her.

He trailed his way back up and kissed her cheeks, then he brushed away her tears with his hand. "Please, let me treat you like the goddess you are."

She buried her fingers in his hair and pulled his mouth to hers, parting her lips to welcome his tongue. Her moan as his hands grazed her body was all the answer he needed.

Chapter 39
Chrissy

Sunlight streamed into the bedroom from the living room as Chrissy's eyes peeked open. Adam curled against her back with his arm draped over her hip, her hair tickling her neck in his breath. She closed her eyes again and smiled as memories of last night scrolled through her mind like the best romance movie she'd ever seen. *How is this real life?*

She looked around the room for the first time, as she'd been a little preoccupied the night before. Much like the rest of the apartment, Adam's bedroom exuded five-star luxury. Her attention was drawn to the pictures on his dresser. Adam wore graduation regalia in one, his arms slung over the shoulders of a middle-aged man and woman she assumed to be his parents. In another he held up a giant fish while standing on a pier, and another showcased him shaking hands with the governor. Amongst the snapshots of a picture-perfect life, a single frame sat off to the side, flipped face down.

Easing herself forward, she slid from under his hand and let it gently fall to the bed. She tiptoed over to the dresser, glancing behind her with every step, then reached out but stopped her hand an inch from the frame.

Second-guessing her snooping, she looked back at Adam again, watching the slow rise and fall of his chest that she'd caressed and kissed a hundred times. He knew her deepest, darkest secrets. Surely that earned her the right to see whose picture he turned face down.

Lifting the frame, she came face-to-face with a pretty brunette nestled in Adam's arms. The world froze, and Chrissy's heart stopped. A brilliant diamond sparkled on the woman's ring finger, and Adam held a beer up in celebration. The air left Chrissy's lungs as if she'd been punched in the gut, and her stomach lurched.

She hurried to her makeshift bedroom and pulled on a long-sleeved shirt and her painting overalls. Then she grabbed her purse and slammed the door behind her as she tried to outrun her broken heart.

Adam

A slamming door jolted Adam from the best sleep of his life. He frowned at the cold, empty bed beside him and rose up on his elbow, scanning the room.

"Chrissy?" Nothing but silence met his ears. He crawled out of bed and started for the kitchen but froze in his tracks. His blood turned to ice as the face of his fiancée smiled up at him from within the silver frame.

"Chrissy?" he shouted as he ran to her room. The chair that usually held her overalls and purse sat empty.

"Damn it." He growled and tugged at his hair, not angry at her but with himself. He should've told her the truth. All of it. But he had needed to accept the truth for himself before opening his heart like that to her. He should've dealt with his feelings long ago rather than bury them. Instead, he'd been stubborn and waited too long.

He sprinted to his closet, pulled on the first thing he grabbed, and sped out of the door. On the way to the lobby, he called her phone. "Please pick up." But she didn't. And he couldn't say he blamed her.

As he jogged to the parking garage, he pulled up Luke's number. Nothing. Next he tried Lilly's, to no avail. He jumped into his car and slammed his hand on the steering wheel. "Damn it. Why did I have to be such a coward?"

He had to find a way to come clean and regain Chrissy's trust. One thing was certain, he couldn't give up. He pulled the car out of its spot and sped off to find her.

Adam slowed to a stop in front of Lilly's bakery and slouched against the steering wheel. All day, he'd tried every phone number and every other location he could think of but had come up empty-handed. The only reason Luke had spoken to him was to say "I told you so." Everyone saw his name pop up and put their phones down, not that he could blame them for ignoring a cowardly idiot. At least Aria told him Chrissy wasn't at their house, which left one last option. If only he could find a way to talk to Chrissy.

The bakery door opened as a man walked out carrying a bright-pink box. Through the large front window, Adam saw Lilly cradling a phone on her shoulder as she jotted something down on an order sheet. A singular ray of hope appeared in the form of a bakery phone.

Adam dialed the number for The Gilded Lilly and held his breath as he saw Lilly pick up.

Lilly's upbeat voice rang through the phone. "This is The Gilded Lilly, the sweetest bakery in town. How may I help you?"

"P-Please don't hang up. This is Adam." He didn't care how desperate he sounded. Watching Lilly's smile fall away at the sound of his name filled him with shame.

"What do you want?"

"I just need to talk to her. Please. I know I screwed up by not telling her the truth and she never wants to see me again, but I need to explain myself. I swear I didn't mean to hurt her." He clutched the phone as if it could stop him from sinking in the emotional quicksand.

Lilly cupped her hand over her mouth as she glanced at the customers eating in her shop. "How did you think she would feel finding out there's another woman in your life? One with a diamond ring, to boot."

Adam's forehead dropped to the steering wheel. He pushed his words through a tightening throat. "I-I didn't mention Bethany because she's not in my life anymore. She's dead."

Lilly's gasp rasped through the line, followed by silence. Adam raised his head from the steering wheel to see if Lilly had hung up.

She still held the phone but chewed her lip in thought. "Okay. I'll talk to her, but I can't make any promises."

"R-Really?" Adam burst above the surface of the quicksand, and his heart gasped for air. "Thank you so much."

Lilly hung up and disappeared to the back of the bakery, beyond Adam's sight line. His heart pounded against his ribs with wild abandon as he stared at his phone, willing the universe to let Chrissy's name light up the screen. Time ticked away, minute by agonizing minute, each one bringing him closer to going under the quicksand again.

His phone buzzed to life, his brain unbelieving. Putting the phone to his ear, he uttered a cautious "Hello?"

"Hello, Adam." The coolness in Chrissy's tone was a dagger to his heart.

"Chrissy, I-I'm so sorry. Please let me explain."

"I'm listening."

Adam sighed, filled with self-hatred as he froze. This was his one chance to make things right, and he still couldn't muster the strength to relive the past. "C-Can we please talk face-to-face? This isn't easy for me to say, and if I could just see you, maybe it wouldn't be so hard.

I know you don't owe me anything to make things easier for me, but please."

More agonizing silence before she spoke, her voice broken. "Where are you?"

He bobbed to the surface of the quicksand. "I-I'm parked in front of the bakery."

"Just a minute."

Chapter 40
Chrissy

As Chrissy walked up to Adam's BMW, memories of her other times in that car rushed back to her. The tender care he'd given her after her fainting episode and Damien's attack made her heart ache. Maybe meeting in his car was a mistake. She couldn't make a scene in the bakery, though, and the street would just lead to more tabloid fodder.

The door popped open as she reached for the handle, revealing Adam leaning across the car. The anguish in his features pulled at her heartstrings. He looked as miserable as she felt, maybe more so.

"S-Sorry I didn't get out to open your door. Traffic is pretty bad this afternoon. P-Plus, I was afraid if you saw me, you'd turn around and leave." Adam's mouth curled in a sad smile, his eyes filling with sorrow.

"Are you sure it's okay if I sit in the front seat? Someone might see and get the wrong idea about us." Adam's car smelled good, familiar, and Chrissy hated how much she had missed it while they had been avoiding being seen together.

"I don't care about that right now. All I care about is explaining everything to you."

"I'm listening." Chrissy crossed her arms over her chest, forcing her eyes forward and away from his tormented face. She wanted to convince herself his pain was an act, but the stutter served as a dead giveaway of his stress.

Beside her, Adam inhaled and exhaled as if mustering his courage. "The picture you saw..." His voice cracked, and he cleared his throat. "The woman in that picture is Bethany. My fiancée."

Chrissy's head whipped around as she sucked in a breath. Fiancée. That word punched her in the stomach and broke her heart. "Why didn't you tell me you were engaged? Why did you let me believe you cared for me?"

"Because she's dead."

"What?"

"And I'm the one to blame."

The world spun around her, and she clutched her door handle to steady herself. Her brain screamed for her to run, but her heart refused to believe her ears. *Adam, a murderer?* "What? How? I don't understand."

Adam rested his forehead on the steering wheel and took several measured breaths. "I know I told you that I'm not a workaholic, but that's not entirely true. After Bethany died, I regretted so many things, and I told myself I'd never be a workaholic again. The only problem was that work was all I had with her gone. I threw myself into my work to numb the pain, keeping my brain occupied and my heart quiet. Until you came along."

Chrissy's heart softened, and an urge to rub his back almost won. Instead, she shook the thought from her head. "But what happened to her?" *And how are you a murderer?*

"I mentioned before how I had to get a new car two years ago, but I didn't tell you why. It wasn't because I wanted to. I was a workaholic when I met Beth, but she loved me anyway. She had a similar background as me and similar ambitions, so she understood. She'd worked her way from barely getting by to being just a few years away from becoming a partner at her law firm. One of my first purchases when I started getting my big paychecks after college was a luxury car. I wanted that status symbol to let the world know I'd made it, you know?"

That sentiment resonated with Chrissy. Her benchmark for success was to have her name on an apartment or home of her own. Though she hadn't reached that point yet, when she did, she'd want the world to know.

He scoffed and shook his head. "I was young and stupid. The only place I ever went was the office, and grabbing a taxi was so much easier. After a little while, the brake light came on, but since I didn't drive it much, I ignored it. Beth's law firm decided to do a team-building retreat at this resort in Wisconsin. It was on a lake and in October, so with the fall leaves it would've been a beautiful place. Romantic like the movies, so Beth wanted me to go with her. All week leading up to the trip, she'd ask me every day to make sure I was going. It was kind of annoying at the time, but looking back I can see why she didn't have confidence in me. Work came first. Sure enough, the day we were supposed to leave, I got tied up in meetings. I lost track of time, and we missed our flight with no more available until the next afternoon. Beth had forgotten to renew her license, thanks to our hectic schedules, so she couldn't drive herself. I told her as soon as my work dinner was over, we would drive there. I would drive through the night if I had to so she wouldn't miss the opening address."

The tears in Adam's eyes gripped Chrissy's heart like a vise.

"She asked me about the brake light, and I told her it was fine. I'd been driving it that way for months, and the brakes worked fine. With the crazy work schedule I'd been keeping, Beth didn't think I should be driving at night like that, but I insisted I wanted to. I had to make it up to her for making us miss our flight. She knew I always drank at dinners, so she asked me if I was okay to drive. I told her I knew my limit, and it was fine." He slammed his hand into the steering wheel.

Chrissy startled at the sudden rage but stayed silent.

"About two hours into the drive, there was an accident. I don't remember much of it, honestly. Just an intersection, a bunch of noise, and then waking up on the shoulder of the road. I learned that we'd been T-boned by a semitruck after running through a red light. I looked around for Beth, but there were so many emergency vehicles and people standing around, I couldn't make sense of anything. I asked how she was, but no one would tell me."

Unable to resist any longer, Chrissy reached out and rubbed Adam's back. "Oh, Adam. I'm so sorry. That must've been so hard."

If Adam felt her hand, he didn't show it. Instead, he balled his fists. "For hours, no one in the hospital would tell me anything about Beth. Maybe it wasn't hours. I don't really know how much time passed. I finally begged a nurse to tell me what happened to Beth. When they said she didn't make it, I thought about all the things I should've done differently. It was later determined that the brakes had failed. My car, the one with the brake light I ignored for months, was her cause of death. It was all my fault."

Every ounce of anger in her dissipated at the sound of his sob. "It was an accident. You didn't know the brakes would fail."

He turned her way, his expression wild. "Every decision I made led to her death. If I hadn't let myself get stuck in another meeting, we would've been on a plane. The brakes failed because I didn't take the car to get checked. I told her everything would be fine and not to worry. I was exhausted from working sixty hours that week, so it's possible I nodded off at the wheel. I can't remember the moments leading up to the accident, so maybe that's why. If I hadn't drunk at dinner, maybe I would've reacted quicker and been able to stop it all from happening. My blood alcohol level was just below the legal limit, but just because it was legal doesn't mean it was okay. It doesn't mean the alcohol didn't cause issues with my reaction time. It's all my fault. There are so many things I could've done differently, and she'd still be alive. My choices killed her."

Chrissy's heart shattered as he buried his face in his hands. Words to ease his pain escaped her, so she slid her arm around his shoulders and leaned her head against him.

"I couldn't stand to live in the apartment we shared, so that's when I moved into the condo. I gave all her things to her parents except for the picture you saw in my bedroom. It was lying down because I couldn't stand the guilt when I saw her smiling back at me and the celebratory beer in my hand, but I couldn't bring myself to get rid of it. For the longest time afterward, I wished I had died with her. Or better yet, that I had taken the brunt of the impact so she could've lived. She deserved her life much more than I do."

Those words hit deep within Chrissy, all the way to her soul. She knew that kind of pain all too well. Sliding her arm from his shoulders, she took his hand in hers. "Listen to me, Adam. You deserve to live. Beth didn't deserve to die, but neither do you. Things happen beyond our control sometimes, and it sucks and is painful, but all we can do is keep surviving day by day. Or minute by minute if you have to. I know those feelings of hopelessness and being unworthy of life." She let go of his hand and pushed up her sleeve. "I've been at rock bottom. But I've also climbed out of it, just like you did."

He shook his head and scrubbed his sleeve across his face. "I don't think I ever really did, though. Instead, I just threw myself into my work and ignored everything. Then you came along and stirred everything up, waking up parts of me that I thought died with Beth. As hard as I tried to ignore it, I couldn't stop myself from wanting to see you. My heart wouldn't listen to a single word my brain told it." He raised his eyes to hers for the first time since his story began. "I'm so sorry for hurting you. I swear I never meant to. It seems like anyone I love gets hurt in one way or the other, and it's my fault for letting things go too far. I should've told you a long time ago, but I was selfish and unwilling to face my own past. Thank you for letting me explain myself, and I hope it eases some of the pain I caused."

His phrase "anyone I love" stuck in her mind. "I'm kind of at a loss for words."

He cupped her hand in his as his brows furrowed with sorrow. "You don't have to say anything. I understand. As much as I'd love to try, I didn't come here to win you back. You need to focus on your own mental health, well-being, and recovery without adding my baggage on top. Telling you everything was just to help you maybe hurt a little less, and I knew going into it that I'd be leaving without you. It's okay, I promise."

"Are you saying you don't want to be with me?" A knot formed in Chrissy's stomach. Though she'd come into the car thinking the very same thing, after hearing his story, the thought devastated her.

Adam sighed as he stared at their hands. "No. I'd love nothing more than to be with you and see where this thing takes us. But I know I broke your trust by hiding so much from you, especially my past with alcohol. You've been so open and honest, and you deserved the same from me."

Chrissy leaned back, taking full inventory of the man before her. A broken, humble man sacrificing his happiness for what he thought she wanted. His strong features hardened by torment juxtaposed with the achingly soft vulnerability in his eyes.

Her mind traveled back to the moments she'd bared her soul to him, letting him into the deepest, darkest parts of her past. The raw nakedness she'd felt then was what Adam was experiencing, his darkest moments taking their turn under the harsh glare of the spotlight. Rather than running from her pain, he'd enveloped her in compassion and taught her to love herself again. She couldn't abandon him to wallow in his pain.

Lacing her fingers through his, she peered through the window at the bright and cheerful bakery. "You know, they say food can't solve your problems, but Lilly's bear claws are so good, they come pretty close to creating world peace. They're as big as my head, though, so I can never finish one. Would you want to maybe split one with me? It's a shame to waste it."

When she turned to Adam, an ounce of light shone through the dark storm in his eyes and confusion creased his features. "You want me to come share a dessert with you?"

"Everyone needs to eat, and I'm assuming you haven't eaten much today."

He cocked his head to the side with a nod. "You got me there. I haven't eaten anything at all today. But I'm surprised you'd want me to join you."

"How about we just go have a snack and see what happens?" She winked, and her heart soared to see Adam's features soften and hope return to his eyes.

A renewed hope blossomed within her as well. The whole time she'd known Adam, she'd placed herself beneath him as unworthy of love from a perfect man. But at that moment, the illusion of a perfect man lay shattered at her feet, leaving in its place a raw, genuine version, with major flaws just like her. Perhaps she didn't belong beneath him after all. And perhaps the true, flawed Adam was actually the perfect man for her.

Chapter 41

Adam

Taking a sip of his water, Adam thanked his lucky stars. After Chrissy had fled the condo, he thought he'd lost her forever, but there he sat across the table from her in Lilly's break room.

Other customers of the bakery had come and gone as Adam and Chrissy talked for hours. At first the wounds of the past bled and throbbed as the conversation ripped them open, but as time passed a healing began. The once terrifying task of opening his heart became liberating, and he found himself letting down walls he hadn't even realized he'd built.

"One thing you're still avoiding is telling me about your parents." Chrissy popped the last piece of the bear claw in her mouth and looked at him, expectant.

Rip it off like a bandage, he told himself before clearing his throat. "Well, they were huge fans of Beth's." He peeked up in time to see Chrissy's face go guarded. "We dated for almost five years before we got engaged, so they'd known her for six years when she died. They took it really hard since they'd considered her their daughter-in-law for years." He stopped to sip his water and give himself some time. "They say tragedy can either bring you closer or tear you apart. It's safe to say it did the latter for me and my parents."

Chrissy's hand wrapped around his, and her eyes filled with sympathy. "That must've been so hard for all of you."

He nodded and peered through the window to the darkened world outside. "Yeah, it was. Especially since I'm pretty sure they blamed me. I know for a fact Beth's parents blamed me. They flat out told me so, but my parents didn't exactly try to hide it either. When Beth died, so did their visions of my future family, of grandkids. As I spiraled inward, instead of reaching out they backed away and let me fall farther. I needed them in my corner, but they couldn't be bothered to leave Beth's. I haven't talked to them since about a month after the accident."

Chrissy squeezed his hand. "Leaving you in your grief was wrong, there's no doubt about that. But as you said, they were grieving too. Have you ever thought about talking to them now, after you've all processed and healed some?"

Adam scoffed. "Like they'd want to talk to me."

Chrissy shrugged and caught his eye. "You'll never know if you don't try. I can tell you're still in pain, and I'm willing to bet so are they. Maybe talking will help you all get closure so you can heal even more."

"Maybe." Adam swallowed as he blinked back tears. She was right, whether he wanted to admit it or not. Deep inside, he knew he needed to at least try to get his parents back. Maybe he could call them in a few days. No need to have every breakthrough in one night. "My therapist has suggested I reach out to them, even if it's just a letter."

Chrissy blinked. "Your therapist?"

"After you talked about your mom's ashes, I started looking into teletherapy. The last thing I wanted with paparazzi on my tail was for them to see me going to a therapist. But after seeing your self-portrait and hearing you talk more about how therapy helped you, I finally made the call. I've been doing daily sessions during my lunch break."

"Adam, that's amazing." Chrissy gripped his hands.

"I knew I needed to open up to you and to tell you about my past. I tried so many times, but I realized I had to open up to myself first. It's still too early to tell if therapy is helping, but at least I'm trying. I was hoping I could work through things and tell you about

Beth before something like this happened. If I could go back in time, I would get over my pride and get help sooner."

"What matters is you finally did. And as long as you're willing to try, you're making progress."

"Sorry, guys, it's closing time." Lilly hung her apron on a hook just inside the break room door and moved toward the light switch in the kitchen. "I didn't want to interrupt, but I didn't want you to walk out to a completely dark bakery either. As long as the lights are on, people will try to come in."

Adam's heart sank as he pictured walking into his bleak condo alone.

"Oh, okay. Sorry, I lost track of time." Chrissy rose to her feet and hesitated, and Adam wondered if she didn't want the night to end either.

Lilly flicked off one set of lights and moved to the next set of switches. "Oh, Chrissy, I forgot to tell you. Zach had a last-minute cancellation, so I'm meeting him at his office for a date night. I'll be gone for a few hours. You're more than welcome to stay upstairs for as long as you need. My guest bedroom has a seating area that's way more comfy than the break room table."

Before Lilly hit the next switch, he could've sworn he saw her wink.

Chrissy crossed the room and wrapped her friend in a hug. "Thank you."

"Anything for a friend." With the flip of another switch, Lilly left.

"Upstairs?" Adam asked as he rose from his chair.

"Lilly lives on the second floor."

"Oh, right. That makes sense." He scoffed at himself for not connecting those dots.

"I don't know how she survives the commute, the poor thing."

Adam took one look at Chrissy's deadpan expression and burst into laughter, a healing balm on his wounded heart.

Chrissy's shoulders relaxed as he laughed, but then she began fiddling with her fingernails again. "If you don't have anywhere to be, I was thinking maybe we could go upstairs and keep talking."

"All I have waiting for me is a cold, empty condo." *Since I'm an idiot and scared her off,* he added in his head.

A visible relief washed over Chrissy, as if she thought he'd actually tell her no and leave. "All right, then. It's this way."

Following her through the kitchen and up the stairs, he counted his lucky stars for a second chance. He would follow her anywhere if it meant more time with the woman he loved. Not that he could tell her that. Not yet anyway. After the tumultuous day he'd caused, the L-word would have to wait. A premature declaration could send her running for the hills. Again. He'd have to wait until he'd proven himself to be the trustworthy man she deserved.

Chapter 42

Adam

Dust particles danced in the beam of sunshine streaming through the window of Lilly's guest bedroom. Adam's bladder ached, but he didn't dare move and disturb Chrissy. He eased his head up, craning to see the clock on the nightstand. Over an hour had passed since he'd heard Lilly and Zach stirring in the kitchen, and his stomach growled as delightful, sweet smells of baked goods wafted into the apartment. But his stomach and bladder would have to wait. His heart was in the driver's seat, and all it wanted was to soak up every last ounce of bliss with Chrissy snuggled in his arms.

He always loved being with her, but after baring his heart and soul it felt different in the best way. All of their secrets lay out in the open. For both of them. If he had known the immense relief he would feel after telling Chrissy about Beth, he would've stopped being a coward and told her sooner. She knew, and she hadn't judged him. They could work on putting the past behind them and moving forward. Maybe they could help each other every step of the way. A true partnership.

He gave a contented sigh, unable to hold it in any longer.

Chrissy stirred, shifting onto her back and easing her eyelids open. When she saw him next to her in the bed, her features contorted in confusion, and she looked around the room.

"We stayed up talking until two, and you said I could sleep here."

"Yeah, I remember now." She scrubbed a hand over her face. "Sorry. I think I slept so hard I gave myself amnesia for a minute."

"Yeah, you were sleeping pretty good."

Chrissy sat up, stretching her neck. "Want to get some breakfast?"

"Yes, please. Whatever Lilly is baking has been torturing me for over an hour." His stomach growled right on cue.

"You've been awake that long? You should've gone ahead and eaten without me."

"You needed sleep, and my arm was under you. I couldn't bring myself to bother you."

"Oh. Thanks." Chrissy climbed off the bed, but the look in her eye let him know he'd made the right choice.

When they opened the apartment door to head downstairs, they were greeted with a box of muffins and two cups of coffee on the landing.

Chrissy picked up the note on the box and read aloud. "Thought you might need this."

"That was nice of her." Adam picked up the goodies and took them to the table.

Later, with one warm muffin in his belly, Adam peeled the wrapper from a second one. He gulped down half of his latte, willing the caffeine to give him courage. With one last deep inhale, he bit the bullet. "S-So I was wondering..."

Chrissy took a bite of her muffin and waited.

"W-Where does all of this leave us?" The thundering of his pulse drummed in his ears.

She set down her muffin and sipped her coffee. "I've been thinking about that since I woke up."

"Me too." *And all of yesterday and last night,* he added to himself. The muffin and coffee threatened to come back up as he peered at the amazing woman he needed to keep in his life.

Her hand crossed the table and gripped his.

Oh no. Here came the Dear John speech he'd earned through sheer cowardice and stupidity.

"You should've told me the truth from the beginning," she said.

His chin dropped to his chest. "I know. I started to tell you so many times, but it just wouldn't come out."

"But I understand why it was so hard for you to talk about."

A singular ray of sunshine broke through the clouds of gloom and doom.

"We all have baggage and skeletons in our closets. Some are hard to talk about. Honestly, without the therapy I've had since starting my recovery journey, I'm not sure I would've been able to tell you my secrets so easily."

His eyes rose to hers, and if he hadn't been sitting, the compassion flowing from her would've brought him to his knees.

"We've both had bad things happen in our lives, but we shouldn't let the past hold us back from embracing the future."

"Are you saying what I think you're saying?" A cautious hope boosted his spirits.

"I'd like to see where this thing takes us." She gave a little grin as she repeated his words from earlier.

Within seconds, he'd leapt to his feet, rounded the table, and scooped her into his arms. For the first time in twenty-four hours, he could breathe. He nuzzled her neck and whispered words of gratitude as her hair brushed against his face. "Thank you for giving me another chance. I promise I'll never hurt you again."

Her lips brushed his cheek as her low voice tickled his ear and sent shivers through his body. "I believe you." She pulled away and cupped his face with her hand. "You're a good man, Adam. One mistake doesn't change that."

His fingers threaded through her hair as he pulled her closer and pressed his mouth to hers, letting his body do the talking.

After several minutes, Chrissy broke the kiss and brought his forehead to hers. "Let's go home."

"I'd love to."

Chrissy

Tiptoeing down the stairs, Chrissy listened to the noises of the kitchen. Lilly's and Ruth's voices mingled with the metallic clanking of pans and the whirring of mixers. She waited until Ruth's voice became distant then poked her head into the kitchen.

Lilly turned in an instant, and she gave Chrissy a knowing smirk. "Well, look who it is. Miss Sleepover coming to do her walk of shame?"

Chrissy smirked as she stepped into the room. "It's not like that. All we did was talk. Nothing happened."

"That was a lot of talking." Lilly returned to her task of splatting donuts face down into a bowl of sprinkles.

"Yeah, it was." Chrissy leaned against the counter and stared off into the distance as bits and pieces of their conversation rolled through her head.

"Where is he?" Lilly asked.

"He's freshening up, and then we'll get out of your hair."

"Together?"

"Yep." Chrissy knew her short answers were driving Lilly crazy, but she figured she might as well have fun with it.

Lilly prodded her. "So...?"

"So, what?"

"So, how was it? What did you talk about?"

Chrissy sighed and let her wistful smile spread unhindered. "It was wonderful. We talked about everything. He told me how he grew up really poor until his dad made some cabinets for a prominent rich family and his business took off. Can you believe Adam used to be poor? Then he told me about college and meeting Beth. He also opened up more about the aftermath of the accident. It seems therapy is already helping him work through some of it."

"That sounds like some pretty heavy stuff." Lilly grabbed another tray of donuts and began piping icing onto them.

"I won't lie. It was hard at first. But I think it really helped him to talk about it. Sometimes the most important stuff to talk about is the hardest."

Ruth entered the kitchen to retrieve the finished donuts. "We need some more apple cinnamon muffins. Oh, hey, Chrissy." A knowing grin flashed on her face before she turned back to Lilly. "I'm getting everything packed up to go to the farmer's market, and Zach is manning the register. Need me to help with anything before I go?"

Lilly surveyed the kitchen. "I don't think so."

"All right. I'm heading out, then."

With Ruth gone, Lilly got to work on another batch of muffins.

"Ruth didn't seem surprised to see me." Chrissy watched Lilly gather a clean bowl and measuring cups.

"Yeah, sorry, but I had to tell her you were here. I didn't want her to be scared to death when someone came down the stairs unexpectedly."

"That makes sense. And it's okay." Chrissy joined Lilly at the other counter and began chopping apples.

"Thanks." Lilly measured out the other ingredients. "And returning to our conversation, I'm really proud of you for handling the whole Beth thing so well."

"What choice do I have?"

"It took so long for you to admit you liked him, I was afraid you would use the whole situation as a reason to run away. To let your fear win. I'm happy to see you don't self-sabotage anymore."

"I'm still a work in progress, but I'm trying my best. Besides, I can't let a little bit of baggage stand between me and the man I love."

Lilly stopped mixing and grabbed Chrissy's shoulders. "The man you love?"

Chrissy nodded, her words getting caught in her throat. The memory of him saying "the people I love" when talking about her replayed through her mind, feeding her hope that he felt the same way.

Lilly pulled her in for a hug. "Oh, girl, I'm so happy for you."

"Thanks. Now I just need to find the courage to tell him."

Chapter 43

Chrissy

Watching Adam hesitate at the door, Chrissy couldn't help but giggle and find him absolutely adorable. The entire week since she'd come back to the condo, he never wanted to leave her side. "It's fine, I promise. Go to your dinner meeting. You have to keep working like normal, at least until the mural is done, remember? If you skip something this important, everyone will wonder what's going on. We can't give Mr. Lyones any more reasons to stress out."

Adam's features relaxed some, but not much. "I know, it's just... I don't want to go."

Chrissy sauntered over and threaded her arms under his suit jacket and around his waist. "I know you don't. And it's so sweet of you, but I'll be fine. I can take care of myself."

He moaned and tugged her closer. "I know you can, but that doesn't stop me from wanting to take care of you. And you holding me like this isn't exactly making it easier for me to leave."

"Oh, well, I can take care of that," she teased as she began pulling away.

"You know I didn't mean it like that." He bent down, pressing his lips to hers.

She gave in, melting into his body until his phone buzzed in his pocket. With a gentle push on his chest, she broke their embrace. "You'd better get going. Can't keep potential investors waiting."

Adam groaned and rested his forehead on hers. "You're right."

She kissed his cheek and stepped back, straightening his suit jacket for him. "Well, I have plans, anyway, so you might as well go to your business dinner and try to enjoy it."

Adam gave a resigned sigh and adjusted his navy tie. "I completely forgot about that. Did Winifred give you any hints about why she wanted you to visit?"

"Not really. She just said to bring my sketchbook. I'm both super curious and petrified."

"She loves you, so you'll be fine. Let me know when you're back home safe." He gave her one last kiss before going out the door.

With Adam gone, Chrissy gathered her purse and art supplies and made her way to the elevator. Knowing she was about to see Winifred's home was exciting and intimidating. Winifred was the most respectable and classy person Chrissy had ever met. She carried herself like royalty but was not at all snobby. The fact that no one really knew anything about her past made her that much more fascinating. Chrissy only hoped she didn't look too out of place. She smoothed her lavender peasant top, inspected her khakis for the third time, and promised herself a shopping trip in the immediate future.

Chrissy punched in the code Winifred had given her to unlock the penthouse floor, and she marveled at how different her life looked within a matter of months. If someone had told her while she lay in the hospital, going through withdrawal, that she'd someday have access to arguably the most expensive penthouse in Chicago, she would've proclaimed their idiocy. Yet there she was.

The doors dinged and opened to an entryway fit for a queen. Green marble glistened on the walls, complemented by a rich darkwood floor. An ornate gold table boasted a grand bouquet of white lilies. Chrissy's mouth hung agape, but she snapped it shut as Winifred breezed through a doorway.

Winifred leaned in and air-kissed Chrissy's cheeks. "Chrissy. So glad you could come. The tea is in the study."

Chrissy drooled over the pink-and-black tweed suit Winifred had donned, and her hands brushed her khakis again. Passing through the living room, Chrissy forgot all about her lackluster clothing as she ogled the rich-green velvet couch set against a backdrop of subtle gold brocade wallpaper.

Just when Chrissy thought she couldn't be more impressed, Winifred threw open the doors to the study. Wooden bookcases lined three walls, with the fourth being a wall of wood-trimmed windows.

"Your study is straight out of a fairy tale."

"Thank you. I quite enjoy it." Winifred paused as Chrissy looked around then waved a hand. "Come this way."

She led Chrissy through the study to another living room that, while elegant, held less grandeur than the first. Winifred took a seat on the plush green velvet couch and patted the cushion next to her.

As Chrissy sat and smoothed her slacks, a fluffy white cat jumped onto her lap. "Oh. Hello."

"This is Anastasia."

"She's gorgeous." Chrissy stroked the cat's silky fur, which prompted a low, rumbling purr. After a moment the cat curled up on her lap and peered at her with its ice-blue eyes.

Winifred looked impressed. "Anastasia is typically a shy cat, not fond of strangers. She seems to be rather fond of you, though."

Chrissy grinned at the feline as she rubbed between its ears and down to its tail. "I'm honored to be chosen by such a beauty. I've always loved animals and wished I could have a pet growing up. That wasn't ever really possible, though. One foster family had two cats, but I was only there for a month or so."

"Well then, that should make your job all the easier and more amusing."

Chrissy's head bobbed up. "My job?"

"The reason I called you here, dear. I would like to commission portraits of my cats." Winifred waved her arm across the room in a grandiose fashion.

As Chrissy followed her gesture, she counted not one but four other cats in the room, lounging on various luxurious cushions. Winifred telling her to bring her sketchbook made much more sense. "Oh—"

"I was told you're experienced in portraits. I came across your social media a few days ago, and the images you've shared suggest so as well."

"Yes, but of people." Chrissy watched a sleek black cat stretch and saunter over to a golden water bowl. A ball of orange fur lay on a white cushion in a beam of sunlight, the gentle movement of breathing the only sign of it being an animal rather than a cushion itself. A blur of gray zoomed past the couch and up a climbing post disguised as a plant.

"Animals are no different. If you can capture the soul of a person, you can do the same for an animal." She smiled at the black cat stretching beside them. "Adam also mentioned that you wanted more subjects for your portfolio and social media. You may share anything about my commission except my name."

Of course, the plan was always for Chrissy's online presence to bring in jobs, but she hadn't expected it to happen so soon. And she definitely didn't expect a job so big from someone so important. Panic swirled beneath the surface as Chrissy surveyed the animals again, and she had to force herself to think of it as any other job. "That would be amazing. Thank you. Were you thinking of one portrait all together or separate ones for each cat?"

Winifred bent and stroked the fur of a fluffy black-and-orange cat. "One for each so you can fully capture their personalities. You'll have to get to know them first, of course. Anastasia is a cautious girl, but once she knows you're safe, she's a sweetheart. She's a true princess at heart. Athena here is the complete opposite. She embodies the tortoiseshell attitude, especially if she doesn't get her way. That's why she's named after the goddess of war. You won't find Athena curled on anyone's lap."

Chrissy held her hand down toward Athena, who then sauntered over and sniffed Chrissy's fingertips. After a few sniffs, Athena bumped her forehead against Chrissy's palm.

"She gave you permission to pet her." Winifred's voice held a touch of surprise in her announcement. "It's very encouraging to see them take to you so readily, I must say."

With one hand petting Anastasia and the other busy with Athena, a calmness enveloped Chrissy. Being chosen by Winifred's cats meant more than it logically should have. Their approval bested that of most of the people she knew. "I have to admit, this sounds like the best job in the world. I'll probably have to do the actual painting at home, though. These beauties wanting attention will definitely hinder my progress. Who can say no to these faces?"

"Indeed, I never can."

Chapter 44

Chrissy

Clutching her stomach, Chrissy willed her breakfast burrito to stay put. A few deep breaths did zilch to ease the swarm of butterflies in her stomach. No, it couldn't be butterflies. Her current level of nerves called for something more substantial. Maybe bats. One glance at Adam told her he battled his own demons in the seat next to her. She reached across the console and gave his hand a squeeze.

He glanced her way with a start as if he'd gotten so lost in his own storm of thoughts, he'd forgotten she was along for the ride. He let out a nervous bark of a laugh. "I don't know about you, but I've got a stampede of elephants in my stomach right now."

Ah, yes, elephants fit perfectly. She mustered the most confident smile she could. "They agreed to see us and even sounded happy after the initial shock. It will be fine."

Please, let it be fine, she begged the universe, especially since Adam had told his parents that he was dating her during their phone call. She had asked him afterward if that was wise, given them needing to keep a low profile, but he had assured her his parents had always avoided the media like the plague. She sure hoped he was right.

Another nervous laugh. "Yeah. It'll be fine."

As they pulled up to the tan ranch-style home, Adam's face paled whiter than Chrissy had ever seen it, a stark contrast against his navy polo. She caressed his back as her brows knit with worry. "Are you sure you're going to be okay? You look like you've seen a ghost."

Adam shook his head but kept his gaze locked on the house. "I don't know if I can do this. Maybe it's too much too soon."

At that, the front door opened and a plump woman with cropped brunette hair stepped out, followed by an older version of Adam.

"Ready or not. Remember to breathe." Chrissy inhaled and pushed the car door open.

Adam followed her lead and rounded the car as she smoothed the skirt of her new sage-green dress. He clung to her, gripping her hand a little too tightly as they ascended the walkway.

Adam's mom cupped his hand between hers. "Adam, it's so good to see you, son. Isn't it, Steven?"

Steven, a living glimpse into Adam's future looks, mumbled under his breath, the tension between the two men palpable.

Adam cleared his throat and threaded his arm behind Chrissy. "Mom, Dad, I'd like you to meet Chrissy."

Adam's mom took Chrissy's hand the same way she'd taken Adam's. "Hello, Chrissy. It's so nice to meet you. I'm Theresa, and this is Steven."

Chrissy gave them both her sweetest smile and a nod, praying her anxiety wasn't marring all her features the way it was destroying her insides. "It's so nice to meet you both."

An awkward silence followed with everyone avoiding eye contact, and Chrissy willed the porch to cave in and swallow them whole.

Theresa broke the silence. "Please, come inside. I made some chicken club sandwiches for lunch."

"That sounds delicious." Chrissy's words whooshed out in a breath of relief as Theresa held the hunter-green door open for her and Adam.

The weathered oak floors moaned beneath their feet as they made their way to the dining room and took seats at a heavy, ornate mahogany table. Drawn to its beauty, Chrissy ran her hand along the rich, smooth wood.

"Like the table?"

Chrissy spun toward the deep baritone of Steven's voice. "Yes, it's gorgeous. The craftsmanship is remarkable. Is it an antique?"

Steven stood straighter, and a smile cracked the hard lines of his face at last. "It's not an antique unless I am."

Chrissy frowned and looked to Adam for clarification.

Adam hooked a thumb toward his dad. "He built it."

She studied the table with renewed appreciation. "You built this? That's amazing."

Theresa entered the room carrying a tray of sandwiches. "What's amazing?"

Steven puffed up like a peacock showing off his feathers. "Adam's lady friend was admiring my handiwork."

"Her name is Chrissy, Dad," Adam said with a low tone.

If Theresa heard the tension, she breezed past it like a pro. "Oh, yes. This table is his pride and joy. He gave it to me when we got married. It was such a surprise, and I felt so bad I didn't have a gift for him."

"You were the gift, dear." An actual twinkle lit Steven's eye as he beamed at his wife, a heartfelt look Chrissy hadn't thought possible when she'd first seen the grouch on the porch.

Theresa gave his arm a playful tap then busied herself with doling out sandwiches. "I'd hoped to pass the table on to Beth, but her style was much more modern." As her words settled, she gave a small gasp, and her wide eyes shot to Adam and Chrissy. "I mean... I'm sorry, I didn't mean to..."

Adam's harsh lines softened a bit, but his expression remained guarded. "It's okay, Mom. She knows about Beth."

Theresa's frozen body creaked back to life, and she returned to the task at hand. "Oh. That's good."

With the food distributed, Adam's mom sat back down, and the unbearable awkward silence returned.

Theresa, who was the obvious brave one of the bunch, broke the silence again. "Adam, I'm so glad you reached out to us. I don't want to dampen the mood of your visit, but I'd like to get the elephant shoved out of the room before it takes over again."

Adam reached for Chrissy's hand under the table as Chrissy's pulse raced at breakneck speed. She hadn't expected this level of confrontation so soon. Theresa sure didn't beat around the bush.

"We're sorry we weren't there for you the way we should've been. We were both in a bad place after the accident, and it was just so hard to wrap our minds around it all. My therapist says I put up walls to try to hold the pain out, but all I accomplished was holding it in. It took me a while to see what she meant, and by that point the silence between us was so big, I..." Her voice cracked. "We tried calling a few times, but when you didn't answer we figured you needed space. After a year, we wanted to reach out again, we really did, but we weren't sure you'd want to talk to us." Adam's mom looked over at his dad and took his hand.

Adam's dad gave a curt nod and cleared his throat. "Your mom is right."

Adam sat motionless for a moment then frowned and shook his head. "I don't know what to say. All this time I thought you hated me. That you blamed me for Beth."

Theresa gasped, her forehead creasing. "What? No. Of course not. How could you think that?"

Adam tossed his hands in the air. "I don't know. Maybe because the last time we spoke, you hammered me with questions about why I did or didn't do this or that. Then you gave up on me and ghosted me for two years."

Chrissy laid her hand on Adam's knee to comfort and calm him before he said something he'd regret.

"No, we weren't blaming you. We were just trying to make sense of it all. No one can prepare themselves for such a tragedy. I'm so sorry it came across like we were blaming you. We didn't give up on you. We tried to call." Theresa reached for Adam's hand, but he pulled it away.

"No one ever asked me how I was doing." Adam's thick voice cracked as he stared at the floor. "I didn't call you back because all you wanted to talk about was Beth. She wasn't the only one in the car. I was there too. I had injuries. I know my experience pales in comparison to Beth's, but it wasn't nothing. But how many times did anyone ask me how I was doing? Zero."

"That can't be right." Theresa pushed away from the table. "Lots of people tried to console you."

"Telling me they're sorry for my loss as they shake my hand isn't the same as asking how I'm doing."

Theresa's mouth hung open. "I'm so sorry, Adam. I never realized it felt that way to you. You didn't want us to stay with you while you recovered, so I thought having stuff delivered to your apartment showed how much we cared. Then when the deliveries started being rejected as a wrong address, we took it as a sign and stopped. I'll admit we should have been more persistent, but we didn't know how to handle all the emotional stuff at the time. We love you, son. We always have and always will. I'm sorry I wasn't equipped to help you through your pain." Theresa stood and rounded the table then bent and wrapped Adam in a hug. Adam returned the hug, his shoulders shaking. After a moment she went back to her seat.

Adam dried his face with his napkin. "I guess I never realized how much I pushed you both away. It was just so hard having every conversation center around Beth, I kind of blocked out everyone who knew her. For so long I let my anger build without ever really considering my part in it all, and I'm sorry. I started therapy a couple of weeks ago to try to let go of some of the guilt and resentment. I understand it was a lot for you to deal with, but I had to tell you my point of view before I could really start to move past it."

Theresa reached for Adam's hand, and he let her take it. "I'm proud of you for seeking help. I hope we can all move forward now."

"Me too." One corner of Adam's mouth ticked upward, and he lowered his sights to the sandwich on his plate. "Thanks for making lunch, Mom. Your chicken club has always been one of my favorites."

"That's why I made it."

Seeing the healing smiles around the table, Chrissy blinked back her tears of both happiness and grief. Adam reconciling with his parents filled her with joy for them and also joy for herself as she would now get to experience a taste of family life. But a small part of her also mourned never having had that for herself. With her parents dead, she'd never get to experience having a parent care. Playing pretend with Adam's parents was the closest she'd ever get.

Adam

I t was real. All of it. The soothing trickle of water in his mom's fountain and the familiar creak of the porch swing weren't a dream. And he owed it all to the magnificent woman sitting next to him. Without Chrissy's urging, he might never have reached out to his parents. He scooped up her hand and laced his fingers through hers, which prompted a smile so sweet his mouth watered.

"How did you two meet?" Theresa asked, setting a tray on the little table beside the swing.

Adam chuckled as he remembered that first day at the mural. "Actually, I startled her while she was painting."

"So you're an artist?" Theresa took a seat across from them.

"I'm attempting to be." Chrissy's voice came out less than confident.

"She's being modest," Adam said. "She's almost done with the biggest mural in Chicago, and she'll likely be painting the riverfront concert area next, along with a couple other murals the city has planned."

Theresa's eyebrows shot up. "Wow. I'd say that's a bit more than just an attempt."

Chrissy's entire face turned crimson, and Adam squeezed her hand. With his other, he tugged his phone from his pocket and pulled up the album he'd made of all the mural pictures. "Here's the one that's almost done."

Theresa leaned into Steven so they could both see the screen as she scrolled through the pictures. "This is beautiful. You're a very talented young lady."

"An artist, huh? No wonder you admired my table. You have an eye for beauty." Steven's face crinkled with a smile.

"Oh, that reminds me. What's your style, Chrissy?" Theresa asked.

That's an odd question, Adam thought.

"My style?" Chrissy glanced at him, but he had no clue either.

"You know, do you like modern furniture or traditional or rustic or... What else is there? Gothic?"

"Oh, uh, I guess I haven't really thought about it," Chrissy stammered.

"What kind of pieces do you tend to buy?" Adam's mom must've finally picked up on Chrissy's uneasiness because her expression turned apologetic. "Sorry, with my husband being in the cabinet and furniture business I'm always curious about a person's style. I didn't mean to put you on the spot."

Adam watched Chrissy pick at her unusually subdued pale-yellow fingernails, a sure sign that her nerves were sparking. The realization that Chrissy had likely never bought furniture in her life smacked him like a ton of bricks. He opened his mouth to come to her rescue, but she spoke first.

Chrissy straightened her spine and looked Theresa in the eyes. "To be completely honest, I've never had the chance to select my own furniture. If I think back, though, there've been pieces I admired along the way. At the children's home where I grew up, the small white dresser was my favorite piece because it was the one and only place my things had ever belonged."

Adam's heart shattered, and one look at his parents let him know theirs lay broken on the floor as well. At the same time, his pride knew no limit for Chrissy for owning her truth in front of his parents, two people whose approval he suspected she desperately craved. If he was honest with himself, he craved their approval of her too.

"The next special piece I can think of is the plain oak table at my brother's house because Luke's is where I reconnected with my long-lost family. At the halfway house, I loved my rickety old metal-frame bed because my life had given me a newfound appreciation of a safe place to sleep. And right now, I love all the clean lines and plush fabrics of Adam's apartment and the wrought-iron bistro set on the roof. And obviously your dining room table is a work of art. All those things are very different, though, so I don't really know my style, I guess. Does that make me eclectic?"

Theresa whisked a tear off her cheek, and her lips curled into a soft smile. "Eclectic fits, but I'd say your style is sentimental. It sounds to me like you're drawn more to the heart of the piece, the feel rather than the look."

Chrissy nodded. "Yeah, I'd say that's true. I never really considered that a style."

"It's my favorite kind." Theresa winked.

"I like that. You did good, son. She's a keeper." Steven's unexpected declaration turned every head in his direction.

Adam coughed and laughed at the same time. "Oh, uh, w-well, we haven't really... I-It's only been..."

"Right now, we're just seeing how this goes," Chrissy said with surprising calm, rescuing him from being a rambling idiot.

Theresa held her palms up in front of her. "Say no more. We get it. You can't rush these things."

"Yeah, sure," Adam said, his tone disbelieving. *They would probably marry us here on the porch this very moment if I let them.* They'd always wanted him to settle down, and they especially longed for grandbabies.

"But when the day comes, she gets my table," Steven said. "That way I know it'll be appreciated after I'm gone."

"Whoa. Okay. Can we talk about something else?" Adam scrambled for a new topic before his parents sent Chrissy running. "Oh, I forgot to mention my friend Winifred is having Chrissy paint portraits of her cats. Do you want to see some of the pieces she's working on?" Getting out his phone again, he pulled up more pictures and sent out a prayer to the universe that his parents hadn't scared Chrissy off.

With the car door secure between him and his parents, Adam puddled into the seat. Though reconciling had been easier and better than he'd ever anticipated, he wasn't mentally prepared for the deluge of parental love after years of its absence. The sweet silence untangled his thoughts and unknotted his muscles. He peeked over at Chrissy as her soft hand cupped his.

A sympathetic smile curved her luscious lips. "You okay? That was a lot to process in just a couple of hours."

He groaned as his mind tortured him with replays of the most cringeworthy moments. "I'm so sorry to put you through that. I don't know what came over them. After Beth, I honestly thought they'd resent you."

She scrunched her nose. "Honestly, I was expecting that too. I figured they'd hate me, especially since the first time they saw you in years was with me on your arm. But I'm so relieved they don't."

"They made that clear enough." He scrubbed a hand over his face, wishing it would wipe away his embarrassment. "I hope that didn't scare you off."

"Are you kidding? They're wonderful."

He peered over at her as if she'd lost her mind. "Wonderful? Try embarrassing. I'm surprised Mom didn't pull out my naked baby pictures."

Chrissy giggled. "She actually took me on a tour of the hallway picture gallery while your dad had you out in the shop. I never would've guessed you had an awkward teenage phase."

His ninth-grade picture flashed into his mind's eye, all braces, acne, and wiry geekiness. "Oh man."

Another giggle. "I loved every minute of the visit, even the hard ones. Sure, your parents can be a little overbearing and intrusive, but it's just because they love you. And the fact they welcomed me with open arms into that kind of love... Well, I'll take it for as long as I can, even if it means an occasional barrage of uncomfortable questions."

A rush of air came out of him on a laugh. "Really? I was afraid we'd go home and you'd start packing your bags."

Her lips curled in a sassy grin. "You're not getting rid of me that easy. In fact, how about you put this car in motion so we can go home and celebrate?"

Adam quirked a brow. "Oh really?"

She nodded, and Adam cursed the console between them as she leaned over it to press her lips to his. The second she pulled back, he shifted the car into drive.

Chapter 45

Chrissy

Please let her like them, Chrissy begged of the universe. She pushed a cart filled with the finished cat portraits into the elevator for delivery. She drummed her fingers on the cart handle, watching the elevator numbers tick by as it climbed to Winifred's penthouse. Her phone buzzed in her pocket.

A text from Adam. "She'll love them. Are you sure you don't want me to come?"

He knew her so well. "Thanks. I'm sure."

She dropped her phone back into her pocket as the doors opened. The cart clanked over the threshold, announcing her arrival.

Winifred buzzed into the entryway, her face aglow as she air-kissed Chrissy's cheeks. "Come, come. I can hardly contain myself."

Following Winifred to the informal living room, Chrissy drooled over her outfit. Every single time Chrissy saw the woman, her clothing choices exuded impeccable taste, and today's high-waisted black pencil skirt and red blouse were no exception.

As soon as Chrissy pushed the cart into the room, Winifred spun on her designer heels. "I simply can't wait any longer."

With sweaty palms, Chrissy lifted the cloth covering the canvases. She attempted to swallow but found her throat was too dry, and she was certain her blue blouse must be fluttering with her heartbeat. She had worked nights and weekends on the paintings, but she'd made sure not to rush. Every detail needed to be perfect. Not only was it her first substantial commission, it was for Winifred. On an exhale, she lifted the first canvas.

Upon hearing Winifred gasp, Chrissy wondered if she'd failed, and she couldn't bring herself to look the formidable woman in the face.

"It's magnificent."

Chrissy's eyes shot to Winifred, who stepped forward and gingerly traced Anastasia's whisker on the portrait.

"You like it?" Chrissy asked, scared to believe it.

"I love it. You captured her regal beauty with a touch of softness and intrigue. It's perfection. It's Anastasia."

As if on cue, the white ball of fluff rubbed against Chrissy's leg, prompting a grin from Winifred. "It appears Anastasia approves as well. You simply must show me the others."

One by one, Winifred fell in love with each of the five portraits. She had Chrissy line them up along the wall and stepped back to admire them. "I've never seen a finer collection of paintings."

Such high praise from someone like Winifred was something Chrissy had never expected. Seeing Winifred of all people gushing over her work, Chrissy could die happy.

Without a word, Winifred crossed the room to a desk and retrieved an envelope. "I realize we didn't discuss payment, so I hope this is sufficient."

Chrissy blinked. "Oh. Actually, I didn't even think about it. I was just happy you gave me the chance, and it's something else I can add to my portfolio."

"Poppycock. You're an artist, a talented one at that, and you should demand payment for your work."

"You don't have to pay me. I consider you a friend, and I was doing you a favor. And since it's cats, I'm sure these portraits will help grow my followers when I post about them."

"I insist." Winifred thrust the envelope toward Chrissy with more force.

Chrissy gave in and took it. "Okay. Thank you."

When Winifred turned her back on Chrissy to admire the paintings again, Chrissy's curiosity got the better of her. She peeked in the envelope, and her knees buckled as she zeroed in on the amount written on the check it contained.

"Are you serious? This is too much, Winifred. I can't accept this." Chrissy gaped at Winifred's back, waiting for a response.

"You're simply unaccustomed to receiving compensation equal to your worth." She finally turned to face Chrissy and motioned to the couch. With both of them seated, she continued. "I know you won't believe this, but we aren't as different as you think. Long ago, before I became the woman I am today, I knew all too well the struggles you've faced. Much like Anastasia, here, underneath this refined exterior lies a cautious, wounded soul, and I can see the same in you. Your wounded soul is partially why you're such a good artist, and why I had every confidence you'd capture my babies perfectly."

Talk about hitting the nail on the head. Having Winifred see her truths and speak of them so casually brought a storm of emotions swirling to the surface. Chrissy stared at the envelope in her hand, containing a check with more zeros than she'd ever thought she'd see at one time.

"That moment when your bank account jumps from next to nothing to an amount you never imagined possible is one you'll never forget. I still remember it like it was yesterday."

Chrissy found her voice at last. "But this is too much for five portraits."

"These portraits are worth much more than that to me. These cats are my children, and all I have to show from my marriages. They're my world."

"I'm glad I could be the one to paint them for you, and I loved every minute of it. I still think it's too much, though." A sidelong glance from Winifred piqued Chrissy's curiosity. "What are you not saying?"

Winifred scooped Anastasia up and placed her on her lap, seemingly uncaring that long white hairs clung to her black skirt. "I'm glad to hear you enjoyed your time with them. As I grow older, I fear for their safety when I'm no longer able to care for them. I have no family to speak of, and therefore no one to care for them."

Chrissy had a sneaking suspicion as to where the conversation was headed.

"I haven't had anyone take an interest in them through the years, at least no one I would deem worthy. There was always a compatibility issue of some sort. Until you. Seeing the way they each accepted you, it is clear they've chosen you."

"Wait. Are you saying you want me to take care of your cats?" Chrissy knew her mouth hung open in the most unladylike manner, but she was powerless to snap it shut.

Love radiated from Winifred as she peered down at Anastasia purring in her lap. "You mentioned you've always wanted a pet. How do you feel about inheriting five cats someday?"

The air rushed from Chrissy's lungs in a mix of shock and laughter. If she'd been honored beyond belief to have Winifred admire her paintings, no words existed to describe how she felt upon hearing Winifred trusted her with her most beloved pets. "Winifred, I don't know what to say. I'm flattered and shocked."

Octavius, the aloof orange tabby cat, chose that moment to jump onto Chrissy's lap and meow a forceful hello. Both women laughed, and Chrissy scratched his favorite place under his chin.

"I'll give you some time to mull it over," Winifred said. "However, I do have another matter to discuss before you go."

What more could this woman have in store?

"I am a longtime supporter of the arts, so I happen to spend a good deal of time talking with people in the art community. It seems there is buzz about a new artist on the scene."

Chrissy wondered what any of that had to do with her. *Hopefully someone didn't take my place on the future murals.*

Winifred continued, seemingly oblivious to Chrissy's panic. "A dear friend of mine just so happens to own an art gallery to which the artist's portfolio was submitted, and she was showing me their work. Perhaps you've heard of Blue Orchid?"

"Of course. It's the most renowned gallery in Chicago." Whoever that new artist was sure was lucky if Blue Orchid was interested.

A satisfied smirk lit a twinkle in Winifred's eyes. "Yes, that's the one. I must say, many of the pictures she showed me looked very familiar."

Chrissy's heart stopped, and her mouth gaped open again as she read between the lines. "Wait. What are you saying?"

"I'm saying you should keep an eye out for a phone call from Blue Orchid in the near future."

Inhaling to speak, Chrissy choked on her own saliva, coughing and sputtering until both Anastasia and Octavius fled to find a quieter place to nap. Winifred disappeared, returning with a glass of water.

Chrissy gulped the cold liquid as if it could quell the panic, shock, and excited buzz riding on the coattails of the adrenaline coursing through her veins. She waited for the golden light to appear because, surely, she'd died and gone to heaven.

At last, she formed words, though her voice came out shaky. "Winifred, I can't even begin to fathom how I'll ever be able to thank you enough."

"Thank me for what, dear?"

"Well, for starters, for this paycheck." Chrissy held up the envelope.

"You earned that fair and square. I've paid far more for far less."

Chrissy tried to shake the disbelief from her head. "But the Blue Orchid? That's going to make a whole new career for me. Thank you so much."

Winifred brushed away Chrissy's comment with a wave of her hand, her diamond ring glinting in the light. "Oh, that wasn't me, dear. That was all you."

"But you said you told your friend about me."

"No, I said my friend told me about you. She saw the portfolio you submitted and looked at your work online long before I talked with her. When I saw the pictures and she verified it was you, I pled for the chance to tell you the news. I'm simply the messenger."

"I can't believe it." Chrissy exhaled, her mind a storm. For so long, she had felt like things just happened to her in her life, and she never had control over it. Then when she'd finally gained some control, she'd made one horrible choice after another, ruining her life more than mere circumstance ever could. But after all the blood, sweat, and tears of her recovery journey, the time had finally come for her to make good things happen in her life. Not just good, but fantastically life-changing.

Winifred gripped Chrissy's hand. "I understand what you are feeling right now. One can grow too accustomed to despicable things. I even married a few, but that's a story for another day. The beauty of life is that things can change, and we can set that in motion for ourselves. You just need to let yourself believe the good as strongly as you believed the bad. Good people deserve to be rewarded, and you're a good person, Chrissy. I know you don't see it, but Adam does. He sees the good in you the same way you see it in him."

The way Winifred knew Chrissy better than she knew herself gave her chills. Adam was one hundred percent correct. No one in the world was a better person than Winifred, and with the way she saw through people she might possibly be a witch.

"Can I hug you?" Chrissy asked.

"Of course, dear. You're my honorary granddaughter, after all."

Adam

At the sound of the door unlocking, Adam jumped to his feet. Waves of relief crashed over him as Chrissy walked in, and he rushed over to her.

"I was starting to worry. What took so long? You were up there for hours."

She turned to face him, her eyes rimmed with red.

Oh no, he thought. "What's wrong? Did she not like the paintings?"

She shook her head and spoke at last. "Nothing is wrong. Just the opposite, actually. She loved them."

He scooped her up into a bear hug. "I knew she would. You're amazing."

When he set her back on her feet, she radiated an energy he'd never seen before. "Is there something else?"

"She's friends with the owner of Blue Orchid, and they told her they're interested in showing my work."

"What? That's amazing." He pulled her in for another hug and kissed her head, his heart swelling with pride. "This calls for a celebration." He sprinted to the refrigerator and pulled out a bottle of sparkling cider, then he poured two glasses and handed one to Chrissy. "Here's to you, my majestic, brilliant artist."

Chrissy clinked her glass but stared off into space rather than taking a drink. "I can't believe I'm going to have a showing at Blue Orchid. I figured I'd have to start small, but this is pretty damn big."

"That's because all your hard work is paying off." Adam set down his glass and took her hand. "You deserve all the good things happening to you. No matter what comes, don't ever forget how amazing you are."

"How can I? You tell me that multiple times a day." Though Chrissy teased him, she appreciated his affirmations more than he'd ever know.

"Of course I have to stay focused on finishing the mural for now. Squeezing in Winifred's cats wore me out. But once the mural is done, I'll be able to really throw myself into pieces for the gallery." She gasped. "I need so many more paintings. Do you have any idea how many it takes to fill a gallery?"

"Can't you use some of the ones you've already painted?"

Chrissy set her glass on the counter and wrung her hands. "Winifred said I could use the cat portraits. She already sent pictures of them to the gallery. She mentioned they'd talked about doing half portraits and half landscapes."

"I'm sure you won't have any trouble with that. You already have half a dozen landscapes finished at least."

"I'll have to find more subjects for the portraits." A devilish grin crossed Chrissy's face, and mischief danced in her eyes. "You know, you'd make an excellent subject with your devastatingly handsome good looks."

Adam struck a pose with his muscles flexed. "Is that so?"

Chrissy giggled and cocked an eyebrow. "I can think of a few poses I'd like to see."

Adam bit his lip as he slid his arms around her. "Oh, really?"

"How about we go test them out?" Chrissy rose onto her tiptoes and brushed her lips on his neck just below his jawline. A moan rumbled in his throat as she pressed herself against his ever-tightening joggers.

"I'll do whatever you want."

"I like the sound of that," Chrissy said with a wink.

Chapter 46

Adam

"Chrissy, it's almost time to leave. Are you ready?" Adam glanced at his phone again as the minutes ticked by. They needed to leave pronto if they were to have any chance of avoiding being late. He surveyed himself in the mirror one last time, straightening his purple tie and smoothing his gray suit.

Chrissy rushed out of the bedroom. "Ready. How do I look? I think the lace sleeve covers my scars really well."

The time was forgotten as he drank in every delicious detail. The deep-purple dress clung to her curves, the one-shoulder style and knee-high slit giving tantalizing glimpses of her creamy skin. Her golden waves were piled on her head with delicate tendrils taunting him as they tickled her neck and shoulders, his mouth yearning to follow their lead.

"You look absolutely spectacular." He closed the gap between them and pulled her into his arms. Unable to resist any longer, he bent and nuzzled into her neck, planting little kisses along the way.

A soft moan rose from her parted lips, but then she gently pushed him away. "I better stop you right there or we will never make it on time."

His hungry gaze raked over her again. "Who cares if we're late?"

"You do." She gave his arm a playful swat and strode to the door.

He groaned as he watched her go, every movement making his pants grow tighter. "How am I supposed to survive this evening with you taunting me in that dress?"

She peeked over her bare shoulder at him. "You can keep reminding yourself you get to help me take it off later."

He adjusted his pants and groaned, which elicited a giggle from Chrissy. "I don't think that's going to help me any."

The whole car ride, it was all he could do to keep his focus on the road instead of ogling Chrissy.

As they arrived at the gravel lot, Adam couldn't help but marvel at how much his life had changed since the first time he'd pulled in there a month and a half ago. He'd begun the journey a broken, guarded man, and now he held the door open for an incredible woman he had the privilege to bare his heart and soul to.

"It's weird getting out of your car here now. Is it okay if we're seen coming to the party together?" Chrissy asked as she climbed from the passenger seat.

"For the fourth time, it's fine. I promise." He wanted to tell her why but made himself wait.

Beside him, Chrissy inhaled as they made their way to the mural. One glance at her face stopped him in his tracks. "Are you okay? You look like you're going to puke."

"That's probably because I am about to puke." Chrissy laughed nervously as she stared at the crew putting the finishing touches on the party setup.

He stepped in front of her and took her hands in his. "There's nothing to be afraid of. This party is for you, to celebrate all your hard work. The mural looks amazing, and so do you."

"I've never been to a fancy party before, let alone one celebrating something I accomplished. And knowing people actually paid a hefty price to come just adds to the pressure." She pulled her hands from his and wrung them.

With a gentle finger, he lifted her face so her eyes met his. "Don't worry for one second about the ticket price. Everyone who paid to come knew their money was going to future projects. You don't owe them anything. Okay? They paid that price because they want to be able to brag about going to an exclusive event put on by the city. You painted the mural that's being unveiled, so you are responsible for giving them bragging rights. If anything, they owe you."

The creases in her forehead softened, and a slight smile graced her lips. "Thanks for talking me off the ledge."

"That's what I'm here for." He lowered his mouth to hers for a soft kiss, careful not to smudge her makeup. That would come later. "Now let's get to your party."

Chrissy

The sea of partygoers grew by the minute, but three particular faces remained missing from the crowd. Even the extra three inches from her gold stilettos couldn't help Chrissy find them. Instead of the faces she wanted to see, a sour older man stalked toward them, people parting to make a path like he would bite if he got too close.

When the man reached them, he shook Adam's hand and nodded a greeting to Chrissy. "I didn't think it was possible, but you finished the mural, and it doesn't look half bad. And finally we have some good press about it. Congratulations."

"Thank you," Chrissy said, but it came out sounding more like a question.

Adam shook the man's hand again. "Thank you, Mr. Lyones."

Chrissy sucked in a breath as the man walked away. "That was your boss?"

Adam's face scrunched. "The one and only."

"Does he always look like he wants to murder someone?"

"Pretty much." Adam's hand gripped her shoulder. "You can relax now. That was the worst part, and it wasn't so bad, was it?"

"No, I guess it wasn't." Chrissy shook her hands, trying to dispel her nerves.

Adam tapped her arm and pointed to her right. "They made it."

Luke's head bobbed above the crowd, and she glimpsed Ben's blond curls following along behind him. Luke gave a low whistle as he, Ben, and Aria broke from the crowd. "Man, you guys sure know how to throw a party."

Chrissy wrapped him in a hug. "Thank you so much for coming."

Aria swooped in for her hug, her brown hair tickling Chrissy's cheek. "Are you kidding? We wouldn't miss it for the world." She let go and held Chrissy at arm's length. "And you look like a million bucks. That dress is insanely gorgeous."

Chrissy had to admit that in that moment she felt like a million bucks. "Thanks. You look beautiful, as always."

Aria fluffed the skirt of her pink-and-white floral dress, then she caught sight of Adam. "Nice to see you, too, Adam."

"Where's the food?" Ben asked, prompting chuckles from everyone.

Adam cocked his head in the direction of the hors d'oeuvres table. "Come with me."

Chrissy smiled after him before returning her attention to Luke and Aria. "I'm so glad to see you guys. Other than Adam, I don't know a single person here so far."

A conspiratorial gleam shone in Aria's blue eyes as she leaned closer. "Speaking of Adam, how are things going?"

Chrissy cut a glance to Luke's serious expression but couldn't wipe the grin from her own face no matter how hard she tried. "Things are great, actually. No more secrets, and no more hiding who we are."

"That's fantastic. I'm so happy for you." Aria let out a little squeal and pulled Chrissy in for another hug.

Luke cleared his throat, the hard lines of his face softening. "I'm happy for you too. Adam is a lucky man."

"I certainly am." Adam rejoined them and slid his arm around Chrissy's waist before kissing her temple. "Lilly says hi and that she'll be done setting up the desserts in time to join us for the dinner."

Chrissy scanned the crowd to see if anyone was looking their way then leaned in so only Adam could hear. "I thought we weren't supposed to act like a couple in front of anyone."

Before Adam could respond, Ben appeared beside them with a plate loaded with snacks. "The party is kind of lame, but the food is amazing."

Aria gave his arm a nudge. "Ben, don't be rude. The party is beautiful."

Ben shrugged and took a bite. "Maybe for grown-ups. Hey, what is this?"

Aria cradled her forehead with her palm. "Don't talk with your mouth full, Ben."

Adam laughed. "That's a smoked-salmon rillette."

"I'm going to go get some more of those," Ben said.

Chrissy giggled as Aria trailed after Ben, her heart the lightest it had ever been. She caught sight of Winifred's silver hair and dark gunmetal-silver gown at the edge of the crowd. Every single person who mattered to her gathered in one place to support her and show their love. *Who could ask for more?*

Chapter 47

Chrissy

"**I** made it." Lilly sank into the seat beside Chrissy. "Oh my gosh. You look heavenly."

"Thanks. You look great, as always." Chrissy meant it too. Lilly always seemed to know the perfect way to compliment her fiery-red curls, green eyes, and ivory skin. Her emerald-green halter dress was no exception.

"I'm so sorry Zach couldn't make it. He's been swamped lately."

Chrissy gave a dismissive wave. "It's okay. I'll have plenty of time to talk with him, because I'm not letting you go again."

Lilly leaned toward Chrissy and lowered her voice. "Speaking of never letting go, has Adam said the L-word again?"

Chrissy glanced around to see if anyone was listening then leaned in. "No. I don't even know if he realized he used that word in reference to me. He was so caught up in telling me about Beth."

"Realized it or not, he said it, and I can tell by watching you two together that he feels it."

Chrissy lowered her voice even more. "We're supposed to be acting like nothing is going on. I don't know what's gotten into him."

A waiter set plates in front of them, interrupting their whispered conversation.

As Chrissy finished her meal, Liz walked up to the table, her black-and-red blouse tucked into black leather pants. "You did a good job, Chrissy."

"I couldn't have finished it without you." Chrissy rose to her feet and held her arms out for a hug. "Thank you for being the best assistant."

"I didn't really have much competition." Liz gave a playful smirk.

"That might be true, but it doesn't take away from your awesomeness. In fact, I'd love it if you'd be my assistant on my future murals."

"Sounds like a plan." Liz reached out a hand to shake Chrissy's.

"I'll text you when I know the official start date." Just then Chrissy saw Abilene and her dad approaching. Chrissy greeted them and made introductions. "Liz, this is Abilene. She came to the mural on a field trip with her class, and I've been helping her develop a portfolio for art school applications. She's going to be my apprentice on the river wall mural."

Wonderment shone on Abilene's face as she took in the scene around them. "Thank you so much for inviting us. I can't believe it."

"The next party will be for both of us." Chrissy couldn't wait to take Abilene under her wing and help her build confidence. Maybe give her a boost toward her dream career. The only thing better than achieving her own dream was knowing she could help someone else chase theirs.

"Time for dessert," Ben said in passing as he rushed back to his spot at the table.

Chrissy laughed. "I guess that's our cue to return to our seats. Trust me, you don't want to miss dessert."

After parting ways with Liz, Abilene, and Abilene's dad, Chrissy found her way back to her seat.

Adam stood and pulled her chair out for her, his face alight. "There you are. I thought you'd snuck home without me."

"Never." She leaned in so only he could hear. "Besides, I need you to help me out of my dress, remember?"

"How could I forget?" Adam's hand found her knee under the table. "Maybe we should skip dessert."

Chrissy looked at him as if he'd lost his mind. "I will never skip dessert, especially if Lilly made it." With a laugh, she grabbed her fork and dug in.

Pushing the plate away, Chrissy rose to her feet. "You really out-did yourself tonight, Lilly. That cheesecake is divine. I have to admit I'm a little upset I don't have room for the chocolate cake too."

"I happen to know the baker. Maybe I can hook you up with a slice to take home." Lilly nudged Chrissy's arm.

"Yes, please."

Adam held out his arm for Chrissy. "Shall we?"

"I'll see you later. Enjoy your evening," Lilly said, winking at Chrissy.

Chrissy looped her arm through Adam's and let him lead her through the crowd. They stopped at the foot of the mural, which was illuminated by floodlights.

"It's a masterpiece," boomed a voice behind them.

Chrissy turned and came face-to-face with none other than Liam Worthington, arguably the second richest man in Chicago, his dad being the first. The swooning she'd have expected when she met the city's most eligible bachelor didn't come. Just months ago she'd swooned at the very idea of this moment, yet here that moment was, and she felt nothing. Her heart belonged elsewhere.

"Ah, Liam. Glad you could make it." Adam shook Liam's hand. "Where's your date? Paige, isn't it?"

Liam shuffled his feet, his posture losing its previous confidence. "I'm only stopping in for a brief moment, I'm afraid. Some issues have come up that demand my attention." He cleared his throat and turned to Chrissy. "My sincerest apologies to the artist. I wanted to let you know that I think you do fantastic work—and that you've officially been selected as the artist for the next three projects at minimum."

Chrissy gasped. She had known she was the likely choice for the next one, but beyond that nothing had been decided. And with all the chaos and scandal surrounding the mural she'd just completed, anything was possible. As she shook the hand Liam offered, she couldn't believe the night had, yet again, topped itself. "Really? That's amazing. I won't let you or the city down."

Liam turned to Adam. "You two will be working a lot together."

It was Adam's turn to clear his throat. "Actually, I'll have to hand my responsibilities over to someone else, I'm afraid."

Chrissy gasped as her brows knit together. Adam hadn't mentioned anything to her about quitting his job. *Or did Mr. Lyones fire him, and it's all my fault?*

Liam cocked his head to the side. "Oh? Why's that?"

Adam gazed down at Chrissy and wrapped his arm around her waist, pulling her snug against his side. "Conflict of interest. I fell in love with the artist."

And that moment, those words, secured that night as the best night of her entire life.

Liam clapped Adam on the shoulder. "No better reason than that, man. Congratulations to both of you." He glanced at his silver watch that probably cost as much as a car and sucked in a breath. "Sorry, but I've got to run. Congratulations again on the mural and everything else. This is your night. Make the most of it."

With Liam walking away, Chrissy turned to Adam and searched his deep brown eyes. The floodlight bounced off his sandy hair and highlighted the strong edge of his jaw. "Did you mean that?"

His palm cupped her cheek, and his fingers tangled in the wavy wisps of hair on her neck. "Come What May," her favorite song from the movie *Moulin Rouge*, played over the speakers, the powerful melody filling the space. "Every single word. I know we've only known each other for a short time, but we've been through so much together. My past taught me how short life is, and I don't want to waste a single moment. And now that I won't be your boss, we don't have to hide anymore. I love you, and I want to find out where this goes."

"Good, because I love you too." She wrapped her arms around his neck and pulled his mouth to hers. Every cell in her body blazed with desire as the world fell away, his touch the only thing reaching her senses.

Adam

A flash of light startled them out of their bubble, both disorient-ed and searching for the source. Another flash and Adam turned Chrissy away from the paparazzi, trying to shield her from their predation as images of that night at the restaurant raced through his mind. They didn't have to hide anymore, but that didn't mean they wanted to be exploited by tabloids.

"It's okay, Adam. I knew going into tonight that complete priva-cy was out the window. What's a fancy fundraising party without lots of pictures for promotion? I've come to terms with this being a part of the life I want, and I'm not ashamed of myself anymore." Chrissy tugged on his arm, nudging him to turn around with her.

Adam hesitated. Allowing the world into their relationship meant not being able to protect Chrissy from everything that went along with that. Her past was well-sealed—Winifred had helped make that happen—but everyone knew tabloids didn't need facts to make up headlines. And if they thought you had secrets, they were out for blood. But perhaps living out in the open would take away the sensationalism of the story. Sure, him dating again would be big news for a week or two, but eventually it would become old news.

It was worth a shot, anyway. Especially if it meant he got to truly be with Chrissy.

Adam stood straighter. "Okay. Let's do this."

They spun around, and she slid her arm around Adam, pulling him close as she smiled for the cameras. After a few waves and questions answered, she tilted her head up and whispered the most scintillating words imaginable. "How about we get out of here and have our own little party? As much as I love this dress, I'm ready to be out of it."

"Sounds like the perfect plan to me." He slid his hand down her back and cupped her butt before trailing his fingertips up her back. She shivered under his touch as he whispered in her ear. "I've already undressed you two dozen times in my mind, so I'm more than ready to do it for real."

Her lips parted, sparking fireworks in his core. Clearing his throat, he threaded her arm through his. Leading her away from the party, he felt himself finally moving forward with his life.

Epilogue
One Year Later
Chrissy

"Where are we going?" Chrissy giggled as she held her hands over her eyes.

"If I told you, then it wouldn't be a surprise, now would it?" Adam steered the car through the streets to their secret date.

Streetlights flashed through Chrissy's fingers, and she peeked down at her lap. All Adam would tell her was to dress nice but comfortably, so she'd chosen the cornflower-blue dress she'd worn to Luke and Aria's wedding.

"No peeking."

She closed her hands back over her eyes with a grin. "I was just looking at my dress. Don't worry, I still have no clue what you're up to."

"Good. By the way, that dress is perfect for tonight."

The car slowed to a stop, and when Adam opened his door, the urge to peek nearly overwhelmed her. She squeezed her eyelids tight.

Her door opened, and she felt Adam's touch on her arm. "I'm going to need your hands, but keep your eyes closed. I'll guide you."

Gravel crunched under her white sandals as Adam helped her from her seat. Possibilities rushed through her mind. Maybe he was bringing her to one of the murals she'd painted. Or maybe a new project site.

He tucked her arm in his and led her down a gravel path. "Don't worry, you're safe with me."

"I've known that from the beginning." Her heart fluttered at those familiar words, which rang even more true almost a year later.

The gravel gave way to grass beneath her feet, and a faint melody teased her ears. As they drew nearer, she recognized the music and smiled. "I love this song."

"Me too. It's the song that was playing when we first said, 'I love you.'"

She could hear the smile in his voice. "What are you up to, mister?"

His lips brushed her ear, sending shock waves through her body. "Open your eyes and find out."

Chrissy did as he said, and her hand flew to her chest. They stood at the edge of the pond in the park, the city lights twinkling on the water's surface like a thousand fireflies. To her left, the picnic table they claimed on every visit held a candlelight dinner for two.

Adam took her hand and led her to the table. A white tablecloth and fine china transformed their favorite picnic spot into a space worthy of a five-star restaurant. Garden party lights twinkled in the tree overhead as their song drifted from a speaker on the table.

"Oh, Adam. It's beautiful."

"Not as beautiful as you," Adam said and tucked his hand behind her head as he brought his mouth to hers.

The love and wanting in his kiss fueled her desire, and she whimpered when he pulled away.

He rested his forehead on hers, his breath ragged. "As much as I'd love to skip ahead to that part, there're other items on the agenda first."

"Are you sure we can't skip?"

"I'm sure. Trust me, it'll be worth it." With a grin and a bow, he waved his arm toward the table with a flourish. "And on that note, have a seat, my lady."

As Chrissy slid into her seat, Adam opened an insulated box beside him. "For the main course, garlic cheese fries from City Club Café and the bacon grilled cheese from Cheesy Pig. I figured there's no need for an appetizer when we have this for the meal."

"You know the way to my heart." Her stomach rumbled, and her mouth watered as he placed the food on her plate.

He beamed across the table, pride evident in his squared shoulders. "I love hearing you say that. Let's eat."

After a few minutes of devouring the delectable food, Chrissy took Adam's hand in hers. "You've really outdone yourself tonight. This is amazing."

"You're in luck because it's not over yet." He pulled out a pink-and-gold box from The Gilded Lilly and lifted the lid to reveal two bear claws. "I know you can't ever finish one by yourself, so the second one is for later."

Seeing Adam's mouth twitch as he placed her half on her plate made her brow quirk upward. "What are you up to now?"

Nervous laughter tumbled out of him. "Okay, you caught me. The truth is, this bear claw has a secret ingredient. The other one is a regular one, just in case you don't like this one."

The thought of a new recipe from Lilly piqued her curiosity. She sank her teeth into the sweet dough, cinnamon and sugar dancing on her tastebuds. "Delicious as always, but I don't taste a secret ingredient."

Adam frowned and took a bite of his half. "Hmm, you're right. Maybe I grabbed the wrong one."

As he reached for the pastry box, Chrissy took another bite and closed her eyes, savoring every sweet morsel.

"I found it."

She opened her eyes and froze. Instead of a pastry, a light-blue box rested in Adam's palm. "What's that?"

"The secret ingredient." He lifted the lid and revealed a dazzling pink sapphire surrounded by sparkling diamonds set in silver.

"Adam, I..." All words fled from her mind as her heart thundered in her ears.

"Chrissy, when I met you, I was dead inside with no hope for the future. My course was set on a self-destructive path. I was a broken man. But then you breezed into my life. You were my beacon of light during a hurricane, and I was drawn to you from day one, no matter how much I fought it. We've been through so much together, and you've stuck by my side even when I let you see the darkest parts of me. I don't know if you remember, but exactly one year ago today, we had our first lunch here. That was the day I knew I wanted you in my life, so I thought the anniversary of that day would be the perfect time to ask you to become a part of my life forever." His voice broke, and he swiped the back of his hand across his eyes as he rose from his seat and knelt beside her. "I'd love to see where this thing takes us—for the rest of our lives. Will you marry me?"

Tears clouded Chrissy's vision as she struggled to form words. So many emotions crashed through her, and so many thoughts swirled in her mind. Choking back a sob, she nodded.

Adam sprang to the bench beside her. "Is that a yes?"

She flung her arms around his neck and nodded. "Yes. A thousand times, yes."

He pulled back, his hands cupping each side of her head, and his mouth crashed onto hers for a deep kiss. Then he pulled her against him as if he'd never let go. And she knew he never would.

Acknowledgements

First and foremost, I must thank my husband, Dustin. Without your support, this book wouldn't exist. This series wouldn't exist. You have endlessly supported me throughout every dream I've chased my entire adult life. Every time I tried to disappear into a puddle of tears, you gave me a life raft. You helped me carve time out of our hectic schedules so I could write and edit and market and all the other hundreds of tasks that come along with trying to make a name for myself in the book world. You refused to let me give in to my fears and insecurities as I broke out of my introvert shell.

To my kids, Bella and Levi, thank you for your patience. Nothing makes my heart happier than seeing you both excited about seeing my cover for the first time or opening the first author copies. I hope I make you proud.

Thank you to my best friend, Chelley, for once again being my cheerleader. Your abundant confidence in me and my abilities buoyed my spirits time and time again. My perfectionism and self-doubt never stood a chance against you.

Several others helped me cross the finish line, and I appreciate you all. Thank you, Emily G., for being such a supportive friend. Your excitement for my books combats my nerves at every step. To Linda at the Bloomfield Library, thank you for being there during all the ups and downs and for always being there when I need to talk.

I wouldn't be where I am today without the encouragement and support of my fellow authors. I'm beyond grateful for the advice and friendship of Barbara Conrey, Katie Mettner, Laura Kemp, Kerry Evelyn, and Linda Milo Martin, just to name a few. You ladies are not merely amazing authors but are amazing humans in every way.

To those who helped shape my story, I am forever grateful. I'm indebted to my wonderful content editor, Rashida, who endured my type A personality like the true professional she is and helped shape this story into the best version of itself. I must thank my line editor, Laura, for helping polish this manuscript until it shone. Many thanks to my cover designer, Erica, for creating such a beautiful cover. And lastly, a huge thank-you to Lynn for believing in me and my writing again. I'm honored to be part of the Red Adept Publishing family.

Finally, thank you to the readers who helped turn my dreams into reality. Without you and your support, I wouldn't be here today. Thank you for letting me share these stories with you and for all your kind words that keep me writing. I have so many ideas waiting to get onto the page and into your hands.

About the Author

Twila Mason has been writing her own stories since she learned how to read. She is a writer of romance, women's fiction, poetry, and short stories. Her work explores raw emotions and the complexities of life while finding hope within every obstacle.

She lives the rural, small-town life in Missouri with her husband, two kids, and menagerie of animals. After obtaining a PhD in Cell and Developmental Biology, she's switching gears to follow her life-long dream of putting her fictional stories out into the world. When she's not reading or writing, Twila can be found crafting, farming, doing home improvement projects, or going on adventures with her kids.

Read more at https://www.twilamason.com/.

About the Publisher

Dear Reader,

We hope you enjoyed this book. Please consider leaving a review on your favorite book site.

Visit our site to find more quality books!

Read more at https://RedAdeptPublishing.com.